TO THE PERSON WHO CHANGED MY VIEWS, AND TOOK ME BY SURPRISE.

CONTENTS

Prologue i
Chapter One 1
Chapter Two 15
Chapter Three 26
Chapter Four 36
Chapter Five 52
Chapter Six 65
Chapter Seven 79
Chapter Eight 102
Chapter Nine 115
Chapter Ten 135
Chapter Eleven 158
Chapter Twelve 174
Chapter Thirteen 185
Chapter Fourteen 198
Chapter Fifteen 221
Chapter Sixteen 241
Chapter Seventeen 254
Chapter Eighteen 265
Chapter Nineteen 279
Epilogue 292
Acknowledgements 303

PROLOGUE

I WAS LOOKING TO MAKE A CHANGE. To get out of the rut I'd been living in. What I found was an ad that sparked my curiosity.

SEEKING ROOMMATE:
2-Story 2/bdrm apartment. Male tenant seeking roommate. Must pay $400/mo., half electricity, and water will be split. Cable and internet included in rent. Must pay bills on time. Prefer a male roommate, but will consider female. Please contact Dodger @ 555-3890 to schedule an appointment.

Sounded normal enough, didn't it? Not misleading, not out of the norm. Just a regular ad. Except it was misleading, and what I got was *so* not normal. In fact, I had no idea what I was getting myself in to....

CHAPTER ONE

"Keegan, I am going to need you to pick up your sister today from ballet practice. My boss called, and they want me to work an extra hour this afternoon," my mom called from inside the kitchen.

"Mom, I can't. I have a study group that is meeting right after my A&P class, and I can't skip this one. Can't you ask Uncle Murphy to get her?" I didn't mean to sound whiny, but honestly, I've had to miss out on the extra help, because my mom's job always seemed to need an extra hour.

She poked her head around the corner, her wild head of dark brown curls twisting every which way. "Seriously Keegan, I need you to do this for me. Your uncle has a life outside of us, and you know I can't tell my work no. We need the money, and I need this job."

Always the same guilt trip, just laced with different words. Rowan Phillips, my mother, has been a single parent since forever. My dad, aka-the sperm donor, left her when they accidentally got pregnant with me. When she told him, he ended up leaving town, and she never heard from him again. My mom had to drop out of school when her parents refused to help her. So as soon as she gave birth to me, she got a job. Growing up, it was always just my mom and me. It was an 'us against the world' sort of thing. But then one day when I was twelve, she sat me down and told me that she was pregnant. I remember that the words didn't make sense. I had a barrage of questions swirling around in my head, but only one that kept sticking out. How could she be pregnant again when she wasn't married? In fact, screw married, she wasn't even *dating* anybody! She explained to me that she'd been seeing a guy, mostly lunches here and there. Apparently my mother wasn't aware that there were methods to prevent getting knocked up. Now here we were, eight years later, and my little sister was bounding down the steps in purple leggings, a blue long sleeved top, and a yellow bow that bunched all of her hair, identical to my mom's wild mane, on the top of her head. She had my mother's eccentric tastes. I was surprised that she didn't get teased more at school.

I crinkled my nose at her outfit and sighed heavily. "Fine. But I can't miss another study session, okay? I'm already barely pulling a C in that class, and if I have any chance of getting accepted into nursing school, I really need to make sure I get some help. This has to be the last time."

She gave me her usual grin that let me know when she'd gotten her way. "Thanks kiddo."

"Sarah, you need to sit down and eat some breakfast." I poked her in the ribs as she passed by me, causing her to squeal. "With all of that dancing, I need to fatten you up."

I loved my little sister dearly. Hell, because my mom worked so much, I was practically raising her. She'd been a blessing in disguise that I'd never take back. I might get aggravated at our situation, or the fact that I had to take time away from something that was really important to me—school—but I *never* blamed her for it. And as much as I'd like to be mad at my mom for our lot in life, I just couldn't. I loved our little family.

"Do boys like skinny girls?" Sarah's question took me by surprise.

Raising my brow at her when we both sat down at the small kitchen table I asked, "What do you care if boys like you?"

She took a big bite of some oatmeal my mom had placed in front of her. "Well, some of the girls in my class said that boys don't like fat girls, and they only like the skinny ones. So why would you want me to be a fat girl? I want a boyfriend *someday* you know?"

I looked up at my mom who had her back to me. She was clearly laughing, because her shoulders were moving up and down. "Sarah, listen to me. Boys like girls of all shapes and sizes. If they all liked the same kind of girl, this world would be a boring place, and everybody would try to look exactly the same. And what I said was only a figure of speech. I don't really want to *fatten you up*, I was just saying you need to keep eating because you're so tiny." Why did I feel like I was digging an even deeper hole that held more questions?

My little sister sat there for a few moments, pondering over what I'd just said. It was amazing how the logic of a second grader worked, and you could actually see the wheels turning in her head. I was literally waiting for questions to be thrown at me. All of which involved the usual suspects: who, what, when, where, why, and how come.

"So do boys like girls to be tiny?"

My head hung down, and I let out a frustrated breath. "Mom, you can jump in any time now."

She chuckled as she placed the last dish in the dishwasher. "Now why would I do that? You seem to be handling yourself just fine."

Shoveling a few large spoonsful of my own oatmeal into my mouth, I stood up and dumped my bowl in the sink. "Sorry, but I don't have time for this right now. I'm going to be late for class." My mom could field the questions. As I walked out of the kitchen, Mom hollered at me not to forget about Sarah this afternoon. "I won't," I shouted back in annoyance.

Walking down the hall, I went into my bedroom to get dressed. I had class in thirty minutes. I wanted to take a shower, but I didn't have time too. Looking in my mirror, I sighed, threw my long blond hair up in a messy bun, and put on a white tank top with skinny jeans. The outfit would probably look cuter with boots, but I slipped on my flip flops instead. Grabbing my satchel, I headed out the door.

I pulled into the student parking lot with five minutes to spare, and thankfully I found a spot around the corner from the science building. I loved this campus, but the University of Georgia was huge, and finding parking wasn't always a picnic. Today was apparently my lucky day. Getting out of my car, I all but sprinted to my class. My teacher, Dr. Christensen, was a tough cookie, and if you were late, she made no exceptions. One minute past starting time, she locked the doors, and you couldn't come in. One missed day of Anatomy and Physiology and you were screwed! I've never been late, not once, and thankfully I made it just in time. As I passed by her when I walked through the door, she said, "Cutting it close Keegan."

"Yes ma'am. I'm sorry, it won't happen again." I kept my head down, scurried to my seat, and class began as usual. We went into great detail about the cardiovascular system and how the blood pumps through the heart. By the time I walked out, my head was spinning, and I wasn't sure how I was going to be able to keep the valves, atrium, and ventricles straight. This was why I needed my study group. Frustrated, I pushed out the door and into the sun, making my way to the Bulldog Café on campus where I met my best friend, Macie, for lunch every other day. This time of day was fairly quiet, because it wasn't quite lunchtime, and most classes were still going on. I went through the line, getting a small personal pizza and a soda before grabbing a table to wait for Macie. No sooner had I sat down than she came around the corner with a tray and a pissed off glare that told me I was about to get an earful.

Dropping her tray on the table, she flopped down into the chair across from me. "So last night, you know how I was supposed to go out with Mark from the basketball team, right?"

"Hello to you too," I said sarcastically.

"Seriously Keegan, are you listening to me? Skip the pleasantries and ask me about my date," she replied impatiently.

I smirked at her, knowing full well that she was only going to get more irritated if I didn't indulge her. "How was your date last night?"

She flung her arms up in the air in the most dramatic fashion and said, "Oh my God, it was awful!" I bit the inside of my cheek to prevent myself from laughing at her. "First it started off really great. He picked me up in this really hot car and was being such a gentleman. Did you know that guys who open doors for you still exist?"

"Mace, we live in the South, most of them do."

She was looking at me like I had grown two heads. "None of the ones I dated have."

I raised my brow. "That's because the ones you've dated are only looking to get laid."

"Shhh, I'm telling a story," she said, ignoring my very true statement. "Anyway, he was being sweet all night, opening doors for me, paying for dinner, holding my hand…then the end of the night came. He came inside and things started getting heated. I was really into it, he was *very* into it."

"So where's the problem? I don't want a play-by-play, Mace."

"I'm getting there Keegan. So I was laying down and he had taken off my pants, but just when I thought things were about to get really good....BAM!"

"What? Bam what?"

"His fingers started to go to town like some adolescent who was feeling up a vag for the first time. I mean, what in the hell? He seemed so confused down there."

Okay, now I couldn't hold back the smile that was creeping onto my face. "Confused how?"

"Keegan, he was fucking rubbing my clit like he was trying to start a fire. In fact at one point I'm pretty sure I saw a spark. Oh God." She put her head on her forearm. "My lady parts are so sore today, I'm pretty sure it's going to take a week to heal, and I *know* I'm walking funny."

There was no holding back my laughter. Served her right. Macie and I have been best friends since elementary school. Growing up together had always been interesting, I was the subdued quiet one while she was loud and liked the attention. I stayed back out of the limelight, while she soaked up every little bit of it. Macie was taller than me by five inches. She stood at five-foot-eight and had legs for days. Her long brown hair went to the middle of her back, and she had warm chocolate brown eyes. Guys flocked to her with a simple batting of her curved lashes. I was happy to stay in her shadow. The thing that I loved the most about Macie though, was that she always treated me like an equal to her. Most days I envied her, today however, she proved to me again why it was that I couldn't be in her shoes even if I wanted to.

"Do I need to take you to the store to find some burn cream? I'm not sure it can be put down there, but maybe the pharmacist could direct us…" I stopped talking when she shot me a look that said I'd better shut up. I coughed out a laugh. "Sorry, I'm sure it hurts."

"Yeah, your voice is just oozing sympathy."

"Hey," I said as she looked away from me, obviously more disgruntled than I originally thought. "I'm sorry, Mace, I didn't mean it. How did the rest of the night go? Did you at least tell Mark that he was hurting you?"

"S'okay. Nah, I just faked the orgasm of my life so he would get off of me. I wanted him to go home. Any sweetness was shot to shit with his lack of lovemaking skills. How was your night?" She changed the subject.

"Ugh! I have to head off campus to get Sarah from ballet practice and miss another study session. I'm floundering here Macie. I just got out of A&P, and I don't think I could tell you what way is up or down. I'm so confused, and my mom's constant need for help is going to prevent me from getting into nursing school." I was whining again, but I couldn't help it. If anybody understood my situation at home, it was her.

"I don't know how you deal with it. I love Sarah just as much as you do, but your mom has got to stop relying on you. Doesn't she realize that school is important? Have you told her that you're struggling and need the extra help?"

"Seriously, don't you think I've said something to her by now?"

She held her hands up, palms out. "You're right, sorry. You know you can always call me and ask me to help too. I don't know why you think you have to take everything on yourself."

Sighing I said, "Because you already do too much. I feel like I'm never going to be able to repay you."

She reached over and grabbed my hand, lacing our fingers. "Keegan, I love you. You're my best friend, and that means we are there for each other. You do more for me than you realize. I swear if it weren't for you, I probably would be knocked up already and following in your mom's footsteps. You keep me grounded. There's no such thing as repayment or scorecards in friendship. If you need me, tell me, and I'll be there no matter what." She squeezed my hand when she said that last sentence.

I looked across the table at her, my eyes feeling glassy from unshed tears. "I love you too."

She shook her head, her long brown locks falling over her shoulder. "Ack! Enough of this mushy shit, let's figure out what you're going to do."

Macie released my hand and sat back in her chair. "What do you mean 'figure out what I'm going to do'? What is there to figure out? I'm going to go find my TA after lunch, ask for the study guide, head to work for an hour, and then get Sarah."

"No, I meant in the long term. I think it's time you move out of that house and have your own space. Start living your own life."

I scrunched my nose. "I have my own life." She gave me a stern 'cut the shit' look. "Okay, so I don't have my own life. But that doesn't matter, does it? I have a job where I barely make more than what covers my expenses, let alone my mom's. I couldn't afford a place right now even if I wanted to."

Macie sat there clearly trying to think of a way around my predicament, her perfectly manicured French tip nails tapping on the table. I decided to take advantage of the silence and began scarfing down my pizza. The greasy cheese wasn't going to sit well with me later, but I was hungry and didn't care. I had just reached for my soda when her hand shot out and grabbed a hold of my wrist, startling me.

BENDER

"I've got it!" she shouted a little too loud.

"Jesus Mace, keep it down."

"Sorry." She looked around the still pretty empty space. "I know what's going to solve your problems," she said softer.

"Enlighten me, oh wise one," I said sarcastically.

"You can't afford a place on your own, and I'd totally be your roommate if I could, but Daddy gives me money, so I'm going to mooch while I can." The girl's parents were filthy rich. Her mom worked as a city councilwoman, and her dad was a doctor. I didn't blame her for drinking from that well while it was still providing.

"Okay, so what do you suggest?"

"Well, if *I* can't be your roommate, then let's find you one." She said it like it was the most simple explanation ever.

"Like where, Craigslist? I'm not looking for a roommate on Craigslist Mace. So don't even suggest it."

I was getting up to go dump my empty pizza box in the trash. "Not from Craigslist. Jesus, I don't want you killed by an ax murderer. I meant from ads posted around campus." She grabbed my hand and started pulling me to the Common Center where students went to study or hang out. "I've seen flyers pinned up on the bulletin boards. Let's see if we can find you a roomy."

When we got inside the building there were a few students milling about chatting and others with their nose stuck in a book. As soon as we opened the door, wind caught some of the papers that were hanging right inside, causing them to blow around. We scoured the boards for about five minutes, plucking off the little cut edges that had a name and phone number on them. Honestly, none of them looked promising. They either lived in a crappy part of town, or they wanted more than I could afford.

"Bingo!" Macie grinned while lifting up some papers covering the one she was reading.

I was shuffling the few that I had in my hand and trying to shove them in my back pocket. "What'd you find?"

Macie read the ad, but I didn't understand what about it made her say 'bingo'. "I hate to break it to you, but I'm pretty sure I heard you say they were looking for a male. Last I checked I wasn't sporting an extra appendage."

"No, it said they would consider a chick too. Just think about it. The Ridgewood Apartments are right around the corner from campus, and only two blocks away from your work. Those are really nice, and rent is within the amount you could afford. Plus, it's a guy. Who doesn't want to live with a hot guy twenty-four-seven? It beats living with some crazy-ass female who is constantly stealing your clothes and makeup. Dude I'd cut a bitch for touching my eyeliner."

I rolled my eyes. "Who said it was a hot guy? He could be a complete nerd who wears his pants up to his belly button, a pair of loafers with tassels, horn-rimmed glasses, and be covered in pimples. Better yet, he could be a gamer who doesn't move from the couch and smokes five packs of cigarettes a day, which if you think about it could endanger my life. He could fall asleep with a cigarette in his mouth, and next thing you know, you will be reading about me in the paper and how they could only identify my remains by my dental records."

She tore the number off the bottom of the page and handed it to me. "You're psychotic."

I slipped the paper in my back pocket and told myself I would throw it away later. "Be realistic Mace. None of these seem like they will work. I'm going to have to stay with my mom for a while longer until I can get my feet under me. At least then I could go find my own place and not have to worry if I'm signing a lease with the roommate from hell."

She stood with her hands on her hips, and she watched me for a second before she said, "Has anyone ever told you that you are a very pessimistic person?"

I smiled. "Only you. Now come on, I need to head to work, and you have class."

"Keegan, can you take that stack of papers and file them in the records that I left out last night? I'm so behind!" Marsha asked from her desk.

I worked part-time at a doctor's office in their medical records room. It was usually only Marsha and me that occupied this space. She had been here for almost ten years, and she was the one who hired me to help her out. When Doctor Hill increased his number of patients and hired a physician's assistant, Marsha's workload doubled. She was technically my boss and who I asked for time off or when I needed to cut out early to take care of stuff at home. I was thankful for that because she was nice to me.

"Sure, no problem!" I answered as I grabbed the papers and started the filing. "Ugh, when is Dr. Hill going to move to an electronic system?"

She looked up at me over the top of her leopard print glasses. "Probably never. He's old-school and likes to have a paper trail."

I grumbled as I moved between two tall shelves that housed stacks of medical records. While I filed I asked Marsha, "Hey you don't mind if I head out a bit early do you? My mom needs me to pick up my sister from practice."

"You know I don't have a problem with it."

We continued working for another hour before I needed to leave. I gathered my things and said goodbye before I stepped out into the bright sun. I shivered a little as I walked to my car. It was the middle of fall here in Georgia, and today it felt every bit of crisp and cool. The leaves hadn't started changing yet, but they would soon. This was my favorite time of year. Next month I'd be taking Sarah to the pumpkin patch out in the country so we could pick our own pumpkins for Halloween.

After picking Sarah up, I drove back to campus and met up with the TA so I could get the study notes for class. He went through a few things on the sheet to help me understand it better, but honestly I was more confused and deflated by the time I got back to my car. Sarah had been skipping along happily beside me, and it was unfortunate I couldn't mirror her enthusiasm. My A&P class was very important. The sciences held more weight on your academic record than say, sociology, when it came time to turn in your nursing application for the program. If I didn't walk away from this class with an A I would have to retake it. Looking at Sarah in the backseat bouncing around, I missed the days of being carefree. No worries, or cares other than deciding what I would have for a snack after school. Something needed to change. I was starting to think that maybe Macie was onto something. Could moving out be my answer to getting my life under control? How would my mom take the news? The guilt of leaving her and Sarah to fend for themselves was creeping up my throat and making my eyes sting. The fact that I felt that responsible for the both of them spoke volumes. Well, in my head it did, but the guilt in my heart was what led to me stay. When I pulled up at the house, Sarah unbuckled and went running inside. I sat in my car for a few more moments. My pocket held at least ten ripped pieces of papers with phone numbers on them. The mere idea of calling any of them made me leery. I'd never lived on my own. I knew I could take care of myself if I left, but I worried about what would happen with Mom and Sarah. Maybe I could just call a few of them to see what they were offering and make my decision after that? Who said I would have to commit to any of them just because I called to ask? Yeah, that was what I'd do. I got out of the car and walked inside. The problem: I knew as soon as the thought crossed my mind that I would find an excuse for each one of numbers I called. No matter how perfect they would sound, they just wouldn't work out for me.

 Mom came home an hour later than she said she would. When she walked through the front door, the air from outside blew in past her, and I smelled men's cologne wafting around her. I narrowed my eyes at her, and she knew I knew.

 "Don't start with me Keegan, I've had a bad day."

 "Hmmm... yeah, *smells* like it."

 "What's that supposed to mean?" She came in and set her purse on the table by the door.

 Sarah was in the other room watching television, so I knew she wouldn't hear us. "What it means, is that you are later than you told me you'd be, and I had to make dinner for Sarah."

 "You cook all the time Keegan, what's the big deal?" She spun around and walked into the kitchen. I followed her.

 "The big *deal* is that I had to miss out on another study session because you supposedly had to work late. Where were you?" I was trying to keep my voice down so Sarah wouldn't hear me.

"Jed from the office asked me out for a drink. We weren't gone that long. Cut me a break." She bent over in front of the fridge and started digging around. "Where are the leftovers?"

"There aren't any. I made Sarah a sandwich with chips. If you want something, make it yourself." I was so mad, I had to leave or I'd say something I'd regret. I marched up the steps, and I heard my mom say something about me being dramatic. Oh yeah, we would see who was dramatic. I was twenty years old and still living at home. Sick of feeling like a loser that was going to fail out of college, the papers in my pocket were a reminder of my possible solution. My mom had just pushed me enough that I was ready to take a leap of faith. Sitting down on my bed, I pulled them all out. Starting with the first one I grabbed, I made the call. Taking a deep breath, I heard someone pick up.

"Hello?"

"Umm, yeah, hi. I'm calling about the ad for a roommate."

CHAPTER TWO

THE NEXT DAY I MET UP WITH MACIE for lunch at a local deli. She was going to shit when she found out that I really called and scheduled to see some of these places. What she didn't know was that she was going to come with me to all of them. No way was I walking into a possible crazy person's lair alone and never coming back out. This was my best friend's idea, and by God she was going to die with me if that were the case.

When Macie came in, she ordered her food and slid in the opposite side of the booth. I must have had a look on my face because she immediately said, "What?"

"I called," was all I said.

She took a sip of her sweet tea and said, "Called what?" I sat there staring at her, waiting for her to catch up. I could practically see the light turning on in her head. "Oh my gosh you called!" She started bouncing around in her seat. "So what did they say? Anything sound promising?"

"Well, I don't know yet. I have three places lined up to visit today and I'll see if any of them work out. You're coming with me by the way." A worker came over and set our sandwiches in front of us.

"I am?"

"You are," I repeated. "I need you to come back me up so I don't look like some lonely girl who can be taken advantage of. And considering that two of these places are with a guy, I will need you."

"I thought I only tore off one who was a dude." She took a big bite of her tuna sandwich.

"Nope, but that's okay. I gave it a lot of thought last night. I almost cancelled them both this morning, but I think I'll be fine regardless. I never considered having a male roommate. Who knows, this could be a good thing."

She tilted her head to the side. "Aww, look at my little Keegan, being all grown up and not pessimistic." I rolled my eyes. "So what did they say? When are we meeting them? What spurred you to be all gung-ho about it?"

I sighed. "Honestly Mace, my mom came home late again last night."

"Oh honey, again? I'm sorry. What was her excuse this time?"

"She didn't need one. She reeked of a man, and I snapped. I'm never going to end up in nursing school if she keeps forcing me to take care of *her* responsibilities." I cringed at my own words. Sarah was never a burden on me. It was my mom pushing her off on me was. "I hate that I'm twenty years old and more mature than she is. Maybe me not being in the house for her to constantly depend on will make her realize that Sarah isn't my kid, and she needs to step up as the parent."

"I think I like this new Keegan."

I chewed my food before I responded to her. "This isn't a new Keegan, Mace. I've always thought this way but have never been brave enough to take the leap. Last night I had been studying before she walked in the door, and all I wanted to do was pound my head into the wall because I didn't understand the material. Then my mother waltzes in and acts like I was being ungrateful. I can't even be a sibling to Sarah, because I'm constantly playing the role of mom. It's time that I get myself out from under her so I can get my degree and get my life together." I paused to ponder saying this next part out loud. "I've been thinking that when I'm done with school, I want Sarah to move in with me."

Macie had been sitting there studiously listening to me ramble. My last sentence made her pause with her sandwich up to her mouth and look at me like I was nuts. "Are you kidding me? Keegan you can't take her. Your mom will never let you."

"It's not like I want custody or anything, I just want to give her a more stable living environment. I know what it's like living in a house where you have to raise yourself. And truthfully, I think my mom would take me up on it."

She shook her head. "So you'd rather make yourself live the same life, and play parent to your sister, than make your mom deal with the cards she was dealt in life? No, that's just crazy. I understand that you want something better for Sarah, but she's not your child, and you have your own life to live."

I pushed away my half eaten sandwich and leaned back against the cool plastic seat. I'd never really thought of it that way. If I took Sarah in after I got myself settled, was I just following in her footsteps? It wouldn't technically be the same. I would at least have graduated high school and furthered my education so I could take care of both of us. I closed my eyes and breathed in deep. The smell of fresh baked bread permeated through my nose. I think I needed to think about this some more. Maybe Macie was right.

"Change of subject. Where's the first place we are going to go check out?" she asked, snapping me out of my thoughts.

"It's a few blocks over, near all of the frat houses. The guy's name is Seth. We're meeting him in about thirty minutes," I said looking at the screen on my phone.

"Oh, Seth, me likey already." She wagged her eyebrows at me.

I laughed and balled up my napkin, tossing it at her face. "You're hopeless!"

We both got up from the table and threw away our trash. "Let's take my car. I'm not sure we'll survive the journey in your old rust bucket."

"Hey, you leave Nelly alone. I've had that car since high school, and she's gotten me through some really rough times." I stroked a hand down my fifteen-year-old silver Camry as we passed by it on our way to Macie's brand new Beamer.

"Yeah, yeah, shut up and get in." We laughed as we made our way to the first house.

By the time we pulled into the single car driveway, I was a ball of nerves. I apprehensively climbed out of the car and walked up to the front door. If first impressions meant everything, mine wasn't good. The house was a single story with dirt for a yard and cracked pavement leading up to the steps. The yellow paint on the house was peeling and gave it an old dilapidated look.

As we walked up to the steps, Macie leaned over and whispered, "He sounded normal on the phone right?"

She seemed as nervous as I felt. "Yes."

I knocked on the door twice and stood back to wait. I heard someone moving through the house before the door swung open. A tall, skinny, blond guy stood in front of me with a big grin on his face. He puffed out some air to blow his long shaggy locks out of his eyes and then reached out to shake hands.

"Hey I'm Seth, you must be Keegan."

I held out my hand and said, "Actually, I'm Keegan. This is my friend Macie."

I didn't know whether I should be offended that he assumed Macie was me, or if he had high hopes when he opened the door that my tall brunette bombshell of a best friend could be his potential roommate. Either way, I watched his smile falter a bit, and I knew I was right. Well, that was strike one against him. He quickly righted himself and shook my outstretched hand.

"Nice to meet you Keegan. Please, come in. I apologize for the mess. I just got out of class, and I didn't have time to clean up very much before you got here." He turned and made his way into what I assumed to be the living room.

I looked around the place and saw empty pizza boxes and beer cans strewn all about. It smelled like sweaty gym socks, and his furniture consisted of two lawn chairs and a television that sat atop of a couple of stacked pallets. There was a couch in the center of the wall upholstered in fabric covered with burnt orange flowers. It reminded me of something that would have been popular in the seventies.

Strike two.

"You can have a seat if you'd like." He pointed to the lawn chair.

I looked over at Macie and tried not to laugh. "That's okay. So can you tell me a little bit more about the place, and the room I'd be renting?"

"Room? This house is a one bedroom with a living room, kitchen, and bathroom. I have the bedroom, and you'd get the couch. But no worries about all your clothes and stuff. That closet behind you has plenty of space for those plastic Tupperware drawers."

Was he serious? Judging by the way he was looking at me, he was every bit serious. I swallowed hard. Oh boy, this wasn't good. "Uhhh... would you be willing to give me the bedroom so I could have a little bit more privacy?"

He glanced from Macie, whom he clearly was checking out, back to me. "Look, if you're worried about privacy, don't worry about that. I have a TV in my room so when it's time for you to sleep, I can just go back there. You can change in the bathroom, and I'll make sure the guys from my fraternity don't bother you when they are over. Ground rules will be laid out, and your stuff won't be messed with."

My mouth was hanging open by this point. "You can't be serious. This is a joke right? I'm being Punked. Macie," I turned to look at her, "cut the crap. You set this up, right?"

She bit her lip to keep from laughing. "No honey, I had nothing to do with this. I think Seth here is dead serious."

"What are you two talking about? It's a pretty sweet deal if you ask me. One of my frat brothers wanted the couch, but I told him it depended on what you thought. And truthfully, I sorta wanted a chick as a roomy." He grinned at me.

I shivered, grossed out. He genuinely thought I would take the offer. I didn't know if he was just stupid, on crack, or a combination of both, but there wasn't a woman on earth who would accept no privacy, plastic drawers, and not having her own bathroom.

Strike three.

"Unfortunately Seth, I don't think this is what I am looking for. But I do hope you find the right roommate." I turned to walk toward the front door, and Macie followed behind me.

"Well, if you or your friend ever change your mind, or are looking for a party, hit me up."

Macie turned toward him and gave him a salute. "Will do Sethy."

We shut the door and all but ran to the car. When we got into the Beamer I looked at her as she looked at me, and we both burst out laughing. She was putting the car in reverse, and I was never happier to leave a place.

"Oh dear God," I said wiping my eyes. "I feel sorry for the person who takes the couch. I'm pretty sure I saw the cushions moving."

She was in hysterics. "Stop, stop, I have to pee."

We laughed a bit more before she settled enough to say, "Okay, where's the next place?"

I gave her the address, and we were off to meet possible roommate number two.

This place was a bit better. It was a couple of miles south of the university, which was still okay. I couldn't necessarily walk to school or work, but driving wasn't so bad. It was a smaller apartment complex that appeared to be well kept. Granted, the building was a tad outdated, but that didn't mean the inside was shoddy. If there was one thing I knew, it was to never judge a book by its cover.

"This one is for the girl right?" Macie asked as she got out of the car.

"Yup." I looked down on the piece of paper I wrote her apartment number on. "She said she lived on the bottom floor on the corner."

We walked past a couple of doors before I found the number she'd given me. I knocked, and we waited. And we waited...and we waited some more.

"Are we early?" Macie looked at her phone.

"No, she told me she'd be here. Let me knock again." I put my fist up and pounded on the door with the padded side of my hand.

When the door opened, a short girl with jet black hair and a nose ring answered. Her eyes were caked with black eyeliner and her lipstick was... holy crap was that purple? She didn't say anything, she was just staring. I felt like her eyes were laser pointers, and she was shooting me with her death rays. Ack! I was already uncomfortable. Needing to break the awkward silence, I stepped forward and held out my hand.

"Hi, I'm Keegan, I called about the apartment."

She looked down and then back up at me. "Who's that?" Her head tipped toward Macie.

"That's my friend Macie, she's tagging along."

She looked Macie up and down, and then did the same to me. She must have deemed us acceptable, because she stepped aside and let us in. As I walked through the entryway hall, I heard music, if you could call it that. With each step I took, it got louder and louder. At first I thought, what an unusually long hallway, but when we got into the open living room, the better question was, how on earth did we not hear this racket from outside? There were drums set up in one corner with a guy sitting behind them, a microphone a few feet in front of the drums that another guy with a Mohawk was screaming into, and a person behind a guitar. I couldn't say whether or not said person was a guy or girl... those people Macie and I called Pat. Either a Patrick or a Patty, but you didn't know which. Turning around I looked at the girl who let us in. I oddly found myself hoping she was the possible roommate. She seemed less scary than Drummer boy, Mohawk Man, or Pat.

When the screaming/singing stopped, I asked Goth Girl, "Are you Jennifer?" I almost laughed at the sweet name for her.

BENDER

"Yes. These are my bandmates. I'll just start off by telling you that we practice every single day from three till seven, sometimes later. The manager let us soundproof the space when we moved in."

Macie mumbled under her breath, "That explains it." I bit my lip to stifle my laugh.

"Your room would be in the back. No overnight guests, if your friends have an issue with anybody in my band, you're gone, and I hope you're not a morning person because I sleep till noon."

Why was she still scowling at me like she wanted to pinch my head between her thumb and pointer fingers? "O-kay," I drew out. "Would you mind if I opened the blinds at least? It's pretty dark in here."

If looks could kill... "I'd rather you not. I like the dark. Dark makes me feel things, and then I write about it. The blinds stay closed."

This was obviously not going to work out, and I wasn't even interested in seeing the bedroom. "I think I'm going to have to keep looking Jennifer. I'm probably too much of a morning person for you, I like sunlight, and I'm sure I'd be too noisy. Oh, and I thrive off of country music." I added the last bit because I knew Macie was about to lose it.

"K. You know where the door is." She turned back toward the band, and they started their shouty singing again. Jennifer had effectively dismissed Macie and me like it was no sweat off her back.

I grabbed Macie's hand and hightailed it back down the long hallway and out into the sunlight. I took a deep breath in, not realizing I was feeling claustrophobic in the dark confines of the apartment.

"Holy shit, Keegan, I think you have hit the motherload of weirdos today."

"Geez that was creepy and I was oddly afraid for my life. By the way, what was your verdict on the Pat?" I asked.

Her grin spread. "I'm leaning toward chick. I was close to asking her to drop her pants so I could see."

"Hardy-har." We got into her car and sat there for a few minutes. I leaned forward and put my face in my hands. I dug my palms into my eyes and rubbed hard. What if they were all like this? I'd rather just stick it out at my mom's if they were.

"Stop it. I can practically hear your mind working over there. Knock it off. We have this last place to go to, and they say third time's the charm right?" Macie was trying to be optimistic.

"Or three strikes you're out."

She rolled her eyes. "The last place is by the school right? The Ridgewood Apartments?"

"Yup."

"Well, let's go. I have a feeling about this one."

Yeah, me too. Except my feeling was that I was going to be living with my mother for the next two years until I graduate.

We drove the few miles back toward campus and parked in front of the apartment complex. This was a place that I frequently passed by but had never been to. The grounds were well-maintained, there was a clubhouse that probably housed a small gym, and there was an outdoor pool and hot tub. No way would I be using those part of the facilities. I wasn't a super big girl by any means, but I was pretty average. I wore a size ten jeans and had more than enough tits and ass, but I was very self-conscious about my body and curves. No bikinis for me.

After the last two disastrous interviews, I wasn't holding my breath for this one. The apartment number I was given was on the second floor. I looked at Macie and took a deep breath. Just before I knocked the door opened. Air whooshed around me and I caught a smell that was so mouthwatering my knees almost buckled. It was some sort of soap and a light aftershave. My eyes traveled up the long lean legs that clearly belonged to a man. The further up my eyes went, the more I liked what I saw. Gym shorts covered a trim waist and a plain white Nike t-shirt was stretched over a muscled chest. When I finally reached the face of the person in front of me, all the air that had filled me before left my lungs in a rush. This guy had piercing blue eyes and dark hair that was disheveled from just getting out of the shower. I didn't have to look over at Macie to know that her jaw was hanging open like mine. Mister Hottie Pants gave us a delicious smirk that caused me to reach out for the door frame. He knew he was good looking, and I was hit too stupid to remember that I normally hated these kinds of guys.

More awkward silence ensued before he held out his hand and said, "Hi, I'm Dodger, which one of you is Keegan?"

CHAPTER THREE

MACIE NUDGED ME WITH HER ELBOW. Dodger noticed, and his smirk turned into a full megawatt smile. How was it possible for someone to have teeth like that? All white and shiny and straight... I continued to stare. Macie nudged me again, except harder this time.

I coughed and cleared my throat. Oh dear God I was a deer in the headlights that got smacked in the forehead by some *way* too hot dude who knew I was checking him out. This was my future roommate, and I was ready to sign up. He needed me to sleep on the couch-check. If he needed the house to stay dark during the day-check. If he needed to sleep till noon and bring over guys that looked like him on a regular basis-double check. Oh Jesus, he was still standing there with his hand out waiting for me to take it. *Get with the program Keegan*, I scolded myself.

"Gosh, I'm sorry. I'm Keegan, the one that called about the room." I stood there again with my hand in his large palm. I heard Macie clear her throat beside me. "Shit. And this is my friend Macie." I wasn't recovering from my bout of stupidity very well. "She came with me for some extra support. I hope you don't mind."

BENDER

He released my hand and shook Macie's as well. I watched her looking at him, and I recognized that sparkle in her eye. She was interested. Oh hell no, I was nipping this in the bud fast! No way was she ruining my possible perfect roommate situation because she wanted to jump in the sack with Mr. Hottie Pants. Ugh! And why did he have to look at her like he wanted to be doing the same thing? When they released each other, he turned to glance back in the apartment and said, "Please, come on in. It's pretty picked up for the most part, but then again, it usually is."

He turned around and in a few short feet, we were standing in an open concept living room. Off to the left was a kitchen that had espresso-colored cabinets lining one wall with a granite island. The living room ceilings were large and expansive. They reached all the way up to the second story where there was a small lookout with a wooden rail.

"The place is a two bedroom apartment. Majority of the rent is covered. Your portion would only be four hundred dollars, plus half the electricity and water bills. If you ladies wouldn't mind following me upstairs, I'll show you which rooms are which." His smooth Georgia accent was very evident.

Macie leaned over and whispered, "I'd follow him into a fiery inferno if he asked me to. Did you see that ass?"

Dodger looked over his shoulder and said, "It's from squatting. I could show you good form sometime," then continued up the stairs after winking at her.

For the first time since, well, since I've known Macie, she looked genuinely embarrassed. Her cheeks were pink, and she looked down. Boy she was really crushing on the guy, and it had only been five minutes. *Must be love*, I thought after rolling my eyes.

We got to the top of the beige carpeted staircase and there was once again an open space. I could see the rail that looked down to the living room in front of me. But off to the left there were two doors and to the right was one. Dodger opened the first door, and inside it was semi-dark because the shades were closed and heavy curtains blocked any light. A king-size bed in the center of one wall had a dark blue comforter and across from it was a large television mounted on the wall with a dresser just below. There was memorabilia on almost every single surface that I could see, but it was too dim to see what it was for.

"Here's the master bedroom. Sorry, obviously it's going to be a bit bigger than your room," Dodger said.

"Oh, that's not a problem. At least this one has a door."

Macie let out a little giggle. Dodger looked confused. She looked over at him with a smirk. "Don't ask."

He walked in front of us and crossed the space to the second closed door. "Here's the bathroom for upstairs. Unfortunately it'll have to be shared. But it shouldn't really be an issue. Well, unless you are wanting to put all that frilly pink shit on the toilet seat and a rug." I grinned and shook my head. "Okay good." He closed the door and went to the last opening. "Here would be your room. There's a lock on the inside, if you feel like you need it. Although I can tell you that your privacy won't be interrupted. Have a look around, and I'll be downstairs in the kitchen."

He turned and left. I stepped forward and turned on the light. The room was a clean slate. It wasn't huge, but it was bigger than where I was currently sleeping. My bedroom at home only had a bed and a dresser. But this room, this one I could put a bed, dresser, television on the wall, and a desk so I could finally have a place to study. I was mentally decorating the place and getting excited about all the possibilities. The only issue was that I wouldn't be able to bring any of my furniture from my mom's house. Even though it was mine, it technically belonged to her, and I still wasn't sure how she was going to react to me moving out. With all of the thoughts flying around, I realized that I really wanted to move out. It wouldn't take but a few months to earn enough money to start buying my own things. In the meantime I'd sleep on an air mattress. This apartment seemed perfect and almost too good to be true. College students didn't typically live in places this nice. There was a nagging feeling that there must be some kind of catch. Like, did Dodger walk around the house naked? That didn't really seem like a hardship I couldn't handle. Did he bring girls over every night? Again, I could just close my door and ignore it. Was I going to be forced to cook for the both of us? I already did that at home so it wouldn't make much difference.

"So what do you think?" Macie asked in a hushed voice.

I looked around again and glanced at the door. "It feels like I'm missing something. Like it's too good to be true, if that makes any sense."

She rolled her eyes. "Pessimist. Dodger was pretty straight forward with what's expected. I think you should take this one. Could you imagine going to anymore places like the last two?"

I shivered. "I'd rather fail A&P and live with my mom." She chortled. "It just seems too cheap though. I mean, four hundred dollars for a place like this? I mean, I know he said most of the rent is paid for, but why not split it evenly?"

Macie shrugged with indifference, and it frustrated me. Sometimes it was hard to remember that money meant nothing to her, and that was because she'd always had it. "Take what's being offered to you, Keegan. If you don't, some other college girl is going to swoop in and snatch this place up."

"And would that be because of Mr. Hottie Pants downstairs?" I raised my eyebrow at her.

"What? No! I'm not interested in Hottie Pa… I mean Dodger." Her cheeks were turning pink for the second time today. She grabbed my hand. "Listen to me, this isn't your typical college dorm room, or frat house, where you have no doors and bands screaming in your ears. This is a good shot Keeg, take it. Get out from under your mom's manipulation and start living your life. Mr. Hottie Pants just makes this place's rating go from a perfect ten to an eleven. He's just a bonus. But this place will be perfect for you."

I smiled at her, knowing she was right. "*If* I take it, you can't be sleeping with my roommate, Mace." She scrunched her nose up like she was going to argue. "No I mean it. You're my best friend, and I don't want you to come over here if things go sour, and it be awkward for everyone. Dodger is off-limits."

She huffed. "Fine. Can we go downstairs and at least give him the good news?"

I quietly clapped my hands like a young teenage girl. "Yes!"

She grinned big and tugged me toward the stairs. When we got downstairs, Dodger was sitting at the table that made up the dining room. It still opened to the living room and kitchen, but it was separate from both spaces. He had a couple of papers in front of him. As I approached, he must have read my face, because he gloriously smiled at me and slid the papers my way. It was seriously a sin to look that good.

"Here's the contract stating what you are expected to pay, the dates that everything is due, and a few other minor things that we didn't really go over. Like no painting the walls crazy colors, having overnight guests without letting the roommate know... blah, blah, blah, that sort of thing. Majority of it is basically taken verbatim from the lease that was signed to live here. I'm sure you understand." His blue eyes sparkled with excitement.

"Yes, I understand." I bit my lip to keep from reciprocating the grin.

"Okay then, here's a pen, and I put tabs where you need to sign." I took the pen from his hand and sat down in the chair next to him. Just as I pressed the tip against the paper, the front door opened and in walked a man that blew Dodger's good looks straight out of the water. He was tall and built. He was wearing gym clothes, and I assumed that was where he'd just come from. His brown hair was short, but spiky, and it was wet with sweat. The clothes he was wearing were clinging to him like a second skin, and I could see the outline of sweat across parts of his shirt. My eyes took in every inch of him as he stepped inside and set his gym bag down near the kitchen. I gasped when he bent over, and I got a good look at his backside. Ever heard of the term 'buns of steel'? I think he gave it new meaning. When he stood back up, he grabbed a water bottle from the fridge and started chugging as he slowly turned around. He must have finally sensed that there were people in the room watching him. When I got a good look at his face, I gasped again but more audibly. Dodger was trying not to laugh beside me, and Macie's mouth was once again gaping open like a fish. His face looked so familiar and yet not. His cheeks were high and sharp, and his jaw was perfectly square. What stood out to me the most were his eyes. Almond shaped and dark chocolate brown eyes were narrowed, looking at me and the pen in my hand. I gulped. He looked almost menacing how he watched me.

"Dodger, you fucker, you can't interview people without me here." His voice sent a shiver down my spine. It was deep, and it resonated inside my chest.

He held up his hands. Still smiling like this guy had no effect on him. "You told me to interview, so I did. And," he looked over at me, winking, "I've found you a roommate."

"Excuse me?" His hard brown eyes turned back to me. "You just gave her the contract to sign without discussing with me if it was okay?"

The way he said '*her*' made me feel like I was small and insignificant.

"She's just what you're looking for. I figured you wouldn't mind."

Dodger's nonchalant attitude about the situation was putting me on edge. My brain was having trouble catching up with the conversation, but when it did, it all clicked into place.

"Wait a second. You don't live here?" I aimed my question to Dodger.

"Nah, that dickhead does." He nodded toward Mr. Tall, Dark, and Angry. "He's my brother. I'm here a lot more than my other brothers, so I took on the role of interviewer."

An excited sounding Macie said, "There's more of you?" I kicked her under the table. "Ouch!"

Dodger's head tilted to the side, but he smirked at my friend. "Yes, there's four of us." He was well-aware of what he was doing to her.

"Wait, wait, wait. You made me think *you'd* be my roommate."

"You assumed I'd be, but I never once said I lived here." I scowled at him. "Alright, I supposed I wasn't exactly forthcoming with the info but my brother here can be kind of temperamental, and he's scared off a few others who have come to see the place."

Yeah, no kidding. His arduous eyes watching me, I could see the tick in his jaw as he ground his teeth together. "Dodge, get your ass in here, we need to talk."

I glanced over at Macie, and her expression was dancing with delight. Yeah I bet she was excited. A little bit of drama with a couple of good-looking guys thrown in the mix, she lived for this stuff. Me on the other hand, my stomach was churning, and I felt like getting up and leaving. I kept playing over and over again how Dodger showed me every room, but he really never did say that it was *his* room, *his* bathroom, *his* apartment. My head was starting to hurt. Rubbing my temples with my fingertips, I had my elbows on the table to support me. This wasn't going to work out. This was the ball I knew was going to drop. Nothing ever went right for me. I could hear Dodger and his brother, whose name I hadn't yet gotten, speaking low but loud enough to catch.

"You dumb bastard, it's not you living with a stranger, and I need to approve of them," the brother said.

"You wanted a fuckin' roommate, well I happen to think she's perfect. She's quiet, she's going to school at the college, she hasn't indicated that she has a boyfriend who will be coming over, and she has a steady job, what more could you want?" Dodger sounded like he was getting frustrated.

My face heated up with embarrassment. I would have preferred that my singlehood stayed private and not be broadcasted. "Which chick are we talking here? The pretty one, or the chubby one?" the ice cold voice said a little louder, and I knew he knew I could hear him. My head snapped up, and I glared. He was looking right at me.

Dodger spoke a little softer but was definitely menacing in his words toward his brother. "The blonde. Her name is Keegan, and she's signing the goddamn papers. I'm not going through this again, brother. Go meet your new roommate and take a fuckin' cold shower, you stink." With that he grabbed some keys that were laying on the counter and walked toward the door. Before he left he addressed Macie and me, "I hope you like the place. We'll be seeing a lot of each other." He looked at his sibling and pointed. "Play fuckin' nice." Then he turned and walked out.

 I kept my eyes level and didn't remove them from the guy who was still staring at the door. I could have sworn I heard him growl. Resigned, he scrubbed his hand down his face and back up again into his messy hair. When his arm dropped by his side, he turned to face me. Straightening my back, I accepted his scrutiny. I wouldn't show him that his words stung a bit harder than I should have allowed. This guy was clearly a gym rat. His muscles had muscles, and I haven't stepped foot in a gym since… well since I was in high school and was forced to participate. I refused to let someone make me feel less than what I was and certainly not this asshole. His eyes remained on me the whole time, never once looking at Macie. That had never happened before. She was always the noticeable one. I blended into the walls. He'd obviously formed some sort of opinion about me, because he shook his head and walked over to stand in front of the table. He loomed over the two of us before he finally spoke.

 "Sign the papers. No boyfriends, no chick parties unless I know about them, I'm the one who goes grocery shopping and does the cooking, and no loud music. You stick to those rules, and we won't have any problems with each other." His eyes narrowed the slightest little bit at the corners.

 "And what if I don't agree to them?" I asked, addressing him for the first time since he walked in.

 He placed his large hands on the table and leaned in so he was closer to me. I could smell his sweat and some other delicious scent that invaded my senses. "Believe me Blue, you won't find another place like this with my same offer. You'd end up paying twice what I'm asking. So sign the fuckin' papers. There's a spare key in the basket by the sink." He stood up and started walking upstairs.

My head was swirling. "Wait, Blue? My name is Keegan. And I didn't even get yours."

It was all I had to argue with. He knew he had me, and I was going to sign regardless. Hopefully we didn't end up killing each other before the year was up.

He paused a few steps up but didn't turn around. "Nothing to explain. And the name is Camden." Then he continued upstairs, and I heard the shower running.

"Holy shit on a stick, this is going to be fun," Macie said, smiling bigger than I'd ever seen.

Holy shit was right.

CHAPTER FOUR

My first week in the apartment was a bit sketchy. The night I signed the papers I went home to tell my mom and sister I was moving out. My mom didn't have much to say. I think she realized what was in store for her, and her partying and days of relying on me so much were going to be nonexistent. She looked at me, simply said, "I hope you're happy," and walked away. I wasn't sure how to take those four words. She was either being flippant and snarky, or she was sad and didn't know what else to say. Sarah, on the other hand, didn't take the news well at all. She cried and ran into my arms. As sad as it was, I explained to her that I was an adult, and I needed to be out on my own. I made sure she knew that she could come see me anytime she wanted, and she could have a sleepover if she missed me too much. When I told her that, my thoughts drifted to Camden, and I mentally high-fived myself. His little rules didn't include no sleepovers with little sisters, so take that to the bank. I brought her over to see it a couple days later. Mom didn't want to come, which was fine, and thankfully Camden was out. Sarah fell in love. She ran all over the place and dove onto the couch. I laughed at her silly lightheartedness. She was going to be fine, and I planned on bringing her over as much as possible.

I found out after a couple of days living here that Camden was a gym owner. I'd gone over and over in my head how a college student could possibly afford to live here and ask so little for my portion of the rent. I chalked it up to the same situation as Macie. I figured Mommy and Daddy paid for everything. I was very much off my mark. I never pegged Camden as being a business owner, and it turned out he wasn't a college student. I would question him about it, but he was hardly ever home. And when he was, he never had much to say. I had scolded myself those first few times when I heard the front door open, and my heart would pick up its pace, knowing who it would be. What he said to Dodger that first day was etched into my memory, 'the chubby one'. I hated that I found him attractive, but any attraction I felt for him faded quickly when he brought a girl home and had flaunted her right in front of me. Unfortunately she wasn't the first one, either. Like all the others, she was the exact opposite of me. Where I was just over five-foot-tall, she was statuesque at around five-foot-ten. My hair was long, wavy, and blond, while hers was short and jet black. I was slightly on the more curvy side, but this chick was stick thin. He walked in, and her hand was in his back pocket, following slightly behind him. I had been sitting on the couch studying for a history exam when they had stopped in the kitchen. He went to the fridge and began digging around for something. When he turned around he had a can of whipped cream and a bottle of wine. He gave her a sexy smirk, and she giggled at him. Camden handed her the items and opened the cupboard that had the wine glasses. That was when she finally turned in my direction and saw me sitting there, watching them. Her eyebrows rose as though slightly startled.

"Who's she?" the woman asked. Her tone was confused and slightly put off.

Camden had two glasses in his hand as he faced where she was looking. He looked at me, his brown eyes boring into mine and replied, "Nobody, just my roommate."

She accepted his answer as all the explanation she needed. They both made their way upstairs to his room, and I heard the door close. I didn't need much of an imagination to know what was going to happen. I sat there playing his words over in my head. I was nobody? He hadn't even bothered to try to get to know me. How could I possibly be *nobody*? Was I that offensive to him? The more I thought about it, the angrier I became. Instead of extending any olive branches to him, I'd be more than happy to be 'just the roommate'. No friendship was required for our living arrangements. I'd hoped I could be friends with him, but it seemed that he wasn't interested. Closing my book, I picked up my stuff and went upstairs. Shutting my door quietly, I thanked the wall gods for making ours a little thicker than normal apartments. I couldn't fathom having to hear them getting it on. I'd probably puke.

Flopping down on my air mattress, I curled under the covers. I looked around the still very empty space of my room. I was able to buy some curtains to cover the window, and a mirror to lean against the wall, but any other purchases would have to wait. I'd like to get an actual bed, because this blow-up bed was hurting my back, but it wasn't a priority right now. What I needed was a laptop so I could do my school work from home, a dresser, and some hangers for my clothes. *Then* I'd get a bed. I figured it would take me a few months to make all of the purchases, but I was okay with that. It would be mine, something that I would have worked hard for and paid for with my own money. For now, this would have to do.

BENDER

Lying there I ended up deciding that I'd live here like I was the only person. When my rent was due, I'd leave it on the counter, along with any of my other bills that needed to be paid. I would go out tomorrow and buy a lock for my door, so I could ensure that I had the privacy that I required. I didn't need any of Camden's bimbos wandering into my room thinking they could take whatever they wanted. I'd also keep any communication with him to a minimum. If I was nothing to him, then he'd be nothing to me. Feeling more settled in my plans, I scooted further down into my uncomfortable bed and drifted off to sleep.

The next day I woke up and took a deep breath in as I stretched my arms above my head. I smelled something that made my stomach growl. What was that, bacon? I got out of bed and rubbed my eyes with the palms of my hands. Throwing on my ratted pale yellow robe, I went downstairs. I was sure my hair was all over the place, but since I'd decided I no longer cared about Camden and what he thought of me, it didn't matter what I looked like. As I hit the bottom step, I saw him in the kitchen with his back turned, and he was flipping eggs in a pan. He either heard me or sensed me because he turned around and saw me standing there. The chick who looked like a model was nowhere in sight. I wondered if he made her go home last night after he was done with her. It wouldn't surprise me. I squirmed a bit at Camden's perusal of me. His eyes went from my messy hair and traveled the length of my body, taking in the robe and my bare legs that showed. Wherever his eyes touched felt like a caress against my skin. Why was he looking at me like that? I shook my head. I was sure he was wondering how he got stuck with someone like me for a roommate. My appearance was less than fabulous this morning.

Unsure what to do, at first, I stood there chewing on my lower lip. I liked his eyes on me, but I also hated what I knew he saw and thought. He looked like he'd already run a marathon, or whatever the hell he did in the mornings. His hair was sticking up every which way, and he was wearing a black shirt with the sleeves torn off. His tanned arms flexed like they knew someone was watching. His blue shorts were long and went to his knees, the mesh material forming over parts of him that I shouldn't be thinking about right now. Straightening my back, I moved forward toward the kitchen. *Do not go there Keegan.* Coffee was on my mind, and there was a fresh pot already brewed. I stepped around Camden as he stood in front of the stove and went to the cupboard that held the coffee mugs.

"Morning," he said, his voice deeper than normal. I gripped the mug tighter.

I didn't turn to look at him, nor did I reciprocate his greeting. I went to the coffee pot and filled my mug. Opening the fridge I grabbed the milk and poured a few splashes. The canister of sugar was next to the fridge, and I put two teaspoons in my cup and began stirring. I felt Camden's eyes on my back, but I refused to look at him.

I heard him sigh and then he said, "I've made breakfast. Whole wheat toast, egg whites, and turkey bacon. I'll put your plate on the breakfast bar." I heard the clink of the plate as he set it down.

If he was waiting for an acknowledgement from me, he wasn't going to get one. I was shocked he even thought to make me a plate. Then again, with what he made, he was probably trying to put me on a diet thinking I wouldn't notice...or he poisoned it. Screw him. Despite my growling stomach I took my mug and started walking out of the kitchen. I'd get breakfast in town on my way to get Sarah. She was coming over to spend the day with me, and we were going to veg on the couch.

"You're seriously not going to eat?" he asked before I could start upstairs.

This time I did turn to look at him. "Why cook me anything? I'm just the roommate right? Cook for yourself." With that, I went upstairs. A few seconds after I closed the bathroom door, I heard a crash, and the front door slammed. Fantastic…I pissed the grizzly off.

After getting showered and dressed I headed downstairs. I looked in the sink as I passed by. The plate of food he made me was dumped and broken into a few large pieces. Sighing I took the broken glass out and threw them away, then shoved the food down the disposal. I wanted to feel bad for what I said to Camden, but I couldn't. He needed a lesson on how to treat people, and I refused to be uncomfortable in my own home.

I'd gone to get Sarah after cleaning up the mess, and we'd picked up a few movies from the store as well as a bag full of candy. I had a serious sweet tooth, and I had yet to find an eight-year-old who didn't have the same problem. She wanted to watch *Despicable Me* first. Popping the movie in, the previews were just starting when the front door opened. Dodger came walking in, and he got a load of the candy spread on the coffee table. He smiled big.

"Hey girls, whatcha doing?"

Dodger had already met my sister, and they got along good. "Watching a movie, wanna watch it with us?" Sarah asked.

He nodded.

"You can have Keegan's Laffy Taffy, but you can't have my Nerds. I don't share those."

He laughed and ruffled her wild curls as he sat down beside her. "I'm actually eyeballing those Snickers."

She gave him a hard face. "You can have *one* but no more."

"Fine, one is plenty. But what about the other candy?"

"Are you kidding? You eat more than that candy bar you'll have a tummy ache!"

"Well, then I'd better just stick to the one." He smiled at her.

I was grinning at their exchange. Dodger was very much like a kid. His carefree attitude and fun spirit was exactly why I loved having him over all the time. I saw him more than I saw Camden. I really wished it would have been him who lived here. The three of us watched the movie together and laughed when I did impersonations of Steve Carrell's voice. When it was over, I put in the next one and let Sarah start it. I took advantage of her zoning out and grabbed a bag from the counter and headed up to my bedroom door. I'd bought a new door handle that had a lock on it so I could lock it from the outside. I'd assumed Dodger had fallen asleep when I started the next movie, but apparently I'd been wrong. I heard him behind me clearing his throat.

"What are you doing?"

I startled. "Gah! Could you not sneak up on me like that? I have a screwdriver in my hand."

He smirked. "I see that. What's wrong with the doorknob that was already on there?"

I looked at him for a few seconds before turning back to the task at hand. "I'm changing them out so I can make sure I've got complete privacy, especially when I'm not home."

He chuckled. "I can assure you, Camden isn't into chicks' clothes."

"Ha, ha smart aleck. I'm referring to the Amazon women he brings home every night. I don't trust *them* to not come in and think it's a free-for-all in my room and take my things," I grumbled.

Dodger touched my shoulder. "Wait, he's been bringing home women?"

My eyebrows drew together. "Yeah, he's brought at least three here since I've moved in. Why?"

His face looked confused. "Nothing, don't worry about it." He stood behind me, completely quiet as I worked. When I stood up, I opened the door so I could test the lock. I heard Dodger groan.

"What the fuck, Keeg." He pushed me aside and hit the light switch on the wall.

"Hey, what are you doing?" I tried to maneuver in front of him and shove him back out. He wouldn't budge. His eyes took in every bare inch of the room. By the time they met mine, he looked confused and mad. "Where's all your furniture? I thought you said you were all moved in."

My shoulders drooped, and my voice got quiet. "I am. This is all I have."

His head was shaking back and forth. "This isn't cool Keegan. You don't even have a goddamn bed!"

"Why are you shouting at me? It's not like I don't plan on getting more furniture, I just can't afford it right now. And my mom wouldn't let me take the stuff from my room." I kept my eyes down, and I couldn't look at him. Why did I feel so ashamed?

He tipped my chin up so I was looking at him. "I can buy you a bed, Keegan. It's not a problem."

I jerked my head away. "No! I'm not a freaking charity case, and I'm working for what I have. I'll be able to get everything I need in a few short months, so stop worrying about me, and wipe that look off your face."

His mouth thinned in a frustrated line. "You know I'm going to tell him."

"Tell who?"

"Camden."

My stomach dropped, and I immediately became defensive. "You tell that bastard anything, I'm gone. I'm not dealing with your pity, and that asshole's judgment being thrown in my face. I may not have a set of parents who give me whatever I need, but I'm capable of taking care of myself. Camden doesn't need to know anything about me. He passed judgment on me the moment he set eyes on me. So please, keep this to yourself, okay?"

He watched me for a few short seconds before he scrubbed his hand down his face. "Fine, but you know he's going to notice this at some point."

"No he won't. And even if he did, he wouldn't care." I knew he wouldn't.

He shrugged. "If you think so. But I have a feeling it would bother him more than you think."

"Whatever. Let's go back downstairs so I can finish this movie with Sarah and get her back home."

As I shut the door and used my new lock, I heard the front door open and close.

"Who the hell are you?" Camden's deep voice boomed through the open space.

"I'm Sarah, who the hell are you?"

Dodger was already at the bottom of the steps chuckling at my sister's response, and I was trying to shove the key in my pocket and race down the steps without falling.

"Sarah!" I scolded. "Watch your mouth."

She shrugged indifferently. "What? He started it."

I seriously hoped my mother wasn't letting her talk like that while I wasn't around. Camden looked over at me as my feet hit the last step and started to glance back at Sarah but did a double take at Dodger and me standing together. I gulped. I had an idea of what it looked like since we'd both come from upstairs.

His jaw worked back and forth. "She belong to you?"

My mouth opened, then closed, then opened again. I wasn't sure how to respond to his sudden anger. His tone was clipped and the way he referred to my sister was as if she were an inanimate object. "If by *belonging* to me you mean, is this my sister, then yes, she *belongs* to me."

"Huh," he grunted. "I didn't know you had a sister."

I took a defensive stance, crossing my arms over my chest. "You might if you were around more. This is the third time she's been here."

His eyes flared. When it came to Sarah, I never held back. I'd played mama bear to her on more than one occasion. This was no exception.

"Yeah well, I work. You know, going out and earning a paycheck." His sentence was dripping with sarcasm, and it ruffled my feathers.

"Excuse me? I work. How do you think I pay for this place?"

"Doesn't matter how you earn it. As long as you're paying, I don't care."

"Oh well that's a real fantastic attitude to have about someone living in your house."

"It is what it is, Blue." He shrugged, and it made my blood go from a slow simmer to a boil.

"Seriously, what's with the nickname?" I nearly shouted.

"Hey," Sarah piped up over the top of the couch. "Trying to watch a movie here."

"Yeah, she's trying to watch a movie, keep it down," Dodger cut in. I'd totally forgot he was still standing there, and he was looking highly amused by the heated argument Camden and I were having.

"Shut up Dodge," Camden clipped.

His younger brother just chuckled. "No way man. I agree, the kid is watching a movie, and you two are making it difficult to hear." He looked between us. "Shew! There's some serious sexual tension in this room."

Camden growled and ran his hands through his sweaty dark hair. "Christ, you don't know when to fucking quit."

"What's sexual tension?" Sarah's curious eyes peered at me.

I turned to glare at Dodger and Camden. Flinging my hands up in the air and slapping them back down on my legs. "Oh my gosh!" I exclaimed, grinding my teeth together. Whispering really low, I pointed to both of them. "Thanks a lot. And watch your mouth. She's only eight." I moved toward the couch and said, "Sexual tension is just when everyone is really happy and having a good time."

I heard someone snort behind me. That was it, Sarah wasn't coming back here until I gave both of them a talk about how to behave in front of my little sister. I could picture it now. Sarah was at school, and my mom gets a call because my little sister was loving the sexual tension on the playground. I sighed.

"Wellllll…this has been fun, but I have places to go, chicks to meet," Dodger said before Sarah could ask anything else.

He put his hand on my shoulder as he walked past me. He bent down and kissed me on the top of my head. I don't know why it didn't seem odd, considering he hadn't known me that long, but Dodger made me feel comfortable, and I knew it was just a friendly gesture. "Be good," he whispered in my ear. I nodded slightly and watched him walk out the front door.

I risked a glance over my shoulder at Camden. His eyes were fixed on me. Why was he looking at me like that? He closed his almost russet eyes and breathed in through his nose. When he opened them again, he focused on my sister. "Hey kid," he tilted his head toward the TV, "what're you watchin'?"

Sarah eyed him skeptically. "Beverly Hills Chihuahua, wanna watch it with me?" Clearly his demeanor didn't intimidate her.

"Depends, is it any good?" He started moving toward her, passing me on the other side of the couch.

"Duh, it's about dogs. Anything with dogs is good."

His body nearly brushed mine as he walked by. I involuntarily breathed in, and his scent crashed into me like a ton of bricks. It was so clean, and yet he was still sweaty. I gripped the back of the couch.

He sat down on the opposite side from her and continued to talk. "Do you have a dog?"

She shook her head. "No, Mom won't let me have one. She says they're too much work."

He nodded. "I grew up with dogs, and they are a ton of work. But maybe someday you will get one."

As angry as he made me, his softer attitude toward Sarah was a refreshing change. Having a man in the house who was always irritable and broody made my normally happy disposition negative. In the week that I've lived here, I found it exhausting. Looking at Camden sitting with Sarah watching a totally ridiculous movie, I felt like the universe had tilted. How on earth did my baby sister penetrate his 'don't mess with me' shell? Maybe he liked kids. The two of them looked pretty settled. I ran my hand through my long hair. It looked like I'd better get comfortable, because I wasn't expecting my night to take this turn.

Three hours and another movie later, Sarah was passed out cold. It was almost eight o'clock, and I needed to get her home. I stood up and stretched my arms high above my head. My back popped, and I groaned. It felt better after sitting so stiffly for so long. I refused to look at Camden when the movie was over. He had seemed on edge with me, and I wasn't in the mood for another showdown tonight. Stepping over to Sarah, I was about to bend down to pick her up when Camden shifted and lifted her in the air before I even got a chance to. I raised a brow at him, questioningly.

"Open the door for me, would ya?" His voice rumbled, but no longer held the edge that it had earlier in the evening.

I went to the front door and opened it. Moving in front of him, I walked out to my car and heard him following behind me. Pushing the unlock button, the lights flashed in the dark parking lot. I opened the back door and watched how careful he was with her. The way he gently tried not to jostle her was almost endearing.

Almost.

When he closed her door he turned and faced me. His hard eyes had a softer feel, and yet they were still intense. A moment seemed to pass between us in the few short seconds we silently regarded each other. He began to open his mouth, but closed it, almost as if he'd thought better of it. Shaking his head, he opened my door and stood back on the sidewalk. I climbed in and started the car. When I backed out I watched in my rearview mirror and noticed Camden hadn't moved. As uneasy as he'd made me feel since the moment I met him, I appreciated his help with Sarah, but it grated my nerves that I'd need to thank him for helping me out with her when I got home.

By the time I'd gotten Sarah back and tucked her in, I had exchanged a few words with my mom. She was yelling at me for keeping her out so late and said I should have just let her stay with me. It only served to flip a switch and tick me off. I accused her of only saying that because she wanted to go out and party, and she couldn't if I was bringing Sarah back home. Her arguing escalated, and I decided that I no longer had to listen to it. I moved out for more than one reason, and this was one of them. It was almost eleven when I'd gotten back home. I was exhausted and ready to go to bed.

Walking into the apartment, the downstairs was completely dark. Camden must have either gone to bed, or he was out again. My stomach dropped at the idea of him being out with another girl, but I quickly squashed the disappointment. I had no claim to him, nor did I want one. He was my roommate, and that was it. Definitely wouldn't be thanking him for helping me earlier. I fumbled up the steps and was just unlocking my door when the bathroom door opened. Camden stepped out into the hallway and steam floated out around him. He had a dark blue towel wrapped low around his waist, and there were still water droplets descending down his perfectly chiseled abs. There was a very defined V with a trail of dark hair that went beneath the towel. I found myself taking in every inch of his perfect form. And when I said perfect, I meant there wasn't a single flaw to be found on him. I had no idea how long I stood there nearly drooling on the carpet, but when my eyes reached his, he had a half a smirk on his face. *Oh God, please don't gloat that I was checking you out, please.* My overtired brain couldn't take it.

Instead, he stepped forward till we were almost toe to toe. His dark chocolate eyes roamed my face, like he was trying to find something. I stood completely still allowing him to search my features. My breathing had picked up, and the rise and fall of my chest was a bit faster than normal. If he noticed, he didn't indicate it. His breathing was still normal, and I sank a little that I didn't have the same effect on him. Being this close, I couldn't look in his eyes. I didn't know what I'd see in them. Eye contact without anger felt too personal. I didn't want to be personal with him. At least I didn't think I did, so my eyes remained on his chest. But then he did something that seemed so out of character, it startled me. His left hand came up and he tucked a few strands of my blond hair behind my ear. It was so subtle and yet very intimate. I sucked in a gulp of air, and my knees almost buckled when I caught the scent of him. It was so clean and warm that it made me want to wrap myself up in it and get lost. I'd been in the shower plenty of times, and I knew what his soap smelled like. This was soap and something that was just him.

Intoxicating.

"Glad you made it back safe. You were gone for a while," he said quietly, almost as if his words were going to shatter the trance he'd put me in.

I couldn't speak. My mind was a blank slate, and no words could be formed. He'd officially rendered me speechless. Between his closeness, his scent, and the burning trail that his fingers left on my skin, I was lost. He had to know what he was doing to me. Nobody that looked like him didn't realize how they affected people. In this moment, if he told me to jump, I'd say, "how high?"

Instead of reeling me in further, he broke the spell he had put me under. He quietly said, "Night Blue," and he turned to walk into his bedroom.

When his door shut, I sagged against the wall. My poor little synapses were firing in all different directions, and I was trying regain my footing. What in the hell just happened here? And seriously, where had he picked up the name Blue? I shook my head and went into my room, locking the door behind me. It wasn't that I didn't feel safe, especially with Camden across the hall. But I wasn't sure that I wouldn't have some crazy dream and sleepwalk my way into his room and rape the man. He was getting to me, and I needed to nip that in the bud quick. His hot and cold behavior was too much. It had only been a week, and I wasn't sure I could deal with it for an entire year without losing my mind. Dodger stating that there was sexual tension was laughable. I might have felt the urge for the first time tonight in the hallway, but there was definitely *nothing* registering on his side. Tomorrow, I was going to have to set him straight. No more Asshole Camden, and definitely no more Touchy Feely Camden. I wanted to be able to walk into my house and know who it was that I was going to be coming face to face with every day. There, it was settled. My nerves were shot, and my body was needy for something, but I had to ignore it. I'd settle it all tomorrow when I got up. Hopefully I'd catch him before he left for the gym. Closing my eyes, it took forever for me to nod off. When I finally did, I dreamed of towel clad Camden and all the naughty things I'd like him to do to me.

CHAPTER FIVE

I HADN'T GOTTEN MUCH SLEEP last night due to a certain male in the house inducing butterflies in my stomach and giving my brain whiplash. Being up before Camden wasn't an issue this morning. I decided to stop tossing and turning at around five and went downstairs to read a book. I heard creaking upstairs about an hour later, and it didn't take long till a groggy looking Camden came trudging into the kitchen to start a pot of coffee. He was wearing a pair of dark grey sweats that curved over his perfectly toned ass. His upper body was bare of any clothing. The defined muscles in his back moved as he filled the pot with water. All tan and smooth skin, my mouth went dry with his every movement. *Why must he walk around half naked and be all delicious?* I nearly groaned when he turned around and faced the living room. He had yet to see me, and I was thankful because it spared me a few extra seconds to scrutinize his every inch. Camden leaned down and placed his elbows on the counter, resting his head in his hands. He was a picture of perfection. Looking at him now, I only hoped that I'd be able to speak to him without making an issue out of how he'd treated me during my first week here. The coffee pot behind him beeped, and he rubbed his hand through his unruly hair and tugged at the ends. Standing up, he was about to turn when he caught me looking at him.

"Morning," I said shyly. I looked down to the book I'd closed and rested on my lap.

When he didn't reciprocate my greeting I glanced up at him. His dark eyes were on me, but I couldn't tell what kind of mood he was in. "What are you doing up?" His normally deep voice came out rough and scratchy.

"Couldn't sleep."

He regarded me before turning away. "Coffee?"

"Please," I said, getting up from the couch. I walked over to the island and sat down. He poured two cups. He made my coffee just as I had the other day; splash of cream and two teaspoons of sugar. I hadn't realized he paid that close of attention.

He passed the mug to me and I said, "Thanks," enveloping my hands around the almost too hot cup. The silence was making me squirm, and I felt as though I needed to start this conversation before I chickened out. "Are you always up this early?" I took a slow sip of the steaming joe. He'd made it perfectly.

I noticed his eyes were watching my mouth as I licked any stray drops of coffee from them. "Usually."

"Are you going for a run?"

"Probably."

"You're quite the conversationalist in the mornings," I mused sarcastically.

He grunted at me. "And you talk too much."

Was he teasing me, or was he being serious? This was exactly why I needed to talk to him. I knew nothing about Camden, and I didn't really know how to gauge his behavior and responses. I gave him a small smile to show that if he was teasing I picked up on it. If he wasn't, well, at least I seemed to feign indifference.

"Just trying to figure you out."

He set his mug down, and he leaned against the opposite counter from me. His arms folded over his chest making him appear even larger than he already looked. He crossed his ankles, and I noticed his bare feet. I swallowed, hard. What was it about a man in sweats or jeans with bare feet that was so tantalizing?

"Alright Blue, what do you want to know?"

I raised my eyebrow at him and took another sip of coffee. "Well, for starters, what's with the nickname? You've barely spoken a few short sentences to me since I moved in here."

"Isn't it obvious?"

"Obviously not," I retorted, being a smartass.

"Next question," he said, disregarding the first one.

"You're not going to answer?"

"Nope."

I grumbled under my breath. I noticed the side of his mouth twitched up but quickly went away. Did I just catch him trying not to smile at me?

"Fine. How about telling me about your gym?"

He seemed to roll his eyes at the question. "Dodger told you?"

"No, not really. He said you and your brothers owned one, and that you were the manager of it. That's all I know. I don't know where it's at, or anything about it."

He sighed and released his arms. "I'm surprised. Dodger likes to run his mouth. The gym belonged to my dad until he decided to retire early and pass it along to us. He and my mom wanted to travel so the gym is now ours. I was the one who showed the most interest in it, more than my other siblings. It's the one a few blocks over, The Dugout." He shrugged. "Well, except for Dodge, but he's not interested in managing the place, he just likes to train."

I felt like I had been slapped stupid. This was the most that Camden had spoken to me since, well... ever.

What was even more surprising was him being so forthcoming with the information. I only expected responses from him similar to what he'd given me so far this morning. Short and clipped.

"Hmmm, I've actually driven past it a few times. But I'm catching a theme here; The Dugout, Camden, Dodger... your parents have a thing for baseball?"

"You're quick." His mouth tipped up in a smile.

"So are your other two brothers also named after something baseball-ish?"

"They are."

We're back to being short. "Care to share?"

"My older brother is Turner, and my youngest brother is Wrigley."

I grinned. "Some pretty unique names. So your parents named everything after baseball?"

"Something like that." He regarded me with wary eyes. "Is it my turn?"

I glanced down at my coffee cup. Steam was still rising from the surface of the liquid. "Your turn for what?"

"To ask questions."

My heart picked up its pace. "What do you want to know?"

A look of mischief danced behind his eyes. "Why such a large age gap between you and your little sister?"

I really didn't want to talk about my family, my mom in particular, but he'd divulged some information so I guess I needed to reciprocate. "My mom got pregnant with me when she was still in high school. My sperm donor—" he cocked an eyebrow at the term, "—left after she told him of my impending arrival. My mom raised me by herself, and then twelve years later she told me Sarah was on the way."

I didn't know if he was expecting more, but I had no intentions of going further. "Is she your only sibling?"

I nodded. His body shifted as he reached for his cup of black coffee, and I openly watched the way each muscle bunched under his skin. His eyes narrowed, and I knew he saw me checking him out. "So, what do you know about The Dugout?" His change of subject gave me pause. Between our very unusual conversation, and him actually being sort of nice, I felt almost put off.

"Well, I've only really *heard* about it. Macie had a membership there not too long ago. She was trying to get the attention of a guy who was going there, but it ended up not working out. Anyway she cancelled it because she didn't want to run into him again and the girl doesn't need to exercise. Her body is already pretty perfect."

He curled his lip as though something I said left a bad taste in his mouth. "First of all, going to a gym to get a guy's attention is just stupid. And second, I don't care *what* you look like, everyone should work out."

I shifted in my chair. This topic felt more taboo than telling him all the ins and outs of my mom's sorted affairs. I was already insecure with myself, but when you couple that with the Adonis standing across from me and eyeing me like he meant that comment for me, I bristled.

"What's that supposed to mean?"

He took a step forward, as though he knew I'd spar with him over the subject. "Exactly what I said, you can be skinny, tall, short, healthy, out of shape, or fat; everyone should be working out."

Was it me, or did my ears pick up on his emphasis on the word *'fat'*? I knew I was probably overreacting, but suddenly I wanted this fight. "Why does it sound like your words are a jab in my direction, Camden?"

He jerked back slightly. "What? I was making a general statement. What are you being so sensitive about?"

I rolled my eyes and hopped down from the stool. Rounding the counter I tossed the rest of my coffee in the sink. "Oh give me a break! I heard you the day I signed those papers, and I've seen the way you look at me. I get it okay? I know I'm not thin, and I don't have the best diet. But who in the hell are you to judge *me* for how I live my life? If I wanted to put my fat ass in a gym, I'd be squatting with the rest of those skinny girls you bring home."

I hadn't realized that I had moved to stand directly in front of him. My stance was completely confrontational, and my hands were shaking in anger. His brown eyes looked menacing as he stared me down.

"I don't know what kind of insecure little girl issues you have going on in your pretty little blond head, but my words were not directed at you. If I have something to say to you, I'd say it."

Pretty? I glowered at him. "You know what?" I stopped to regain my composure. Taking a deep breath in through my nose, I closed my eyes and then reopened them. "Just forget this conversation ever happened. It's obvious that you and I are incapable of being friends. I don't want to live the next eleven months in a house with someone who is cruel and judgmental. So do me a favor. When you see me just pretend I'm not here. I'll stay out of your way, if you stay out of mine." I turned to march upstairs. Before I thought about it any longer, I flipped back around, my hair flying into my face. I was certain I looked like a mad woman. "And another thing, I'd really appreciate it if you'd stop bringing your stick figured, zero percent body fat, fake boob, airhead bimbos in my house. And yes, it's also *my* house. I have a contract that says so." Boom. Now I was done. He said nothing after my rant, and I stormed upstairs and slammed my bedroom door. Sitting on my air mattress, I tried to calm my breathing.

In the few minutes that passed, I tried swallowing down the large lump that was forming in my throat. I'd really gone off the deep end. I let my image issue get the best of me. But I had a feeling that it was more than just me picking a fight with him. From the time I moved in here, the air had been tense between us. The pressure was too much, and I was buckling. I truly enjoyed having my independence and living here despite my few run-ins with Camden. I couldn't break now and say 'screw it' and move back in with my mom. I would make this work. I just wasn't sure how I was going to feel around Camden after my little episode downstairs. And I hated the way he made me feel like I was under a microscope when he was in the same room with me. I knew that had to be mostly in my head, but I'd always put people like him up on a pedestal, which only served to make me feel bad about myself. That had to stop, right…now! He was a normal person, just like I was.

Now the other issue at hand was the draw I felt when he was near. It was more than just attraction. And that really pissed me off. I didn't want to like him. He was very good looking, and that was just something that wasn't going to change. But the air between was so electric it was almost tangible. Last night was something that shouldn't have happened. I let him mess with my head. He was being nice, and he seemed to like to make me want him. Maybe he was one of those guys that got off on the idea that if a girl didn't appear to be into him, he'd lure them in and feel attraction. Had he done it on purpose just to mess with me? I wasn't sure I wanted an answer to that. For now I'd go back to my original game plan. I would ignore him when he was around, and I would do my own thing. Today I'd stay in my room and study for my A&P test later this week and maybe call Macie to see what she was up to.

BENDER

I'd just gotten out of my history class when I heard a familiar voice behind me. I turned around, and Dodger was crossing the hall to get to me.

"Hey there Blue, whatcha doing? Just get out of class?"

I groaned. "Not you too. Care to tell me where that name came from? Your brother doesn't seem so forthcoming."

He barked a laugh. "It's your eyes, Keegan. They're the bluest I've seen, even compared to mine. It fits you."

My eyes? That was where Camden got the nickname from? I shook my head refusing to think too much into it. "Well, I don't think I care for it. Besides, isn't that the nickname for the old guy on the movie *Old School*? You're my boy Blue." I did the worst impression of Will Ferrell.

Dodger was practically in stitches laughing at me. I tried to scowl at him, but honestly the air around him was light, and I couldn't help the grin that stretched across my face. This was why I enjoyed being around him. He was always happy.

He wiped under his eye and stood up straight. "Didn't know you were an impersonator. You got any more you can do?"

I nudged him with my arm as we started walking. "Shut up."

"No seriously, that was great. You shoulda taken off your shirt and ran through the campus yelling it. Would've made it so much better."

My face heated, and I knew I was red. He was still laughing as he slung his arm around my shoulder. "You're unbelievable," I scolded him.

"That's what she said." He wagged his eyebrows at me.

I sighed. He could go on all day, so I quit while I was ahead. I noticed a backpack hanging off his shoulder.

"How did I not know you were a student here? I'm feeling like a crappy friend here."

"The subject never came up. I'm in my third year, going for my physical therapy license."

"Huh, I can see that," I said, glancing up at him. "Would you work out of The Dugout?"

A sly smile spread across his face. "Camden tell you about it?" When I nodded but didn't say anything else he continued, "I figured, why not? I wouldn't have to open my own place, or find some doctor's office to work out of. I'll probably add on to the building so it seems more separate, and I can use the equipment in the gym for what my clients will need."

I winked. "Sounds like you have a good plan."

We walked silently and fairly slowly when he asked, "Where are we going?"

"Well *I* am going to the Bulldog Café. And *you* are more than welcome to join me. I always meet Macie for lunch."

"Macie, huh? What's her story anyway?"

I quirked my brow at him. "Why do you ask?"

He looked straight ahead and dropped his arm from my shoulder. "Just curious is all."

"Uh huh. You are interested in her, aren't you?" When he didn't say anything I glanced up at him. "Mace is my best friend, and I love her to pieces, but she's a bit of a player." I stopped walking and pulled on his arm. "Listen, I get that you are probably into her, but I'm thinking it might be best if you stay away from that one. I hate talking about her like this, but I really like you Dodger, and I don't want to see either of you hurt."

His emotions flittered across his face before he settled on a grin and teasingly said, "I'm not looking to marry the girl, I was just wondering."

"If you say so, just please, be careful alright?"

He reached out and ruffled my hair, and I swatted at him. "You worry too much. Loosen up. Oh, speaking of, so there's this party at one of the frat houses…"

I interrupted him with a gasp. "Oh my gosh I would have never pegged you for a frat guy."

"Well if you would have listened to what I was saying I was getting to the part where I would have said one of my really good *friends* lives in the house that's hosting it. It's going to be a Halloween party so you'll need to dress up, but it would be fun if you came. I could introduce you to some people, and it'll give you a chance to get out and stretch your legs some."

"Stretch my legs?" I giggled.

"Yes, stretch your legs." His smile was beaming. "So far I've only seen you work, go to school, and hang out with your sister and Macie. Get out a bit, Keegan. There's got to be a little she-devil hiding in there somewhere." He squatted down so he was eye level to me and acted as though he were searching.

I blushed. "No, there's not. And I don't want to go to some frat Halloween party where I'm forced to dress like a slutty cop or a sexy nurse. It sounds like a nightmare stuffing me into spandex and something too short. I would look like a can of exploded dough."

His face became stoic. "What in the hell are you talking about?"

"Seriously Dodger, I'm not blind. I know what I look like, and I make no qualms about what I see in the mirror. Squeezing into something that is only going to make me uncomfortable all night doesn't sound like a good time." I stopped talking when I saw him clenching his fists, and his mouth had formed a straight line. Tilting my head I said, "Did I say something wrong?"

He shook his head. "You really don't see yourself clearly."

"What?"

"You have a very distorted view, 'cause what you're seeing is not what *I'm* seeing. You're not fat, or chubby, or whatever else you like to call yourself. You're beautiful, Keegan. And before you argue with me, I'd like to believe that I'm a pretty good judge on what's hot and what's not. You, my friend, are smokin'." His eyes ran the length of me while he gave me a wickedly handsome smile.

I felt like I wanted to go hide under a bush. I had no doubt my face was bright red, and I really wasn't sure how to respond to his misguided compliment. "Ummm...thanks?"

"You say that like it's a question." He placed both of his hands up on my shoulders. "So you're not one hundred pounds soaking wet and as tall as a skyscraper. You have something else that those girls don't have."

Now he'd piqued my curiosity. "And what would that be?"

"Tits and ass," he said it with a casual shrug.

I laughed. "Maybe. But it's just unfortunate that my curves also come along with a hefty spare tire."

He glanced down at my stomach, and all I wanted to do was cover it up. "Once again, you're seeing shit that just ain't there. But now it seems I'm on a mission."

"Oh God, should I be worried?"

"Definitely," he chuckled. "I'm going to prove to you that you are a desirable woman. I can't stand that you have such low self-esteem when you are a freaking ten on my hot meter. It must be fixed."

I rolled my eyes. "Yeah, yeah. You're barking up the wrong tree. But knock yourself out."

"Why don't you come to the gym with me tonight?"

I balked. "So your first order of business is to take away the curves that you say are attractive and turn me into one of those skinny chicks? No thanks, Dodger, I'm not interested." I was turning to walk away.

BENDER

He grabbed my forearm and stopped me. His baby blue eye searched mine. "You're not hearing me. I'm not trying to *change* you, Keegan, I'm trying to help you. *You* think you look a certain way, when I don't see anything wrong with it. My solution is to change the way you see yourself." He looked genuinely unsure about whether he was reaching me.

A few seconds passed before I wiped under my eyes to rid the moisture and straightened my back. "Fine." Dodger was truly not trying to hurt my feelings by saying what he did. "Come get me after six, I should be home from work by then."

He nodded. "Aren't I still coming to lunch with you?"

"No, I need a little bit of time alone with Macie, if that's alright. I don't mean to be rude."

"Not rude at all. I'll catch ya after work. Tell your friend I said hi." And with that Dodger turned and walked toward the student parking.

I continued on to the café, ready to dump all of the swirling negativity on Macie's lap. I wanted to get her take on everything. I really felt adamant about going to The Dugout and possibly running into Camden. He was at the forefront of my mind when Dodger mentioned taking me with him. If I went, it would feel like I was conceding to every word Camden said to me this weekend, and it ticked me off. I didn't want him to think he got his way, and he somehow got his chubby roommate into the gym. I swear I could practically hear him laughing about it now while giving me an 'I told you so' face. I balled my fists until my nails were biting into my palms. Just the idea of it made me feel murderous. I knew Dodger wouldn't let me back out. Little did Macie know, I was going to drag her along. At least she could act as a buffer while I was there. All of the guys would be paying attention to her instead of watching me huff and puff on the elliptical. I'd survive this. I promised I'd go with him tonight, but that didn't mean every night after that. And one evening in the gym wasn't going to change the way I saw myself. As I approached the café, I felt resolute that this was going to be a one-time deal. After that, Dodger would have to find a new way to show me how I should be seeing myself. I'd also be crossing my fingers that Camden had better things to do than be at work that late in the evening.

CHAPTER SIX

I'D JUST PULLED ON A PAIR of black yoga pants when I heard the front door open. Grabbing a rubber band to pull my long hair up, I bounded down the steps. Macie was sitting on the couch, reading some gossip magazine, looking cute as ever in her workout clothes and pristine makeup. Dodger was grabbing some water bottles from the fridge in the kitchen, glancing at Macie over his shoulder. I wasn't sure how I felt about his interest in her, but that was a bridge I'd cross when I got to it.

"You ready?" Dodger asked, while zipping up a gym bag.

I shrugged. I truly had been dreading this all day, and I scolded myself for even agreeing to it. I've been to the gym before, but I was the type that went in once, felt self-conscious, and never went again. I was much more comfortable exercising in my own home, which of course I never did.

Macie stood up from the couch, and I couldn't help but admire her confidence in this moment. She wasn't agonizing over how she looked. She didn't have to. Her long lean legs were perfectly proportionate to the rest of her body. She was wearing a pair of short black spandex shorts with a hot pink, skin tight tank top. Her brown hair was up in a messy ponytail that she pulled off flawlessly. Her body was incredible, and I almost hated her for it. I glanced down at my own body and sighed. Besides my yoga pants, I had on a yellow sports bra with a white tank top over it. I've never left the house wearing tighter clothing. What I was comfortable in was usually somewhat baggy around my middle. Wearing this was completely out of my norm. I was worried people were going to home in on my lumpy stomach. I wanted to dart back upstairs and change into a baggy t-shirt, but Dodger seemed to read my mind and shook his head at me.

"No way are you changing. Besides, the gym isn't the place for a fucking beauty pageant. You're perfect, let's go." He hefted the bag up over his shoulder and held the door open for Macie and me.

The drive to The Dugout was okay. Dodger and Macie were chatting in the front about music and school schedules. Macie seemed just as interested in him as he was her. The music in the car was loud enough that they had to speak over it to hear each other. I tuned them out and watched the scenery pass by. Because we were still close to campus, the buildings were well kept, and the surrounding neighborhoods were manicured. I loved this area of Athens. It was very much part of the city but still had a country feel. Plus if you ever tired of the hustle and bustle it wasn't much of a drive before you were looking at cow pastures instead of concrete. I closed my eyes and let the bass of the music soothe me. Before I knew it, we were pulling into a parking lot, and Dodger had turned around, looking at me.

"You fall asleep, Blue?"

I rolled my eyes. "No, I was just...meditating. And stop calling me that, it's annoying."

He smirked before he got out of the car, and Macie followed behind him. I'd never been given a nickname before, but that particular one really grated my nerves. I knew why, too. Looking around at the parked cars, I tried to find Camden's Mustang, but I didn't see it. I released a breath I hadn't realized I'd been holding. My body automatically released some tension, and I got out of the backseat. Dodger and Macie were waiting for me by the front door.

"When we get in here, there's a women's locker room off to the left. You can go check it out or use the restroom if you need to before we start. I'm going to use tonight for demonstrating and making sure you know how to use the machines and weights. Good?"

Ugh! Why was he always so happy? "I don't even know why you're bothering with this. I'm going to be here once. You're better off putting me on a treadmill and training Macie."

His lip curled. "You're not getting out of this. And I'm not putting you on the treadmill. Well, at least not for the whole time we are here. I want to show you that the gym isn't a scary place where people are here to judge you. Okay?"

There was no sense in arguing with him, so I simply nodded my head.

When we walked in through the glass double doors, there was a desk at the front with an attractive brunette sitting behind it. She looked up from her computer screen and beamed at Dodger, batting her eyelashes.

"Hey you," she cooed.

"Hey." Dodger gave her a friendly smile but really didn't seem interested.

"You looking for your brother?" Reception Girl asked in a sing-song voice. My heart jumped into my throat at the mention of Camden. I thought he wasn't here. "He's in the back doing a class, but they'll be out," she glanced at the clock, "in about ten more minutes."

Fantastic.

"Nah, I'm actually about to show these two beautiful ladies around and get them started on a few machines."

The brunette looked at us as if she hadn't seen us standing there. Her lip curled as she seemed to be sizing us up. I got a quick once over, but she must have deemed me non-threatening. When she saw Macie, her eyes opened a bit wider, and her face looked like she had just sucked on a lemon.

"Well, y'all have fun," she said in a perky, fake voice.

Dodger grunted before leading us over to some blue mats.

"Someone has a crush," Macie said, laughing.

"What are you rambling about?" Dodger asked, while bending over and unfolding some of the mats to make a long rectangle.

"The little tart over there. She was practically fucking you with her eyes. 'Oh Dodger'," Macie chirped a fake, high pitch voice. "'You're so hot. Bend me over this counter and...'" she trailed off.

Dodger shot around and pinned Macie with a look. I wasn't sure what it said, but it was both heated and a warning. Macie didn't back down though. She enjoyed a challenge like this. She thrived on them.

"Careful," was all he said.

She raised a single brow and smirked. Dodger dragged his hands through his messy charcoal-colored hair and turned back around. Macie peeked over at me, and I just shrugged my shoulders. He seemed defensive about Macie's teasing, but then again, who knew what that was all about. Frankly I didn't care. My eyes were too busy darting back to the closed door that I assumed Camden was behind teaching his class. I didn't know he taught. I just assumed he came in and dealt with paperwork all day.

"Okay girls, we're going to stretch first. I can't have you doing anything before your muscles are warmed up, or you might hurt yourself. So down you go. Sit Indian style and keep your back straight, like you have a board behind it." We did as he instructed. "Alright, now, you're going to lean forward with your arms out in front of you and you're going to fold over and stretch out those back muscles." When I rolled forward my back popped twice. I moaned; it felt so good.

I heard a deep sound in front of me that almost sounded like a growl. Slowly rising, my eyes landed on a pair of large tennis shoes. Hmmm...those were some big feet. The further my eyes went up, the more I admired. I knew who those toned legs belonged to. I'd stared at those narrow hips and sculpted arms on more than one occasion. When I reached Camden's eyes, I was shocked to see a frustrated, and somewhat angry, face looking down at me.

"What are you girls doing here?" He spoke low.

"I brought them so I could train them," Dodger said easily.

He was still looking at me. The deep brown of his eyes pulled me in like a drug, begging me to take a hit. They made my stomach flip as though I'd just taken a dive off a mountainside, and I was free falling. In all my twenty years, I'd never met a guy who made me feel so curious, so angry, so pent up with....something. His eyes narrowed as though he were reading my thoughts.

"So, after your little hissy fit, you had the balls to step foot in my gym?" His arrogance threw me.

"Jesus Cam, could you just back the fuck off?" Dodger pleaded.

"What's he talking about? What hissy fit?" Macie asked curiously.

Camden's harsh eyes never left mine. I shook my head. Unbelievable! Was he looking for a fight? If so, I was rarin' to go. Someone give me a pair of boxing gloves and put me in the ring. Every gym had a boxing ring, right? Err, maybe not. Either way, I was pissed that he brought up the argument from the day before and was now rubbing it in my face that I was here.

I looked over and told Macie, "Don't worry about it, I'll tell you later." Then I turned my attention back to him. "Your brother seems to be on some crazy mission. He asked me to come here with him, and I reluctantly agreed. However, I didn't realize I was going to be judged for doing a friend a favor. My mistake." I started to stand up and walk toward the front door.

I heard arguing behind me, and Dodger calling Camden a dick. I was almost to the front when a heavy hand grabbed me by my wrist. Heat scorched through my skin. I stopped in my tracks and twisted slightly toward Camden.

"What?" I hissed.

"So you're going to give up, just like that?" He was standing so close I could smell the delicious sweat still on his body.

"I'm not giving up. I just refused to be spoken to like I don't belong. I'm a fucking human being Camden. I don't take well to people embarrassing me." I bit the inside of my cheek to prevent the tears from forming. I wanted to be angry, and unfortunately when I'm angry, I cry.

He squeezed his eyes shut for a few moments. I watched his features as they scrunched up. He was thinking about something, and his emotions were flitting across his face whether he realized it or not. This was a face of conflict. What he was possibly conflicted about, I didn't know. His hand was still encircling my wrist. A sensation was running up my arm, and it made my legs weak. I didn't think he realized he was doing it, but his thumb was stroking short, sweet circles on the inside of my tender skin. When his chocolate eyes opened and trained on me, they were softer.

"I'm sorry, I shouldn't have embarrassed you. I'm just confused as to why you're here."

His tone took me by surprise, because he meant what he said. I looked down at the ground. His fingers squeezed me as if trying to get my attention. I looked back up. My eyes bounced back and forth between his. "It's fine, don't worry about it. Earlier today I'd told Dodger some things, and he thinks he can fix me s'all."

He took a step closer to me. "Things like what?"

I gulped. "Just, things. Things that I don't like about myself."

"And what don't you like about yourself?"

"It's obvious isn't it?"

"Obviously not." He threw my earlier words back at me. It caused me to half smile.

I contemplated telling him. Here, in this moment, where it seemed to be just me and him, I almost told him. There was a soft pleading in his voice that made it sound like he really wanted to know. A loud clang of weights being dropped sounded behind me, and I jumped. Pulling my wrist from his hand, I turned my face away. Grateful for the distraction, I started walking toward Macie and Dodger, who apparently were having their own discussion. At this point I was exhausted, and I hadn't even started to sweat. My pulse was already up, and all I wanted to do was get this over with and go climb into my bed. Camden was following behind me, and when I got back to the mats, I heard him speak.

"Here's the deal." The baritone of his voice gave me the chills. "You're more than welcome to come here and use the facility whenever you want, but I have two rules." Macie and I were listening intently. "The first one is, when you're here, you're working out. No fiddling around on the machines, and if you don't know how to use something, just ask and I'll help. I can't have people getting hurt in here." I was tempted to roll my eyes. He was speaking to us like he was standing in front of a second grade classroom giving safety tips. I couldn't help but wonder what he'd do if I broke his rule. Spank me? I coughed, which caused his eyes to shoot toward me.

I held up my hand. "I'm fine, I'm fine." I could feel my face heating up.

"Second." He looked at me as though waiting for another interruption. "This isn't a beauty pageant. Nothing chaps my ass more than seeing a girl walk in with her hair and makeup all done up. I don't run a dating service. So if I see it, I'm going to call you out on it, understand?" That was what Dodger had said earlier in the apartment.

He had directed rule two to Macie. She scoffed, "Oh get over yourself. If I wanted to pick up a guy, it wouldn't be some juiced up meathead whose head is too small for their steroid ridden body."

Dodger, who'd remained quiet this entire time, barked out a laugh. His eyes were nearly sparkling at her as though she were something he'd never seen before. Camden grunted once, gave me a short nod, and walked away.

"Could your brother be any more uptight? Maybe that should be my workout of the day. Pulling the oversized steel rod out of Camden's ass." Macie's face was nothing but serious curiosity.

Now it was my turn to laugh. "That would make my night so much better. Not to mention the rest of the year I'm living with him. Could make him more tolerable."

Dodger was chuckling at our comments. "Come on girls, let's get started."

"I can't feel my legs. I think they fell off on the stairs coming up here," I said as I plopped down on the couch.

"My ass is jello. Like, I definitely think I understand why people get their asses massaged," Macie mumbled, face down on the loveseat.

Dodger had just dropped us off at the apartment after he'd nearly killed us. I had quit at least fifteen times through the two hour workout, but he'd tell me he wanted more. I've never pushed so hard in my life. People actually *paid* him to torture them? I was baffled. They needed their heads examined. Yep, I was convinced that people who go to the gym and push themselves to the point of losing a limb were certifiable.

"I need a shower," I groaned.

"I need a wheelchair."

I giggled. We were pathetic. I slowly pushed myself off the couch, almost falling on my face in the process, when the front door opened. Camden came in like a man on a mission. His eyes were trained on me, and I swallowed hard at their intensity. When he kicked the door shut he moved toward me but stopped when Macie cleared her throat. He must not have seen her.

"What the hell?" she wondered, just as confused as I was feeling.

He pointed at her and ordered in an authoritative voice, "You…out."

"Excuse me?" She was taken aback by his tone.

"I need to have words with Keegan, and I'd prefer you gone."

She was about to say something that probably resembled a death threat, but I held my hand up and said, "It's fine, Mace. Just go, and I'll call you later."

Macie kept her eyes pinned on Camden. "You sure? He looks like he's about to blow a gasket."

I nodded my head but didn't speak. I wasn't sure. In fact, my pulse was thrumming, and my hands were slightly trembling. I squeezed them into fists to hide it. Macie stared a minute longer before she conceded and pulled me into a tight hug. She spoke loud enough for Camden to hear. "If he hurts you, I'm going to need your help moving the body."

I smirked at her silliness, but I had the distinct impression she wasn't kidding. When she walked out Camden took two deliberate steps in my direction. "What the hell was that?" he asked, his voice calm and yet not, all at the same time.

I tilted my head to the side questioningly. "What are you talking about?"

Another step. "You know what I'm talking about, Keegan. I'm extremely pissed off right now, so I suggest you answer the fucking question."

The way he said my name made my body shiver. "No, I really have no clue. And I can tell you're mad."

He was still advancing toward me. He seemed to take a deep breath and blew it out. "Let me tell you a little something about me. I like to have control. I control every single facet in my life. It keeps things running smoothly, and there are rarely any hiccups. It appears you didn't listen to me earlier. I told you what I didn't want to happen and yet, it still did. Now I want to know, did he ask you out?"

Oh, now I knew where this was going. But even still, why did it matter? He couldn't possibly think he could control me, or what anybody else did. That'd be absurd! About an hour into my workout a good-looking guy with longer blond, shaggy hair approached me and struck up conversation. I was a disgusting, sweaty mess and never once had it occurred to me that the guy had been flirting. His name was Luke. He had walked over after lifting some free weights and asked me what my name was. He'd commented that he'd never seen me in here before. I was polite, despite my huffing and puffing. He'd flashed me a dazzling smile and chatted away while I lifted my legs and stretched my arms, keeping a steady tempo on the elliptical. I'd noticed Luke in the far corner when I had been scouring the place to see if anybody was watching me. And not like, *watching me* watching me, but looking at me like I didn't belong. Luke's eyes had locked on mine, and I had looked down blushing. I'd never fathomed that he would have approached me. When he had been mid conversation telling me that he was a graduate student, I'd felt a pair of eyes boring into my back. The hairs on the back of my neck stood up, and I had goosebumps despite it being hotter than Hades. My eyes shifted from Luke's, and I locked eyes with dark brown ones that were staring at me warily through the mirrors. Camden looked pissed. It must have been only ten minutes into us chatting, err…well *him* talking to *me* since I couldn't really breathe, let alone talk, that he asked me to go out with him sometime. I told him sure and puffed out my phone number. He blew me away with a beautiful smile and said he'd be calling soon. After he'd walked back to the weights, I looked back up to see if Camden was still watching, but he was nowhere to be seen. Now, standing here with the prowling beast of a man taking slow menacing steps toward me, I wished I were able to speak. Unfortunately, cat got my tongue.

"I'm going to ask you again, Blue, did he ask you out?" The bass of his voice shook in my chest.

I blinked once, twice, three times before I nodded slightly. Camden made another move in my direction, and by instinct, I took a step back. He narrowed his eyes at me, silently daring me to move again. I knew he wouldn't hurt me, but my fight or flight instinct was kicking in, and I wanted to step out from under his penetrating glare. His anger was somehow turning me on, and I could feel the dampness in my panties. Camden was only a few feet away from me and inching closer.

"I need to shower!" I suddenly blurted out.

His mouth tipped up into a half smile. "Did you say yes?"

Bastard, he wasn't going to let this go. Why was it such a big deal? Better yet, why was it such a big deal to *him*? I cleared my throat then responded, "I gave him my number."

I was backing away toward the steps, and he moved with me. We seemed to be in some sort of dance. "What did I tell you about my gym not being a place to pick someone up?"

I perked up. "I didn't pick anyone up, I gave him my number. He asked for it. What's the big deal?"

He ran his hands through his spiky brown hair. "The big deal is you broke one of the rules I gave you. It's not a place for a meet and greet. You go in, work your ass off, and you get out. It's that simple."

"And again, I didn't go searching for Luke, he came up to me. What I'm failing to see here though is it's not like anybody was making out or jumping each other's bones, Camden. He was a nice guy, he asked me out, and then we went on our merry way. But exactly what part of that concerns you?"

Now he was really moving toward me. I turned and picked up my speed toward the stairs. I came to an abrupt halt when his voice boomed, "Stop," through the apartment, and he was less than a foot away. I could hear his breathing. It was ragged and sounded edgy. We stood that way for several moments; the only sound in the apartment was our breathing. When he finally spoke I tensed. He had stepped in, lightly brushing me from behind. My nostrils flared, and I could smell that soapy clean scent of him.

"When I give you rules to follow, you follow them. If my rules are ever broken, there are consequences. There are *always* consequences. I said don't pick anybody up, and yet you somehow did." I wanted to bristle at his choice of wording 'somehow', but chose better of it and kept my mouth shut. "I'm going to let this go for now, but here's how it's going to play out. You ever come back in my gym, and he's there, you ignore him." His breath blew across the outside of my ear, and I nearly moaned in pleasure. "If pretty boy so much as winks in your direction, I'll terminate his membership and kick both of you out." I felt his presence step away from me, and I glanced over my shoulder. He was walking backwards toward the door. It felt like his eyes were burning into me. "Rules, Keegan. Break them again, there'll be consequences."

I wanted to turn around and lash out, then beg him to fuck me. He nearly had me in a puddle of mush on the floor. His hand was on the door leading outside when he called over his shoulder. "And feel free to share what I said to *Luke*," Camden sneered with an emphasis on his name, then slammed the door behind him.

My body gave out, and I flopped down on the bottom step. I felt more exhausted now than I had when I got back from the gym. Camden was being such a hard ass, and he somehow seemed to take great pleasure in fighting with me. How was it possible that a man who showed his clear distaste for me was completely adverse to me exchanging numbers with someone? It shouldn't even matter to him. And what was worse? None of that was what was truly bothering me at the moment. It was even more disturbing than his stupid rules. It was that with one look, one snap of his fingers, one menacing step in my direction, my body became needy for him. Camden made me feel desire unlike anything I'd ever experienced before. I was angry with myself for every single ounce of it. I'd come to realize that I wanted him to touch me, and I wanted more than just his eyes to penetrate me. It was unacceptable.

Sitting here in the quiet apartment, the only sounds were of the AC units outside humming. My long wavy blond hair was draped around me, covering me like a blanket. It felt cold and bereft without Camden's presence. I gritted my teeth and tried to pull myself together. Standing up I marched up the steps and climbed into an icy shower. While the water beat down on my sore muscles, I decided that I was going to go back to the gym. I would face seeing Camden on a daily basis. I'd deal with the fact that I was physically attracted to him, but I would ignore it. I hoped that I would run into Luke, and we could work something out and possibly go do something. I hadn't been on a date in a long time, and I was long overdue for one. My bossy roommate was going to have to deal with *me* and my non-compliance to his stupid rules. I smiled to myself, almost giddy at my determination of defiance. Take your rules and shove them up your perfectly carved ass, Camden. I had other things in mind.

CHAPTER SEVEN

THREE WEEKS HAVE PASSED since Camden's threat. I have pretty much continued my daily routine. I went to school, work, came home, and went to the gym. Yes, the gym. Despite my concern of body parts falling off, I liked how I felt after a good workout. I saw Camden almost every time I went. The first few days I showed he had a smug little smirk across his face. I seriously wanted to beat his face in with a dumbbell. I refrained, because it didn't seem very nice, and frankly I wasn't sure if I could get blood out of my clothes. It aggravated me to no end. It was as if he got his way, and he somehow was the person to convince me to get in shape. There was a time after my second trip to The Dugout that I had thought about adding a laxative to his protein powder. It would have given me great satisfaction to see him running to the bathroom. He was lucky I wasn't a vindictive person. Around my fourth time coming in, he stopped with his shit eating grin and went about his business like I was any other paying customer. I wasn't sure how I felt about that. For starters, I wasn't paying a thing to be a member there. It made me feel a twinge of guilt, because I was already paying so little for the apartment, and now I was taking advantage of his facilities. This was his livelihood. But then his words 'the chubby one' replayed through my head, and I shrugged it off. He owed me.

Sarah has been over at least a dozen times. She seemed to be adjusting well to the change, and she loved coming here. As long as she was happy, I was happy. There was one particular day when Dodger was around that he asked her if she had a boyfriend. She blushed and said, "Yes." My eyes nearly bugged out of my head. But what entertained me was Dodger's response. At some point since meeting her, he'd taken on a protector role with her. He gave her a level stare after grilling her about this boy's name, age, how tall he was, if he had any prior felonies...? To which she replied in a very Sarah like fashion, "He's eight. What's he gonna get arrested for, stealing Spiderman underwear?" He explained that with boys you never know, and then he proceeded to tell her that she was not allowed to kiss anybody until she was married. Dodge said, "You're the best kind of girl out there, Sarah. You make sure you find a boyfriend that cherishes every single one of your smiles and laughs, treats you like a princess, and gives you everything you could ever want." Then he followed it up with, "Things like diamonds, a castle, and a Ferrari, so I can drive it and make sure it's safe." I laughed at him. Sarah smacked him on the arm and said kissing was gross then returned to playing with her dolls. Dodger was sweet to take her under his wing. She lacked a male role model in her life. He was good to her, and I approved of the time they spent together.

Luke and I have gone out a couple of times since he asked me for my number. I remembered walking through campus while eating some Whoppers when my cell phone rang, and I saw Luke's name flashing on my screen. I inhaled my chocolate ball whole and started choking. Thank God for passersby who knew the Heimlich maneuver. What a sad, and yet wonderful, way to die...death by candy. Anyway, after my near death experience, I got the courage to call him back. He asked if I wanted to go grab a bite to eat and see a movie. I said yes, and now here we are.

He's been very nice, and I was certainly attracted to him. Luke has this carefree look about him. He had longer blond hair that was tasseled like he'd just gotten out of the ocean and let it air dry. His arms were very tan, and I could only assume that the rest of him was just as dark. Luke's body was long and lean. Not like Camden's bulky muscled look, but one that showed clear lines and ridges of abs and arms without it being too much. My favorite part of Luke, though, was his smile. It was so easy and warm. His perfectly straight and white teeth stood out each time his face lit up at something I'd say. I found myself on numerous occasions leaning into him when he directed his grin at me. Yeah, I was definitely attracted.

My cell was vibrating and dancing across the table I'd set it on. I was at the library studying for my next A&P test. I'd managed to pull off a B on the last pop quiz, but again, it wasn't enough. I had to push harder if I stood a chance at making it into the nursing program.

Picking up my cell, I propped it between my ear and shoulder while I shuffled some books around. "Hello?"

"Hey beautiful, what're you doing?" Luke's pleasant voice traveled through the phone.

I couldn't help the smile that spread across my face. "I'm at the library studying. How about yourself?"

"I was just at the grocery store picking up some things for the house. Those guys eat at least twenty-five pounds of food a day." I giggled. "If you think I'm joking, you should come watch them sometime. If there's food in the house, they are all like a bunch of bloodhounds sniffing out their next meal. If I was like this at all when I hit puberty, I totally owe my mom for keeping me well-fed." I could hear the lighthearted tone in his voice. Luke lived in the same frat house that Dodger had invited me to for the Halloween party.

"Sounds pretty typical. Aren't y'all still growing boys?"

His voice deepened. "Depends on what you're referring to that's growing." I bit my lip, and I could hear his throaty chuckle. "I swear I can practically *hear* you blushing through the phone."

"Shut up," was all I retorted with.

"Alright, alright, well I'm calling because I wanted to see if you would like to come out to the park with me. I could pack us a picnic and bring a Frisbee or a kite. What do ya say?"

He sounded so hopeful. It still amazed me that I was seeing someone like Luke. People like him never happened to people like me. I must have been quiet, because he said my name. "Oh sorry, I got distracted. Yes, I'd love to, that sounds fun. What time?"

"I'll be there around six."

"Sounds good, see ya then."

We both hung up, and I gathered all of my things, looking at the time. Crap, I had two hours to get ready. I still needed to head home to take a shower and pick out what to wear. Slinging my bag over my shoulder I headed to the elevators.

When I got to the apartment, Camden was sitting on the couch. I wasn't expecting him to be home so soon. He was always at the gym, working until at least seven. It still made me slightly nervous to be alone with him in the same space. Shrugging it off, I came in, took my shoes off, and set my bag on the loveseat.

"Hey, you're home early," I stated simply.

He looked over at me from the television. He was watching some show about muscle cars, figures. "Yeah, I was teaching a class to the seniors when one of the granny's started to go down. I thought she was having a heart attack but turned out she just can't seem to lift the free weights and step up on the platforms." He sighed. "I ended up pulling my quad trying to get to her before she hit the floor."

I looked down, and that was when I noticed the ice pack resting on his leg. I instinctively went toward him to check on it but stopped short. He was eyeing me like he was wondering what I was doing. Instead I walked in front of the couch and around to the back. I was certain I looked like a crazy person walking random circles in the living room, but I couldn't play off that I made a move in his direction.

"Just remember to keep the ice on for twenty and off for twenty."

He glanced at me over his shoulder, a weird look marring his hard features. "I work in the fitness industry, I know how to take care of a pulled muscle."

He didn't mean what he said in a snooty tone, but I sighed. "Are you going to be okay?" I asked moving toward the stairs.

He'd turned away to look at the television. "It's fine, I'm fine. I just need to ice it and work it out."

"K," was all I responded with.

I climbed the stairs and started rummaging through my messy closet. Deciding on a light blue maxi dress that I coupled with some flat sandals, I figured it would be the perfect outfit for the park. I didn't want it to overdressed, but I didn't want to seem like I didn't care either. Hopping in the shower, I cleaned every crevice of my body, shaved my legs, and pumiced my feet. I tended to walk around barefoot a lot so the soles of my feet were on the rougher side. When I stepped out, I wrapped my body in a towel and darted across the hall to my room. I hadn't realized, until I was putting on my makeup and doing my hair, that I was really excited to see Luke. He gave me butterflies. He was also the first person since my high school boyfriend who made me feel pretty.

I styled my hair half up and half down, so it cascaded down my back in long blond waves. The makeup I applied had a natural glow to it. My cheeks were a soft pink, a little mascara was applied on my lashes, and a very light rose-colored lip gloss finished my lips. Looking in the mirror even *I* had to admit to myself that I looked good. I looked…happy, excited, fresh. Luke was doing this to me. It was nice.

As I walked down the stairs, I breezed past Camden who was in the fridge looking for something to eat. I took a quick peek at him and noticed his nostrils flare slightly. Did he just smell the air?

"There's some sweet potato soup in the Tupperware on the bottom shelf that I made the other day if you'd like it. It's healthy so I figured you might want some," I offered, as I sat down on one of the stool and adjusted my sandals.

Camden was looking at me in such an odd way, but he eventually turned back to the fridge and dug out the bowl. When he lifted the lid, he grunted in what I could only assume was approval. "This doesn't look half bad. Thanks for offering."

I snickered. "That's because it's not. I can cook, you know. Just because you like to control everything doesn't mean that others are incapable of making healthy foods for your royal mouth to taste. And…you're welcome."

That honestly all came out harsher than I'd intended, but whatever. He regarded me for a few short moments before he continued moving about the kitchen and heating up the leftover soup. While his back was turned to me he said, "You uh, look nice. You goin' out?"

BENDER

I gaped at him. Like full on, fish out of water, mouth hanging open, gaped. Did Camden Brooks just compliment me? Now that was a strange concept. And it was one that made me flush from head to toe. I wasn't even sure if I should acknowledge it, or if we were supposed to pretend that it never happened. I was also a little curious about the tiny butterflies I'd had in my stomach over thoughts of Luke, and how they had now sprouted hummingbird wings and were fluttering so fast that I felt the need to check my pulse. *Pay attention Keegan.* There was a question associated with his compliment. What was it again? When I brought my head up after fidgeting with the straps of my shoes, I was greeted by that deep chocolate brown color that was becoming all too familiar. His brow rose, reminding me that I still hadn't answered him.

"Are you going out?" he repeated but in a slower way, annunciating every word.

Snap out of it woman! "Umm, yeah. Luke is coming by to pick me up."

He was mulling over something. "You two seem to be seeing a lot of each other."

It was a statement, not a question. I responded anyway. "Yes, we've been out a few times."

The heat of his stare was making me uncomfortable and squirmy. "Hmph."

What. On. Earth? *Just drop it Keegan.* Thankfully a knock sounded at the door and saved me from asking. I answered the door and was handed a beautiful bouquet of wild flowers. Luke was beaming. His dusty blue eyes went from my face, down my dress, and back up again. He smiled approvingly.

"You look stunning, as always." Luke leaned in and kissed me on my cheek.

"Thank you so much. These are gorgeous. Why don't you come in so I can put them in some water and then we can take off?" I stepped aside and let him in.

Luke stopped short just inside the door and was watching Camden inhale his soup.

"What is Brooks doing here?" Luke asked.

Hadn't I told him that Camden and I lived together? I thought about it, but the more I jogged my memory, I'd come to realize I hadn't said anything about it. Oops!

"He lives here. Camden is my roommate." I pushed inside of the kitchen and started digging for a vase. The quicker I got the flowers in water, the quicker we could leave.

"Sup," Camden said in greeting.

Luke gave a curt nod. "I didn't know you two lived together."

Camden's cocky grin was plastered on his face. "Well, you do now."

"Huh." Luke's voice sounded put off.

The two continued their staring contest, while I desperately searched for anything to use for the flowers. Why in the hell did it feel like a testosterone induced battlefield in my kitchen? And an even better question, why was I even bothering to look for a vase in a dude's apartment? I couldn't imagine that Camden kept them on hand for the many times he'd received flowers. Getting a tall glass out of the cupboard I filled it with water and started placing the flowers inside. I looked up at both boys when the room fell silent. Both were looking at each other as though they were sizing each other up. I briefly wondered if I should blurt out that they should just compare their penises so someone could come out a clear winner and I could pass out ribbons. I almost laughed at myself for even thinking it. As much as I didn't understand this weird male ritual that I was witnessing, it still struck me as odd. Camden didn't seem like the type to get intimidated, and yet there was something in his face that made it like Luke was competition. Competition for what, I wasn't sure. We needed to get out of here, now.

Clearing my throat, Luke broke the eye contact and looked at me. "You ready to go?"

He nodded and moved the door. Both guys said their last names as a way to say bye, and we walked out the door.

When Luke and I got in the car, there was an awkward silence that had taken over. My hands were fidgeting in my lap, and I was trying not to lean forward to start fiddling with the dials of the radio or A/C. I'd been alone with Luke on more than one occasion and never was it tense when neither one of us were speaking, although the quiet moments were far and few between. Right now I'd sell a kidney to hear what was going through his head.

"Sooo…" I said but wasn't sure where I was going with it.

He looked at me out of the corner of his eye. "So?"

MmmK, this wasn't going to go anywhere unless I just explained this to him. "Listen, I'm sorry I didn't tell you about my living situation. It wasn't intentional. Camden and I hardly even see each other, because he's always at the gym, or I'm on campus studying. Most of the time it feels like I live there alone. I guess the subject never came up or occurred to me. But, I need to know, is this going to be a problem?"

He sat for a few short beats before he reached over and grabbed my hand. My fingers laced with his and I glanced down, noticing a crinkly spot on my dress. Oh man, apparently I'd stopped wringing my hands together and had taken up fisting my dress. Wonderful, it was all wrinkled now, so when I stood up, it would look like I'd had a death grip on my crotch. I sighed.

"It's fine. I think it took me by surprise more than anything. I just assumed you lived with Macie. But that's what I get for assuming, I should have asked." He spoke quietly, and I could tell he was still deep in thought over it.

"Well, I should have said something. It's really not a big deal. In fact, we shouldn't have even run into him tonight, but he came home early because he pulled a muscle while teaching a class. I really don't see him that much." I gave a sheepish shrug.

He squeezed my hand. "It's okay, Keegan, you don't need to explain yourself. You live with him, and there's nothing else going on besides being his roommate, right?"

"No!" My answer came out more abrupt and high pitched than necessary. "Camden hasn't been the nicest person to live with, but I've made do. I can tell you without a shadow of a doubt he's just my roommate, nothing else."

We were just pulling up to the park, and Luke parked the car. When he got out, he came around to my side and opened the door for me, holding his hand out to help me out. I asked him if he needed any help carrying the blankets or food, but he declined, assuring me that he had it. We walked a short ways to a tree that was by a pond full of ducks. Luke started unfolding the blanket he'd brought and tossed it up in the air, letting the fabric fluff out and spread out on the ground. When I sat down, I sighed contentedly. This whole place was picturesque. The grass was a deep green and cut short. It smelled as though it had been mowed recently. That was one of my favorite smells. The tree we were under was also one of my favorites. It was a weeping willow. I had wanted one in my yard as a kid, because I thought they were magical, but I'd been told by my mother that they were messy, disgusting trees, and she'd never plant one. Sitting under it now, letting the drooping branches cloak us from the beating heat of the sun, it didn't seem as bad as she made it out to be. I found it beautiful, and a perfect place to hide from the world. There were quacking ducks in the background, along with some chirping birds, and kids playing. I felt warm and peaceful, it was nice.

Luke opened a few of the paper sacks he brought. They contained deli sandwiches, chips, two cookies, and some sort of pasta salad. I smiled up at him, and he actually looked a little embarrassed.

"Sorry, I know this isn't exactly diet food, but at least it will taste good."

I giggled. "Just because I'm working out doesn't mean I'm dieting. I still love food. In fact my hips and butt love food more than my mouth."

He laughed. "I appreciate that your hips and butt enjoy the food."

My face felt red, and I knew I was blushing. Luke reached over and tipped my chin up to look at him. "You're beautiful Keegan. I like that you have curves, and you enjoy good food. Between your long blond hair, big bright blue eyes, and sweet as pie personality… you're like the ultimate package. I couldn't even believe that nobody had snagged you yet."

I shied even more. "Nobody's noticed until you."

His eyes studied my face. "Well then, they are fools, and I get the prize. But I have a hard time believing nobody has noticed. Even your own roommate looks at you like I do. Hell, all of the guys at the gym practically trip over their own feet watching you."

I turned away from him. "Okay, now I know your lying." I couldn't help but wonder if he was right about Camden. I'd never noticed any looks from him other than ones of annoyance. Could he possibly be attracted to me?

No, I wasn't even close to his type, and I refused to entertain the idea. Luke was just trying to be complimentary. Camden tolerated me because we lived together, that was it.

He casually shrugged. "Again, you're seriously selling yourself short."

We both unpacked the dinners. Luke and I sat for a long time enjoying each other's company. We talked about our college classes, and the professors we'd shared over the past couple years. He was two years older than me since he was in a master's program, which meant, despite having the same teacher, we'd never be in class together. We talked about how we grew up. He had an older sister who he saw pretty often, and his family still did Sunday dinners. I admired that and wished that I could have had a family who was so tight-knit. When I told him about my mom and Sarah, he listened intently. I saw what looked like sympathy flash across his face at one point, and it made me withdraw slightly from my story. I kept out some of the harder details, like my mom's dating cycle and how I was more of a parent to Sarah than she was half the time. I didn't want him to feel sorry for me. This was the hand I was dealt in life, and I was embracing it. Regardless of the topics we shared, I was feeling closer to Luke than I had over the past few dates. We laughed at his stupid jokes, and it was turning into an all-around great time. The whole time we talked, he was touching me in some way or another, whether it was a gentle brush of my hair behind my ear, laying his hand over mine, or leaning in and kissing my lips.

Luke was lying on his side with his body propped up on his elbow. He glanced up at me through his thick dark blond lashes. His eyes were flirty when he said, "So I brought a Frisbee out, do you want to toss it around a bit before it gets too dark?"

My tummy did flip flops at the way his eyes were smoldering. "Sure, that sounds like fun."

He stood and held his hand out. When I took it his palm was slightly rough but warm to the touch. It gave me chills even though the air was muggy. I tipped my head back to look up at him. He was slightly taller than Camden, but still, I was so short I had to look up at almost everyone. Luke held my hand as we walked out to an open spot near the pond. He gave me a slight squeeze before he released me, and we walked in opposite directions.

"Don't go too far. I can throw a Frisbee, but I'm not sure I can promise it will make it to where you're standing," I casually joked.

He smirked. "Just hold your hand out like this." He bent his wrist and flipped it out without letting go of the plastic disc, to show me how to do it. "The Frisbee will do the rest of the work." Luke lightly flicked his wrist and the disc came sailing in my direction. He did it so easily and precise that it came right to me, and I caught it with grace.

I laughed. "What are you, some professional Frisbee thrower?"

Luke's face lit up. "As a matter of fact, in high school I won an award for the discus throw in track and field."

"Show off," I shouted. I tried to mimic how he had done it only seconds earlier, but I flung it practically straight up, and it came crashing back down almost in front of my own feet. "Oh come on!" I laughed. Luke was chuckling, the back of his hand covering his mouth. "Are you laughing at me?"

He shrugged. "Well, you're pretty cute. You get this look of concentration, and then you somehow managed to toss it to yourself. I can go get another one if you want to play a solo game I guess."

I teasingly glared at him across the open space. Luke barked out a laugh. I threw the Frisbee and it at least went in his general direction this time. He caught it after taking a few steps to his left. I loved the way his eyes danced when he was playing around with me. His long tan legs easily moved around as we continued our game. Luke would brush his blond hair out of his face every other throw, and it looked so masculine that I found myself watching him, intrigued by whatever move he made next. Did he know such basic movements made women gushy? He must, by the way his stare had turned from fun and playful to heated and tense. Luke caught the Frisbee after this last toss, and he made the few short strides across the grass to stand in front of me. My heart picked up its pace. The air between us was heavy, and the feeling between my legs indicated that he was affecting me.

"Why are you looking at me like that?" Luke asked, his voice a little deeper than normal.

"I don't know, you're just... beautiful," I said breathily.

"Beautiful?" He made it a question, but he wasn't offended by the slightly feminine compliment.

My head was tipped back, and I was looking into his cerulean blue eyes. I knew my chest was moving up and down with my breathing because he glanced down and then back up again. Luke brought his hand up and pushed his fingers underneath my long hair and behind my neck. We'd kissed before, but it was always short and sweet. This felt different. The way he was looking at me, I could tell he wanted me. His fingertips were lightly stroking the sensitive skin on my neck. I watched in awe as he slowly bent forward and pressed his lips to mine. It was soft at first, but when I sighed, he pulled me to him and melded my body to his. My eyes fluttered closed, and I let him set the pace. His tongue ran along the seam of my lips, and I opened, granting him access. The warmth of his mouth was inviting, and he tasted like the potato chips we had earlier. I licked the little bit of salt that was lingering on his lower lip. He groaned at my exploration. His kiss was adoring and passionate. It made my body respond in a way that was begging me to let him take me back home and do whatever he wanted to me. But was I ready to go there? In this moment, my answer was yes. He was attractive, kind, and he'd done nothing but made me feel wanted. This wasn't like some high school relationship where I needed to take things slow, because I was still a virgin and wanted to save myself for marriage. I'd already been with three other guys before, and now I was in college. I was an adult, and this felt right. I made the decision quickly. Before I could chicken out, I pulled back slightly, with my eyes still closed.

I whispered to him, "Come home with me. I need to be with you."

He pressed his forehead to mine, his breathing labored. I could feel how aroused he was against my stomach. "Are you sure? I don't want you to think this has to go any further right now."

I opened my eyes and saw the bright shining blue of his watching me. "Positive."

He blew out a breath and leaned back. "Let's pack up and head out then. Besides, it's getting pretty dark."

I nodded, and we walked back to our picnic area and cleaned up. When we got in the car, he took my hand and kissed my knuckles so tenderly. I smiled at him, and we started making our way back to my apartment.

On the way there, my mind wandered to Camden. I hadn't really taken him into consideration when I made the offer for Luke to come stay the night with me. Was it wrong for me to bring a guy to the house with the intention of doing more than just hanging out? As quickly as that thought came into my mind, I brushed it aside. Of course it was. But Camden had already brought home at least a half a dozen girls and never once thought if I'd care that those tramps were in my space. He did whatever he wanted, so I was going to do the same. My only hesitation was when I remembered the look that Camden gave Luke in the kitchen. I didn't want any repeat episodes of a pissing match. In fact I was hoping that he would either already be in his room, or that he'd have left to go do something and wouldn't even see us.

As we pulled up to the apartment, my nerves kicked in. It shouldn't be bothering me so much that I was bringing someone home. We walked up the steps to my front door, and I quietly unlocked the door. I was trying to be as discreet as possible. If Luke had noticed what I was doing, he didn't indicate it. I looked at him over my shoulder, and he smiled at me. If I didn't know any better, I'd say he looked a little nervous himself. What did he have to be nervous about? Luke was perfect. Perfect body, perfect looks, perfect moves…hell he was even a perfect kisser. Maybe I was just reading him wrong.

As we stepped inside, it was notably dark, but I heard a faint beating noise from upstairs. Camden must be up in his room listening to music. I closed my eyes and exhaled. Thank God! Grabbing Luke's hand I weaved him through the downstairs, and we climbed our way up to my room. When I pulled out my keys, Luke raised his brow in question.

"Don't ask," I mumbled.

Just inside my door I turned on the light and shut the door behind him. He was standing still, taking in my personal space, but his brows were furrowed.

"What's the matter?"

"Where's your bed? In fact, where's all your furniture?"

I shrugged. "I'm still saving to get it all. When I moved out of my mom's house, I didn't take any of my things with me besides my clothes. It's really not a big deal."

He regarded me carefully. "But you're sleeping on an air mattress, Keegan."

"Yeah, I know. Is that a problem?"

"Well, yeah. I can't believe that Camden hasn't even offered to buy you furniture. A girl like you shouldn't be staying in a room with nothing in it. In fact, I'd be happy to go and buy-"

I held up my hand and cut him off. "No, you're not buying me anything. Now can we move the subject on to something more pleasant? Otherwise I'm going to lie down and get some sleep." I didn't like that he was even offering. What was it with all these boys trying to fix me?

He'd been standing with his hands on his hips, trying to assess if I meant what I said. I raised my brow, silently goading him to try me. As quick as he could turn me on, this subject had been a mood killer. His graceful square jaw ticked as he clenched his teeth. I could see the war battling within him to be the hero here, but I didn't want a white knight. I wanted him to look at me like he had out at the park. I wanted Luke take me in his arms and be with me. Whatever his decision was, he'd made it. Stepping forward he grabbed my elbow and slid his hand down until he reached my hand. He pulled me to him and wrapped my arms around his back.

"Fine, I get that you are proud and want to do this on your own. But if you ever need any help, please know that I'm here. All you have to do is ask."

I tilted my head to the side. "That's sweet, Luke. I appreciate the offer. Now can we please, like, kiss or something? My knees went a little weak in the park, and I'd like to see if you can do that again."

His answering grin was all I needed. His mouth came crashing down to mine, and clothes went flying. He walked me backwards until my feet hit the air mattress.

When I stumbled back, and my butt hit the bed, I giggled. I was ready to enjoy this.

The next morning I was lying there wide awake. Last night wasn't at all what I was expecting. Luke was wonderful in every way, but when he pushed inside of me...I felt nothing. There was no spark, no chemistry, nothing! I mean, don't get me wrong. My body responded the way that it should when it's been touched and caressed in very intimate places. I even had an orgasm from the sensations, but it fell completely short for me. It was more like a formality than a passionate meeting of bodies. I was almost ready to cry, because something was missing. In the middle of Luke thrusting, I'd briefly wondered if Camden could hear us. I wanted to know if he was jealous, if he wished he were Luke. When Luke's pace started to change, I put my head back in the game, because he was clearly close to coming, and I wasn't even close to being on par yet.

Looking up at this handsome, blond-haired man who I was entangled with, I wondered if there was something wrong with me. I shouldn't have been thinking about my roommate while naked and going to town with someone else. That thought was just wrong! In fact, I was going to do this again. I liked Luke. He deserved to have all of my attention and not just part of it. Well, that was if he wanted to have sex with me again. I couldn't just assume that I was all Miss Super Porn Star and everything he'd hoped for.

"What's going on up in that gorgeous head of yours?" Luke's groggy voice sounded beneath me.

I raised my head from his chest and looked at him. "Mmm...you're awake. Nothing worth talking about." I gave him a small smile.

He quirked a brow. "You sure?"

I nodded, my chin brushing the light dusting of hair on his pecs. "You sleep okay?"

His mouth tipped up. "I slept quite well, thanks to you. In fact, maybe air mattresses are the way to go. This sucker is pretty comfy."

I laughed softly. "Yeah, regular beds are overrated."

His beautiful mouth curved into a grin, and he tapped my nose with his finger. "You're cute in the morning."

I curled my lip. "Meh... I'm going to pretend that you can't see the makeup that I'm sure is smeared under my eyes, and that it doesn't look like a bird is nesting in my hair."

He shook his head. "You don't see yourself like I do."

I tilted my head. "Dodger said the same thing to me."

Luke chuckled. "Well maybe we're on to something." He started to sit up, so I moved. "Listen I don't mean to cut out on you, but I have to get to work in an hour, and I still need to go change my clothes."

"That's fine. Do you want me to cook you any breakfast before you go?"

He cupped his hand on my cheek, and I leaned into it. "Nah. I'll grab something on my way home."

Bending down he placed the sweetest softest of kisses on my lips. Luke stood up and moved about my room getting dressed. I looked at his killer body completely unabashed. I was pretty sure I sighed dreamily. He looked over his shoulder and winked at me. Busted.

I got up from bed too and tied my ratty yellow robe on. I made note that I needed to replace this thing. It'd seen better days.

"I'm going to walk you out."

Grabbing my hand we went downstairs, only to be met by the smell of bacon and a shirtless Camden and Dodger. I didn't know why I'd forgotten that Dodger was going to be coming over to go for a run. He'd asked me to join them, and I declined, saying there was no way I could keep up. I was getting healthier, but in no way was I capable of their stamina.

Luke bumped into the back of me when I paused at the bottom of the steps. Both guys stopped what they were doing and looked up at me. Dodger's shoulders were moving up and down, and I knew he was laughing. I could only assume I was never going to hear the end of this from him. Camden, on the other hand, had a different expression. His mouth was closed, and his eyes zeroed in on the robe I was wearing. I caught a very subtle and brief rising of his brow, before it went away, and he looked like his usual grumpy self. *Okay, keep moving, Keegan.* Just as we passed the breakfast bar, Luke's hand slid to the small of my back in a possessive manner.

"Hey Dodge... Camden." Luke was friendly toward Dodger, but his greeting to my roommate was brisk and cold.

Both boys nodded at him. I made quick work of walking him to the front door so I could say goodbye. When he stopped dead in his tracks, I heard Camden quietly saying, "Nice, doing the walk of shame." I turned and saw a very irritated Luke. Even I bristled.

"What did you say?" Luke's voice was low and threatening.

Camden looked up from his cooking bacon and stared directly at Luke. "I said, how nice, doing the walk of shame."

"Shut up, Camden," I hissed.

He didn't even look at me. Luke's body was tense. I wanted nothing more than to shove him out the front door and deal with this on my own. My face was enflamed, and I hated that not only was one Brooks brother here to witness my overnight guest leaving, but there were *two* of them. And now the macho pig, Camden, couldn't bother keeping his mouth shut?

Wonderful.

Luke attempted to shrug it off in his casual easygoing way. "Yeah well, not all of us can be so lucky to be with someone like Keegan."

I looked up at him and smiled. That was a sweet thing to say.

Camden's nostrils flared. Did we hit a sore spot? He grunted and said, "Keep on walking Luke. Maybe you'll get lucky, and she'll open her legs for you again sometime."

Ouch, talk about a dagger to the gut. That was all it took. Luke lunged toward Camden, and Dodger jumped between them. He pushed Luke back before he was able to land any solid hits on his brother. I was standing there shaking like a leaf. Not from being cold or scared, but because I was furious. I couldn't believe that Camden would say something so hateful. Out of everything that'd come out of his mouth in the past month and a half, that was the worst. He made me sound like I was easy, like I was just like every other girl that he brought home. Luke was the first guy I'd brought into this apartment. *How dare he make me feel like a slut when he was the one carting women in here by the truckload?*

Dodger was seething too. He glared at his brother and said, "What the fuck Camden? Since when do you talk about women like that? Keegan is a good girl, and you know it."

Camden brushed off his comment and stood tall, his muscles bulging like he was flexing. The look on his face screamed that he wanted this fight. He was begging for it.

Luke leaned in as close as Dodger would allow, and he pointed his finger in Camden's face. "You ever talk about her like that again, you'll be lucky if you wake up in a hospital bed. I see the way you look at her. We're not blind. You want her. She's not like anyone else you've ever been with, and it's driving you mad that you can't have her. So you treat her like shit because you don't know how to deal with it." Camden actually growled. "Here's what's going to happen, you so much as look at her wrong or say something hurtful to her again, and I'm coming for you, Brooks. There's no question about it." Luke straightened his shoulders, rolling them to loosen some tension. He looked over at me, his eyes softening. He mouthed the words, *I'm sorry,* before making his way to the door.

I stood there in shock. My emotions rolled around from hurt and extreme anger, to pity and confusion. I couldn't even process what Luke had just spewed. Never had Camden indicated that he was into me... right? I wanted to march up to him and slap him across the face for being so ugly to me. And for some odd reason, I wanted to do the same to Luke, but that was because I didn't like the way he threatened Camden. *Holy moly what a weird way to feel.* I should be thanking him for standing up for me. I really needed to sort out my emotions. I shook my head and looked at Luke who was heading for the door.

"I'll call you later Keegan. Oh and Camden, why don't you buy your roommate some fucking decent furniture. I can't believe you'd let a woman sleep on an air mattress for a month and not at least help. You're a real piece of shit." He walked out the door, slamming it. The sound startled me.

Swallowing hard, I timidly looked over at Camden. I noticed that his eyes went from confused to angry in less than a few seconds. Oh no... why did Luke tell him that?

Camden shook Dodger off of him and took a step toward me.

"What's he talking about?" I kept my eyes on the ground. I could feel the anger emanating across the short space. "I said, what the *fuck* is he talking about?" I stilled at the clipped tone of his voice.

"Cam... chill out, you're scaring her."

Camden turned and started taking the stairs two at a time. Something in me snapped to attention. Shit he was going to my room. I didn't want him in my personal space. It was private, and he didn't deserve to see it. I started moving forward to chase after him. Dodger was hot on my heels. When I reached the top step, I saw Camden heave one quick shoulder into my door and break the lock. When he stood back up, I saw the look on his face. It was pure rage.

Oh. Shit.

CHAPTER EIGHT

I DIDN'T KNOW WHAT CAME OVER ME when I saw him standing in the doorway. All I knew was that I didn't want him in here, and I was willing to do anything to move this mountain of a man. I went at him full speed, and I flung myself onto his back. I expected him to stumble forward or take a steadying step, something, but he didn't move. Not even a little bit. As for me, I felt like I'd run into a cement wall. I made an 'oof' sound when my stomach hit his back. My arms were wrapped around his neck, and my legs were locked around his waist. My weight wasn't exerting him in the slightest. *Seriously, shouldn't his knees be buckling under the pressure?* It infuriated me that he came in here without my permission. Not only did he break my brand new lock, but I was feeling so violated that I was on the verge of tears.

"Get out," I tried growling in his ear, but it came out garbled and weak.

I saw him shaking his head back and forth. Not being able to see his face wasn't doing anything for me, nor was clinging to him like a monkey. Releasing him, I slid down his back and moved to stand in front of him. Maybe I could try and block him from seeing more than he already had. Oh who was I kidding? Standing in front of him, he could easily see over the top of my head. I took in how rigid he was. Camden's eyes roamed the nearly empty space. Not but a few seconds ago, he looked so pissed his veins were bulging from his neck, and his jaw was mashed together. Now his expression just looked... defeated. I didn't understand it.

He swallowed, and I followed the movement of his Adam's apple. "Why don't you have furniture, Blue?" His voice was quiet.

"I just don't."

"Why?"

"Because I don't, okay?"

That was when he tore his eyes away from my room and looked at me. Like, *really* looked at me. I felt so small standing here with him towering over me and no means to defend myself. Not in a physical way but an emotional one. Those eyes held me in a way I'd never felt. He made me feel like I was falling into the depths of him, and as much as I tried to claw my way out, he wouldn't release me. I brought my arms up to wrap around my middle. He followed my movement. It was as if I were exposed to the one person who I didn't want to pass judgment on me. For whatever reason it mattered, coming from him, it mattered to me. In no way, shape, or form was I ready to analyze why. The way his eyes pierced mine, it was like he was seeing through me. It unnerved me.

He shook his head again. "No, it's not okay."

"I don't understand why it matters?"

Camden reached up and ran a hand through his hair. "Because it does."

Sometimes it was so exasperating to talk to him. He was always so short with me, and this was no different. I needed him to explain to me why he looked so upset. I wanted to know why he behaved the way that he did toward me, why he said what he did to Luke. Why he couldn't just act the same way that his brother did. Speaking of which, where did Dodger go?

"That's not a reason, Camden. I want to know why."

Those deep russet eyes burned into mine. "Because you're my roommate, and a chick, and you shouldn't be in a room that's bare."

I shook my head angrily. Not far from stomping my foot at him I fumed, "No, not good enough. *What's the big deal* if I don't have these things? I don't care that I'm a girl, or that I'm your roommate. I want to know *why* it matters to *you*?"

He took a step forward, so I took one back. When he saw I wouldn't let him any closer he mumbled something under his breath, scrubbing his hand down his face.

"Hmmm? What's that?" I pried.

Camden put his hands on his hips and glared at me. I knew whatever was coming was going to be a blow so I braced myself, straightening my back and standing tall. "You matter, okay? You fucking matter. You're more than just a chick, you're more than a roommate. You're kind, and you care about people. You have put up with my bullshit since the day you moved in here, and I've slung a lot of it. I keep waiting for you to break, and yet you don't. You jut your little chin out and deal. So yeah, it fucking matters to me that you are sleeping on a goddamn air mattress, and not the softest bed that money can buy. It pisses me right the fuck off, Keegan. You deserve more."

Holy…what? I was breathing hard and so was he. The intensity of his eyes deepened, and it was more than I could handle. I turned my face away and took a deep breath. Where did I begin processing all of that? I mattered to him? Since when? The man barely gave me the time of day, let alone acted like he cared. I figured I could get run over by a semi and he'd be the dude on the side of the road videotaping it instead of calling 911. That was how much stock I put into my relationship with Camden. Hearing him say I deserved more felt like my undoing. I began walking forward, when I felt him step up behind me. Shivers broke out over my skin at his nearness, and I squeezed my eyes shut tightly. *Block him out, Keegan.* When his hand came up and rested on the spot between my shoulder and neck I jumped, my eyes flying open. His hard callused fingers brushed across the bare exposed skin. I knew he knew what he was doing. His touch was so gentle and unwelcome, yet I found my body leaning back into him for more.

"Don't walk away from me, Blue." He was speaking very subtly but firm.

"What am I supposed to do with that?" I continued to stare straight ahead at the white walls. "You've treated me a certain way since I have moved in here, and now you're telling me that I matter? I don't even know what to say to that."

He leaned down so that his face was only inches away. I felt the heat of his breath blow across the shell of my ear. "This can't stay this way. I won't let it."

What was he talking about? Was he referring to the room? "I don't understand," I responded in confusion.

He didn't even reply. When my room remained quiet for a beat too long, I turned around, and he was gone. That was weird, I still felt him at my back. It was as if the sensation of him was seared into my skin, and the feel of him continued to linger. I sighed loudly. This was too much. All of it was too much. I had no desire to try and break down what just happened. But I knew someone who would. I needed to call my best friend and tell her that this was an emergency. I swear every hair on my body was still standing on end, and my heart had yet to settle down. Macie would know what was going on. She had to. She knew boy code. Was this Camden's weird way of giving me an olive branch? I heard someone moving around downstairs, and I stiffened.

"Keeg?" Dodger yelled upstairs.

I visibly relaxed at his voice. Maybe he'd know what just happened. I stepped out of my room and up to the banister that overlooked the living room.

"Yeah?" I squeaked.

"Hey, I need to take off. Shit to do and all that."

I swallowed, unsure how to ask. But mostly because I felt stupid talking to Camden's brother about it. "Dodger, can you tell me why—"

Holding his hand up, his black hair moving back and forth, he said, "No. You're doing this one on your own. Cam just left, and I'm not getting in the middle of it."

My mouth dropped open. "But I just want to-"

He looked up at me with his piercing blue eyes, and firmly repeated, "I said no. I love you, but this is between you two."

I tipped my head down in understanding. "K." I stood there and watched him grab his keys and shut the front door behind him. My lower lip quivered, and I just wanted to crawl back in bed and pretend that everything that happened this morning would go away. Could I have a do over day, pretty please? Shaking myself out of my stupor, I went back to my room and phoned Macie. We set up a time to meet. She didn't seem at all concerned when I gave her the condensed rundown. She simply said, "We're skipping lunch and going straight to the chocolate cake." I was cool with that. And frankly my thighs would appreciate a little loving at the moment.

"What does it all mean?" I whined to Macie, who was sitting across from me. I'd just finished telling her every pitiful detail of what happened, from the moment I woke up until I turned around and Camden wasn't standing behind me.

Using her fork, she pierced a piece of cake and brought it to her mouth. She shoved it in then shrugged. What in the hell? Why was she shrugging at me?

"Mace, I'm not kidding. I need help here. Why does Camden keep going from hot to cold?"

Licking her lips, she put her fork down. "Well first, why don't you tell me about your date with Luke."

I drew my brows together. "Luke? What does he have to do with any of this?"

Macie had a knowing look on her face, like she knew where she was going with it. "Just tell me about your date, and then we'll tackle the other issue."

I glanced down at the plate. My stomach was so tied up in knots that I hadn't even taken a full bit of the little slice of heaven in front of me. "Well, we went on a picnic at the park then we played some Frisbee. He's really good by the way. Before the game and during the game, things seemed to be heating up between us. Before I knew it, we were kissing, and I was asking him to come stay the night with me."

"And did he?"

I rolled my eyes. "Duh, does he have a penis? A chick asks you to stay the night and you think he'd actually turn it down?"

She shrugged again. Grrr... I've about had it with her stupid shoulders. "You never know. I mean, what if he knew that she slept around and had a serious case of the Hot Crotch?" She picked up her fork again, reaching across the table and diving into my cake. After she took her bite, she pointed her silverware at me. "That, my friend, is nasty. I'm sure he would have said no to that."

"Mace, I have no idea where you're going with this, but eating chocolate cake like you are, and talking about

Hot Crotch is seriously going to make me gag." Not to mention it was making me itchy.

"Never mind. Tell me what happened next."

I leaned back in the booth. "Well, we went back to the apartment, and we had sex."

"Did you orgasm?"

"Of course I did."

"No need to sound offended, Keeg, I'm just asking you questions."

I crossed my arms over my chest protectively. "Yes, I had an orgasm."

"Did you feel anything else?"

"What do you mean?"

"I mean, was there passion, steam, heat, hair pulling, spanking, dirty talk, any and all that good stuff that happens when you're really into it."

"Jesus, do you do all of that stuff?"

Macie stared at me like I'd grown a second head. "Don't you?" I shook my head. "Holy shit, what am I going to do with you? So you simply had sex, and that was it?"

"It wasn't just sex, Mace, it was sweet. He was sweet."

Now she looked irritated at me. "This is what I'm getting at. You have no passion with Luke. He may heat you up, but he only keeps you warm. You want someone who will make you angry, fiery, passionate, and so desperate to have them that it makes your thighs shake." She paused for a few brief moments. "Someone like Camden."

I shot up in my seat. "I have no idea what you're talking about."

Her little smirk stretched across her beautiful face and touched her eyes. "Yes you do. Camden makes you feel all of those things and more. You just finished telling me, not even ten minutes ago, that you were responding to him, and you didn't know why. I bet if you sat back and listened to your body, it'd tell you that you crave your sexy roommate. You want him, Keegan. He may piss you off more than any other man that you've met, but that's the kind of intensity that I'm talking about. Those kinds of relationships are the ones that are explosive in and out of the bedroom. I bet he could make you come just by telling you to do so."

I squirmed in my seat, and she noticed. How embarrassing. I was sitting in the middle of a restaurant pressing my legs together because just the idea of Camden touching me the way that I had physically been craving made me wet. I felt my cheeks heat up, and Macie gave me a full blown smile.

"Okay, so I'm attracted to him. At the end of the day though, none of that matters. He's been nothing but a dick to me, and I don't know if I can forgive him for that."

"Sure you can. After everything you told me, he seems to have a sweet spot for you. In fact, I know he does. I've done some digging with the little brother."

I had a feeling I was going to need some cake for this. I spooned a bite and waited for her to tell me more.

"So Dodger and I have been getting pretty friendly."

"I noticed," I grumbled.

"Oh shut up, and be happy for me. Nothing is going to get weird, I promise. *Anyway*," she emphasized, dropping the subject. "I'd already been noticing some subtle cues from Camden when he's around you. He'd watch you when you weren't looking, or I'd see him blowing off girls that came on to him. I decided to ask Dodger what was up with that. At first he didn't want to say anything. Those boys are awfully tight lipped about everything. But me being me, all it took was a little coaxing, and he started talking." She gave me a brilliant devilish smile. I couldn't help the one that was spreading across my face. "Turns out Camden's a pretty private person. He doesn't date girls, and he never sleeps with them more than once. But when you told Dodge that Cam was bringing girls to the house, he apparently went and asked his brother about it. He accused him of trying to make you jealous. Cam, of course, told him he was ridiculous, but Dodger swears he's never seen him behave the way that he does toward you. He says his brother has gone softer."

"What does that mean, softer?" I questioned.

"I don't know. But if I had to guess, I'd say that Camden's walls are starting to come down, and he's trying to figure out if you'll let him in."

I sat back again, completely confused and unable to respond. Did Camden like me? I wasn't so sure. But I could tell a difference in how he was with me up in my room. His words were sincere. I mattered to him. Maybe he was ready to finally be friends. That had to be it. Maybe Camden had never been close with a girl before, been friends, because he's never trusted them. I was feeling like I was onto something when Macie interrupted my thoughts.

"So what are you going to do about Luke?"

"What do you mean?"

"I mean, how are you going to let him down easy?"

I shook my head in confusion. "Let him down? I'm not walking away from Luke. He's good to me, and we've already made plans for the Halloween party."

She tilted her head. "But we've just established that you and Cam-"

"No, *you've* got a theory. I'm not walking away from something that could be the best thing that's happened to me in years, Mace. I think Camden just wants a friendship with me. Luke doesn't play games, and I enjoy being around him. I'm not walking away from that."

"Even if the sex is mediocre?"

I scoffed. "Sex isn't everything."

The waitress had come by and given us our bill, and I pulled out a twenty to leave on the table.

"Oh young one, I have a lot to teach you."

Standing up I grabbed my purse. "Alright Yoda, you can tell me all about it in the car. Let's go before I order some ice cream to go with that cake you just hoovered." We both laughed as we walked out of the restaurant.

I'd kept myself busy by going to the mall and browsing around. Then I stopped by the house to visit with Sarah and my mom for a bit. When things had gotten too tense, and mom and I were on the verge of an argument, I'd gotten up and left. I'd been avoiding coming home for most of the day because I wasn't ready to face Camden just yet. When I unlocked the door and started to push it open, I saw the light from the television glowing in the darkened space. As I came inside I set my keys down on the counter and slipped off my flats. My heart sped up when Camden came out of the downstairs bathroom, shutting off the light behind him.

"Hey, you're home." He greeted me with his usual deep voice.

"Yeah, I went to meet up with Macie and stopped at my mom's for a bit. I'm pretty tired though, so I think I'm going to go crash." I was covering my mouth to stifle a yawn.

He seemed to be watching my every move, and it was unnerving me. "Okay, have a good night."

"Yeah, you too." I paused for a second, trying to consider what that look on his face meant.

I was too tired for any more mind games, so I turned and trudged up the steps. When I got to my door, I stopped. The knob was different. There wasn't a lock on the outside, and it looked like it had been changed out for this new one. Tentatively I grabbed the handle and twisted, pushing the door open and switching on the light on the wall. As soon as my space was illuminated I gasped.

What. The. Hell. Was. This?

My room wasn't how I'd left it. Freshly painted walls invaded my senses, and I took in every inch that was now different. There was a soft yellow that now colored the walls. It brightened the space even more than plain white did. But I didn't get a chance to enjoy it. My eyes landed on the other offending objects in the room. Up against the wall, where my air mattress used to be, now stood an espresso-colored sleigh bed with two matching night stands on either side. Their sleek glossy finish reflected the light from the ceiling fan. Directly across from the bed was a matching dresser. On the floor was a grey rug that looked so plush you'd lose sight of your toes if you stepped on it barefoot. What in the hell was all of this? I took a few steps into the room and slowly approached the bed. Running my fingers across the polished wood, it felt soft to the touch. I felt my blood boil more with every step I took. I tipped my head back and forth, popping the bones in my neck.

I couldn't believe he did this. That was why he was looking at me so weird. This was my room, and Camden came in and completely invaded it. I plopped down on the bed and considered what I was going to do. It wasn't that I didn't love the furniture, it was that I didn't *ask* for it. With every passing moment, my anger was turning to pure unadulterated rage. *How dare he!* I bet the bastard was sitting downstairs all smug thinking he'd helped the poor roommate that couldn't afford anything. I couldn't sit still. Standing up I began pacing. This was going too far. I could handle nice gestures, but coming into my room and giving me things that I didn't ask for was taking it too far. I wanted it out. I wanted it all out.

Now!

Marching downstairs, I was a girl on a mission. When I reached the bottom step, Camden turned around to look at me. Sure enough, there was that smug, satisfied little grin. I bet he was expecting a thank you for his diluted sense of generosity. Oh boy, was he in for a treat. I smiled back at him, but I had a feeling it didn't look quite right. I was certain I had a crazed look in my eyes, and at this point, I didn't care. My crazy was about to be hanging out all over the place. Now where in the hell was it? My eyes drifted to the corner of the dining room. Up against the wall was a Louisville Slugger, just what I was looking for. I casually walked over to it and picked it up. I knew Camden's eyes were tracking me. The grin on his mouth had slipped, and now he just looked confused. I held the bat in my hand, testing its weight and deciphering my next move.

"What are you doing?" Camden asked.

I looked up at him, sending daggers at him through my eyes. "Practicing my swing."

His confusion deepened. When I saw his eyebrows raise, I knew realization hit him. "Now Keegan, don't go doing something you're going to regret."

The laugh that came from my mouth was pure evil. It sounded bizarre, even to me. "Oh Camden, I'm not going to regret this. I'm going to enjoy it very much." With that I turned on my heels and raced up the stairs. But not before I heard him say, "Shit," and hurdle the couch coming after me.

I made it up to my room before he did. I took a brief moment to breathe in through my nose and back out through my mouth. I was centering myself for my grand swing. Standing before the beautiful bed he had no business buying me, I brought the bat up high and was about to bring it down as hard as I could, when it stopped mid-air. Twisting my head around, I locked eyes with wild deep brown ones.

"Don't you dare," he growled, inches from my face.

CHAPTER NINE

HIS TONE ONLY SERVED TO HEIGHTEN the wildness flowing through me. Sticking out my chin I seethed, "Or you'll what?"

Camden licked his lips, my eyes following its path. "You either drop this bat and step away from the bed, or so help me, I will put you over my knee."

I barked a laugh. "Oh really, I'd like to see you try. I'm so fucking furious with you right now, the moment you let that bat go, I'm going to town and giving everything in this room a facelift. I just might even start with *you.*"

He narrowed his eyes. "Don't test me, Blue."

"Stop calling me that!" I shouted in his face.

"No, I think I'll keep it. If it gets you riled up at me like this every time, I'd say it's worth it," Camden taunted.

"*Let the bat go.*" I spoke through gritted teeth.

"No."

I tried giving it a tug, but it wouldn't move. It was still partially in the air, but Camden had such a tight grip on it, I knew it wasn't going anywhere. Something had to give here, and there was no way I was backing down from this. I felt violated, and the only place I could direct the emotions welling up in me was at the man standing in front of me. He had no business doing this without asking. Instead he plowed in here in typical Camden fashion and did whatever in the hell he wanted. I was sure he thought he was doing a good thing, but he knew nothing about me. I didn't even consider us friends, and yet he decorated my room without any input from me. Did I love it? Yes. Was it exactly what I would have picked out? Yes, but that was beside the point.

"I swear to God, I know you have more bats in this house, and I will go find them. I suggest you let this one go."

Our chests were heaving despite not having exerted ourselves. Camden's eyes were so fierce, so lethal, I couldn't help the dampness that was forming between my legs. The man was damn sexy when he was pissed. I liked it even more, because it was directed at me. The depth of his deep brown irises seared through my soul as I watched them bounce back and forth between my eyes. When I caught him glancing down at my mouth, I tilted my head ever so slightly. What was he doing? Before I even had a chance to register the movement, he yanked the bat out of my hand and chunked it to the side. I heard it hit the wall with a thud, and I glared at him. The damn bully. I mentally calculated whether or not I could dart to the side and grab it faster than he could get a hold of me, but I knew the odds were against me. Watching him watching me caused a shiver to break out over my skin. Camden was challenging me.

He slowly shook his head back and forth, never taking his eyes away from mine. "You just can't fucking let it go can you? I practically see the wheels turning in your head." He leaned in even closer. If I moved a few inches in, our mouths would touch. "You'll never make it." The smirk that was plastered on his face made me want to hit him.

"I hate you," I said with as much venom as I could muster.

He gave me a full blown brilliant smile that nearly made me weak. "No you don't."

"Oh yes I do, I hate you more than-"

He cut me off. His hands moved incredibly fast and dove into my hair behind my neck. He pulled me forward so hard that I had no choice but to crash into him. His mouth came down onto mine with such intensity that I moaned with unrequited desire. His tongue pushed against my closed lips, demanding entrance. I didn't even try to deny him. There was nothing about this kiss that was soft and sweet. This was balls-to-the-wall intense. He was taking what he wanted from me, and I didn't care that he hadn't asked. Which was strange since I was furious at him for doing that very thing to my room. When I opened my mouth, he dove in. His tongue was soft and yet forceful. He was leading this kiss with every thrust, every push. One of his hands buried in my hair moved forward a few inches to rest on my cheek. He tilted my head slightly with his thumb and got a deeper angle. The way his mouth moved over mine was possessive. He was branding me. I openly welcomed any mark he was willing to leave. My hands were grasping the front of his shirt, and I didn't realize he had been walking me backwards until my back hit the wall. With the length of his body pressed into mine, I could feel what I was doing to him. In this moment, I felt powerful. I was turning Camden on, and he wanted me. There was a heady concoction of lust and desire swirling through me. I had no self-control with his lips on mine, and yet I felt like I could weld him to do whatever I wanted.

When his hands came down my back and rested on my butt, I lifted my leg slightly. He took hold of it and lifted me effortlessly. As I wrapped myself around him, I heard him growl his approval into my mouth. His erection was now resting right where I wanted him to be. Pushing against the strained hardness of his pants, I felt the pool of desire at my center. All that was separating us was a few articles of clothing. I wanted them gone, I *needed* them gone. Lifting at his shirt, I tugged it up and over his head, briefly breaking the torturous kiss he was consuming me with. We stilled for a beat, looking at each other, gauging what the other would do next. When I allowed my eyes to drift down his chest, I admired every sculpted curve. Tentatively I placed a finger in the center of his chest and traced the bulging of his pecs, moving down to his abs. He was watching me with a guarded fascination but didn't stop my perusal. I wanted to memorize every inch of this bare skin under my fingertips. The way that my touch was causing his muscles to twitch as I ghosted it over his skin, the way that he held his breath as though he were afraid of me, or that I'd end this. And I did need to end this. I had no idea what I was even doing letting him hold me against this wall, even though he was fulfilling my darkest desires. All I knew was that I was going to take this moment and file it away later when everything went back to normal between us. When Camden remembered that he couldn't stand the sight of me. I'd think back to this, and know that I held the power for a few brief moments, that I was capable of bringing this man to the edge and made him desire me. One of his hands that was between my back and the wall came forward and stilled my hand on his chest, just over his heart.

"Enough," he said so coarsely that I thought he was going to put me down, that he had come to his senses. Instead he came forward again and used his tongue to trace the seam of my lips. I parted them slightly, so that he might push further. A sound of approval rumbled through his throat as he ground his pelvis into me. I couldn't help the shocked gasp that came from my mouth. I felt his mouth tip up into a grin. "Feel good, Blue? I can make you feel so much better." Oh I knew he could. That was never the question. But my brain was warring between stopping this and telling him to get the fuck out and mind his own business, or letting him take me to whatever ecstasy he had in mind. Both choices weren't good. Both would lead us back to the same boat we were in before he decided to kiss me. He was going to regret this, deep down I knew he would.

He carried me over to the bed that I both loved and hated and set me down on my feet. His rough hands snaked their way under my shirt, lifting it until it was right under my breasts. My skin pebbled under his touch. My legs shook from the weakness he made me feel, and I squeezed his shoulder to hold myself up.

"Lie down," he demanded.

"Wha-?" I didn't even get to finish.

"Lie down, or I will put you across this bed myself."

I gulped, my heart was in my throat. Did I really want to do this? Hesitantly, I sat on the edge of the bed and pushed myself back with my arms. When I'd scooted far enough that I could lie down without my feet dangling off the edge, I looked at him. What I saw in his russet depths held no reservations. He wanted this. There was an edge that screamed he was going to take me, and I didn't have a choice in the matter. Did that even bother me? There was no time to think about it because one of his eyebrows lifted, daring me to defy him. Sinking back onto the bed, I was lying completely flat. My body was humming with an energy I'd never felt before. It was like being on a rollercoaster ride. I was on the tracks, making my way to the top. The moment that you were ever so slightly teetering, before the free fall and your stomach was in your throat...that was how I was feeling. It was invigorating and terrifying all at the same time. I stared at the ceiling, knowing he was standing next to the bed, watching me, calculating his next move. The room was so quiet you could hear a pin drop. The anticipation was making me crazy. Squeezing my eyes shut, I waited, counting my breaths while he decided his next move. I heard the quiet rustling of clothing and something falling to the floor. Oh my gosh, was he getting naked? All of a sudden I wasn't ready for this. We weren't even friends, and yet I was splayed out across my bed, waiting for him. I had to stop this before anything happened.

I shifted slightly, making out as if I were going to get up, when I felt the weight of the bed dip next to me. His hand came to my shoulder opposite of where he was sitting and gently pushed me back down. My eyes opened and darted to his. Camden shook his head, telling me I wasn't going anywhere. Mine narrowed back in return, and I saw a flicker of a challenge cross his features. His head tipped to the side, silently daring me to try and move. When his gaze broke from mine, and traveled down my body, I noted that his pants were no longer resting on his hips. That must've been what I heard.

"I'm not having sex with you!" I blurted in a moment of panic.

All motion from him stopped, and he brought those beautiful brown eyes back to mine. "Who said we were having sex?"

"Well, I thought...and you kissed me, you...you took your pants off so I assumed...." I was stuttering, my cheeks flaming.

He gave me a half smirk, as though he were privy to some private joke I didn't know. "I'm lying next to you tonight to make sure you don't destroy your new furniture, Blue. Settle down."

He what? "So wait...you're *not* sleeping with me?" I questioned, now slightly confused.

Chuckling he said, "Do you *want* me to sleep with you?"

"No!" I said, my voice squeaked.

"Riiight." He leaned in so he was looking down at me. "Don't think I don't know what you were feeling a few seconds ago. It's okay that you want me."

"You self-righteous son of a—"

"Are we resorting to name calling? Cause if that's the case, I have a few in mind for you; Vixen, Feisty Kitten, Crazy Bat Lady...the list could go on."

"I don't understand you," I snidely retorted.

"Good, I don't want you to understand me."

"Well, I don't." He had leaned back, and I crossed my arms over my chest like a pouting child. My emotions were all over the place.

"So did you expect me to walk out of here and trust that you wouldn't find something else to beat the shit out of all this?" His arm went out, as if to show the display of furniture. "Nah...I'm not letting you out of my sight."

"You can't just stay in here without my permission."

"The hell I can't. And I'm pretty sure it'd be entertaining to watch you try and kick me out." He climbed into the bed and laid back, pushing his legs under the comforter and placing his hands behind his head. His body was wedged right against mine. Well, more like the bed was so plush that I had no choice but to roll into the side of him.

I was speechless. How did I go from being so furious and wanting to commit murder, to feeling so much lust that I thought I would explode from it? Now I was utterly confused. Unfortunately he was right, I would never be able to move him. My efforts would be futile. "This is unacceptable. Tomorrow morning I'm calling some people and having them remove all this stu—"

"You have no people, Blue," he interrupted me. His eyes were closed, and he was completely relaxed.

"I do to have people!"

"No you don't."

"Yes, I do."

"Dodger already knows that if he even tries to move anything out I'm going to kick his ass. So *no*, you don't have people." He opened one eye to peer at me. I was gaping. "And shut your mouth or I might have to find a way to put it to use."

Unbelievable. How did any of this happen? I had scooted over to the farthest spot on the bed that I could to get away from him. "Crazy bastard, thinks he can come in here and take over everything. Well, I'll show him…" I was mumbling under my breath, my body turned away from his.

"Hmmm… what's that?" he taunted.

"I'm going to pay you back for this. I can't let you buy me all this stuff and not give you the money for it."

I was lying on my side one minute, and the next I was flat on my back with Camden hovering over the top of me. "Listen to me closely, Keegan. All of this, it was a gift. I gave it to you because I wanted you to have it, because I think you deserve to have something nice. You think I don't see how much you struggle; you're studying, working, going to the gym, school. And up until this point, I hadn't known you'd been sleeping on an air mattress. There was no way I was going to sleep across that hallway from you, knowing that, and not doing something about it. What kind of man would I be if I were curled up in an actual bed every night, while you were on the floor? I wasn't going to tolerate it." His mouth formed a thin line. "You will accept this gift from me, and I won't hear any more of you paying me back for it. Do you understand me?"

I breathed in through my nose, taking in his words. It wasn't helping that his body was nearly lying on top of mine, and I still felt the sensation of desire coursing through my veins. "I don't like things handed to me Camden. I work for them, I earn them. I don't want to feel like I'm weak, like I'm some sort of charity case."

"Is that how all of this makes you feel?"

"Yes."

He continued to stare down at me, a look I couldn't decipher etched into his handsome features. When a grin slowly began to spread across his face, I knew I wasn't going to win this argument. Okay, when have I ever won an argument with him? With a casual shrug he said, "Too fucking bad, you're keeping it. And for the record, I don't do *weak*, and you're not."

If anybody asked me whether I knew what I was going to do next, whether it had been an accident or on purpose, I'd lie till I was blue in the face. My knee jerked up and made contact with his balls. He almost fell forward onto me but caught himself before he did. Camden rolled to his back, cupping his precious jewels, his eyes squinting shut.

"Oops! Hope I didn't hit you too hard," I said in the most ladylike voice I could conjure.

He started coughing and moaning. "What the hell Keegan?"

A smile slipped onto my face, and I rolled away from him, again. "Night Camden."

I could have sworn he called me a Crazy Devil Woman before he rolled the opposite direction from me and settled into my new bed. I see another new name had been added to the list.

My body was hot, and I was scissoring my legs, trying to get them out from under the sheets. A hand came around and splayed on the bare skin of my stomach making me pause. Camden's warm breath blew across my neck causing goosebumps to spread over me. His rough fingers traveled down until they barely slipped under the edge of my panties. I turned my face into my pillow and tried to muffle my moan. What was happening right now? It didn't matter, I needed this to keep going. Pushing my butt back into the hard male body behind me, I ground my ass into a very erect cock. My arms moved out from under my pillow, and I grabbed onto his forearm that was holding me. I lightly dragged my nails down the skin to the hand that was ever so close my throbbing center. Helping him push it down further and further, until he reached the sensitive skin that desperately needed attention.

"Please," I begged.

"Please what?" Camden's husky voice resounded in my ear.

"Please, touch me. I want you to touch me."

"Where?"

Grasping his large hand I pushed his fingers between my slick folds. "Here. Oh God, right here."

"Right there?" he breathed as he swirled his fingers over my clit.

My body was shaking, and I was still so warm. Why was it ridiculously hot in here? I tried again to move the covers off of me, but they wouldn't budge. What the hell? When a long finger slid inside of me, all other thoughts went out the window. My hips began rocking against very capable fingers. Stars were dancing behind my eyelids, and I was so close to tipping over the edge. I moaned again, this time much louder. Sweat that was beading up on my skin was now trickling down my boobs and across my forehead. It was too much. I was on sensory overload. Between what was going on downtown and feeling like I was in a sauna, I had to get these covers off of me before I passed out. Grabbing the blankets I threw my arm back, flinging the blazing inferno off of me. My hand connected with something.

"Ouch! Fuck!" someone next to me yelled.

Startled awake, I opened my eyes. When I flipped over, Camden had his hand to his face. I scrambled up the headboard, trying to calm my racing heart. He looked up at me with confusion.

"Seriously, Blue, you have a mean swing. Damn it, that hurt." He was rubbing his nose.

"Why are you still in my bed?" My voice was thick with sleep, my body still pent up with need.

"I told you I wasn't leaving." When he dropped his hand he had an incredulous look.

"What?" I said sarcastically.

"I think the better question would be, were you dreaming about me?"

My face flamed. "No, why?"

An eyebrow lifted, and he smirked. *"Touch me. Oh God right there,"* he said in a voice that was supposed to mimic my own.

I gasped. Had I really said that all out loud? Holy crap that was embarrassing. I tried to school my face and not show how mortified I was. "I was dreaming, but it certainly wasn't about you."

"Oh really, then who could have you been dreaming about? And don't bother lying to me by saying Luke. You and I both know he could never make you pant like that."

I let out a clipped laugh. "And you think you could?"

A rough hand gripped my hip and slid me over to press against his side. He came up over the top of me and squeezed himself between my legs. With a feather light touch, he brushed his finger down the curve of my face from my cheek to my chin. I couldn't help my body's natural reaction to lean into him. When he pushed up with his hips and ground into my sensitive nerves that were already on the verge of combustion, I let out a very guttural moan. My eyes rolled back, and my hands grasped his biceps. The slight quaking of my body couldn't be helped. If he did it just one more time, I was going to burst.

"Yeah, that sounds about right."

I took a deep breath and opened my eyes. "What?" I felt so out of sorts, and pent up, I didn't want to talk anymore. Arguing with him was exhausting. I was in a position to let him win, just this once, if he would give me what I needed.

He was looking down at me, wonder in his eyes. "You're stunning when you need to come."

My brows furrowed. "Excuse me."

"Don't make this so complicated. You were having a dream about me, you even said my name." I did? "I see it in your eyes, the way your body is melting beneath mine. If you want me to finish it, Keegan, all you have to do is ask."

Oh God, I wanted him to finish it, with every fiber of my being I wanted him to finish it. But my brain was screaming at me to tell him to fuck off. The internal battle going on was so strong I couldn't even speak. My mouth opened and closed, and he continued to stare at me. Nothing was going to come out of me. The side of me that was warring to shove him off was winning.

"I can't." I finally managed.

He blew out a breath, frustration settling across his face. "You are such a stubborn woman, you know that?"

I couldn't help the grin that came to my lips. "Hello pot, I'd like you to meet kettle."

"You're sarcasm might be endearing most of the time, but right now, it's annoying as fuck."

I laughed. "Glad I could entertain you. Now will you get off of me, I need to go shower."

He held there a few moments longer than necessary. I had a feeling he was trying to decide if he was going to give me what I was asking for, or what I really *wanted*. And it wouldn't be just me who needed sating. Oh no, I could feel very clearly what was going on with him down there. Decision made, he shifted back and got out of the bed. He moved to the door and was about to walk out when he said, "I'm making breakfast. Toast, bacon, and coffee sound okay?"

I suddenly felt shy. Here was 'kind Camden' again, the one who I didn't know how to handle. "Sure," I responded.

He turned and left my room. I sucked in a much needed breath of air. Good God, last night went *nothing* like I thought it would. I stood on very shaky legs and went to my closet to find something to wear. I had to go to the mall today to get the finishing touches for my Halloween costume for the party that was coming up in two days. And of course, at some point, I'd need to find a time to study. Getting into the shower, thoughts of Camden rolled through my head freely. Before, I had doubted that he had any interest in me. I thought I was just his chubby roommate who he wanted nothing more to do with than collect rent from, ignoring my presence. Never had I assumed he could possibly be attracted to me. I was nothing like the women he brought home. In fact I was the opposite. Maybe that was why he was messing around with me. Maybe he was testing the waters with something different because he was bored. That thought made my stomach turn. Could he possibly be that cruel? The more I thought about it, the more I realized, yes, he could be. Camden had no problem hiding the way that he felt about me when I first moved in. Even now, he kept me on my toes, never knowing what he would say and if it would leave behind a sting. Could I honestly trust what happened last night and this morning as something more than a man pushing to see if he could score with someone like me? Whatever happened last night couldn't repeat itself. I didn't even know what had gotten into me. I was dating Luke. How would he feel if he found out that

Camden kissed me last night? I had a temporary moment of weakness. Camden had been pushing my buttons for a long time now, and last night it had all built up to a fleeting moment of mouths and hands. I wouldn't lie and say it didn't feel good. In fact I'd never felt anything quite like it. When Camden was touching me, my brain seemed to start misfiring and could no longer form logical thoughts. I had to stay away. There was no question. *Haven't I said that before?*

    By the time I'd stepped out of the shower and gotten dressed, I was in a bad mood. Any residual longing I felt for release had drifted away. I brushed my hair and teeth, and started to make my way downstairs. I figured I would eat breakfast with Camden as fast as possible and leave the house before he got me worked up again. But when I reached the bottom step, I froze. The sight in front of me was enough to make any woman melt. Camden stood shirtless with only a pair of black briefs on. He had a set of ear buds in his ears, and the iPod that was attached to it was partially sticking out of the waistband of his underwear. He was bobbing his head, and doing some weird little shimmy shake, while cooking turkey bacon over the griddle. I smiled at how ridiculously cute he looked. Standing back, he hadn't noticed that I was here watching him. In the morning light he looked different, softer somehow. I allowed my eyes to roam over his barely covered body. The sun reflected off his tanned torso. Anybody who saw him like this could admire the work he'd put into himself. Every turn he made, every twist and lift of his body and arms, you could see the defined muscles push against his skin. He was a true work of art, and his body was his canvas. Camden took care of himself, and I found that to be an attractive quality. He turned his back to me again, reaching for something in the cupboard. Unknowingly I walked a few steps toward the kitchen. It was as if everything he did was drawing me in.

I wanted a closer look. Naturally my eyes shifted to his gorgeous ass that was encased perfectly by black fabric. Sweet Jesus, why was I a butt girl? It looked so good, all I could imagine was digging my nails into and nipping it with my teeth.

"*What do you say to taking chances...*" Camden's sudden high-pitched outburst of singing caused me to startle. "*So talk to me, talk to me...*" he sang some more. He turned back toward the rest of the living space and stopped short when he saw me standing there with the biggest shit eating grin on my face. Yanking one of the ear buds out, he actually looked embarrassed. Hmmm...what was that about? "Sorry, I didn't hear you come down."

"Well, I wouldn't think so. You were too busy singing." I eyed him skeptically. Still smiling I asked, "What are you listening too?"

"Music."

"Uh huh, what music? You seemed pretty into it. How about we plug it into the stereo, and we can listen to it together?"

"Nah. It's just rap shit. You don't like that kind of music." He narrowed his eyes at me. "How long have you been down here?"

"Long enough." I took a few steps toward him.

"Blue..." His brown eyes looked nervous.

"Yeah."

"What're you doing?"

I wanted to know what was making him so nervous. He was listening to *something* that was making him hide from me. Determined, I was going to find out what it was. Playing it casual, I walked into the kitchen. Shrugging my shoulders, I picked up a ripe strawberry and took a bite. He was only a few feet away from me, watching me skeptically. "Nothing, just grabbing some breakfast before I leave to go to the mall."

His shoulders visibly relaxed. "What are you going there for?"

Camden still had one ear bud in. I could hear the faint sound of music playing through the one dangling at his side. Pretending to reach for a banana I moved quickly. Grabbing the iPod out of his briefs I dashed around the counter and swiftly put one of the ear pieces in. His face blanched. He started to come toward me, but I put my hands up to stop him. Recognizing the voice singing I burst out laughing.

"Celine Dion? *You're* listening to Celine Dion?"

"Yeah, so what?" He tried to let it roll off as if it wasn't a big deal.

"So what? Camden, you're not the type of dude that listens to the woman who helped make Titanic popular." I kept giggling, and I could tell it was ruffling his feathers. "Are you a closet Celine fan, Cam?"

Shaking his head slightly, I could see light dancing behind his eyes. "I'm going to give you three seconds to come back over here and hand me my iPod like an adult, or I'm coming after you."

"Oh come on. I swear, your little secret is safe with me."

"One." He stood with his hands braced on the counter.

Giggling I took a small step back. Dramatically lifting my arms I held them out to him. *"Never let go, Jack."*

I saw a ghost of a smile cross his mouth. "Two."

"I can totally find you tickets to see her in Vegas, if you love her that much."

"I warned you. Three."

I squealed and dashed for the dining room table. Making it to the other side before he caught me, I turned and saw him grinning from ear to ear. I was breathing heavy but enjoyed taunting him. "I guess I never would have pegged you for a ballad kind of guy. That's sort of sweet."

"You're pushing your luck. I'm going to catch you, and when I do, you're going to wish you'd handed the music over like a good girl."

"It's a good thing you won't catch me then."

We were in a staring contest. Who would jump first? Almost as if we moved at the same time, Camden hopped up onto the table and scrambled across it while I went running back toward the kitchen. A yelp came from my mouth, and I tossed the iPod over my shoulder, hoping he'd give this up if I gave him what he wanted. Arms came around my waist and lifted me in the air. He caught me. I was laughing so hard, I knew I couldn't escape him.

"Gotcha." He spun me around and walked me into the living room toward the couch.

My legs were swinging freely, and I tried to kick away from him. "Let me go."

"Huh uh. For all I know, you're going to run out of here and tell everyone that I like chick music."

Chortling I said, "But you do like chick music."

He dropped me onto the couch and came over the top of me to straddle me. "I swear to God, I will tickle you until I'm sure you'll keep your mouth shut."

I gasped. "You wouldn't."

He raised his hands like claws and wiggled his fingers. I started laughing before he even touched me. "Oh God no, please don't. I hate being tickled."

"Then tell me what I want to hear."

"What do you want me to say?"

He lifted a brow at me. Those darn eyebrows always said so much. "You're going to say, 'Camden, I promise I won't tell anybody what I heard today.'"

I let a few seconds pass by. "I am sure that Macie and Dodger won't judge you for your eccentric musical tastes. In fact I'm sure they'd sing right along with…AAAAAHHHH!" I screamed as his fingers came down and wiggled against my armpits. I was laughing so hard tears were streaming from my eyes. "Stop, stop, stop!"

"Say it." His voice was gruff but playful. He stopped moving.

Taking a deep breath I sang, *"Near, far, wherever you are…"* His fingers began their torture again. "Ahhhh okay, okay…I won't say anything. Just stop! I swear I'm about to pee my pants! STOP!"

He chuckled. Leaning down to get closer to my face he said, "You promise?"

There was a crackling in the air. All of the playfulness was being sucked back and something else was taking its place. "I promise," I stated sincerely.

A calloused finger came up, brushing down my cheek and stopping under my chin. "So beautiful," he whispered.

He continued to hover over me. His eyes seemed to look from my eyes, cheeks, nose, lips, and back again, as though he were searching for something. My heart began pounding in my chest, and I was certain he could hear it. Swallowing, I tentatively asked, "What's happening here?" I'd said it so quietly, I barely even heard myself.

"What do you mean?" he said, clearing his throat slightly.

Did I ask him what was going on between us? Would I be embarrassing myself if I threw out every thought I've had about our relationship, and how it was shifting onto unsteady ground that I couldn't define? Lying underneath him for the second time today, I took note of how he was once again turned on. But was it because he was touching *me* or was it because I was simply a female and that was just what happened to every guy? Deciding better of my question, I changed the subject.

"Are you going to the Halloween party?"

His head tipped to the side, and I briefly wondered if he was going to let me get away with ignoring what he just asked. "No, I stopped going to those frat parties three years ago." I sagged in relief that he let it go.

I shifted under him, and he took the hint to move off of me. I felt the loss immediately and wished he would come back. I loved his weight being on me. "Oh, okay."

He sat with his arms resting on his knees, and he was looking at the ground. "Are you going with Luke?"

"Yes," I replied softly.

He glanced over at me with a seriousness I hadn't yet seen in him. "Be careful with him, Blue."

"What-?"

Shaking his head he stopped me. "I'm not going to say anything else other than, just please be careful. Okay?"

I nodded my head in understanding. I'd seen so many expressions on Camden's face in the past couple months, but this one, this one unnerved me. He was warning me about Luke, but I had no idea why. I sat there wondering what could possibly make him say this to me, but I'd felt nothing but comfortable with Luke. He was warm, gently, caring, and endearing. If I should be worried about anybody, it would be Camden. He was the one who had an air of dangerousness, edginess, and darkness that I'd never touched before. Well, not until last night. I should be scared of the man sitting next to me, because he made me feel like his very essence was a drug. The draw I felt to him was so potent, that even now, I wanted to taste him. I wanted to feel him on me, caressing me, whispering things in my ear that made me blush. Rubbing my hands back and forth on my legs, I needed to get going. Some fresh air and time away from Camden would do me good. I stood on shaky legs and made my way to the door. Camden remained on the couch and watched me walk away.

"I'll be home later," I said over my shoulder.

"Okay."

I opened the front door. "And Cam?"

"Hmmm?"

"You're not sleeping in my room tonight." I leveled a look at him.

That glorious smirk that now made me feel naughty things crossed his mouth. "We'll see Blue, we'll see."

With that I walked out the door and headed to the mall.

CHAPTER TEN

TWO DAYS AGO I'D LEFT THE APARTMENT, and my mind was reeling. After talking to Macie while I found the rest of my Halloween costume, I was no longer questioning if Camden liked me, but rather just wanted to know why? I wasn't his usual M.O. When I looked in the mirror I saw an average girl with curvy hips, somewhat pretty hair, and that was it. When I looked Camden, he was dangerously sexy, the guy who every girl wanted to tame but never could. So I wondered again, why me?

I thought about this while I was putting on my costume that Macie had talked me into and was feeling butterflies in my stomach. Nobody had seen me in it yet, and as much as I told myself I was nervous for the general masses to get a load of me in my barely there nurse outfit, I was mostly terrified of Camden seeing me. He'd already referred to me as 'the chubby one' once before. Despite working out, I wasn't feel overly confident in my appearance. Macie said the costume was made for my body, but, as my best friend, I figured she was supposed to say that. I stood in front of the full-length mirror that hung behind the bathroom door. I had on a pair of black stilettos that increased my height by four inches, fishnet stockings, and a lace garter with a little red bow hugging my right thigh. A black dress that embraced every one of my curves completed the costume. There was no way I'd be able to bend over or sit down without flashing my box of treasures. When I decided to go with a nurse costume, it was really just as a joke since I was in nursing school. There were two options: black or white. Macie told me to go with the black, and we'd make it look like a vampire nurse, so it would be something different; darker, more alluring. My long blond hair was pinned up in a messy bun with some loose tendrils falling down around my face. What was most shocking were my eyes. The color of them were already a vibrant blue, so when I added the dark eyeliner and shadow, they stood out in stark contrast against all of the black. I leaned in a little to get a closer look. Weird…they seemed almost light blue/white. I added a finishing touch of some fake blood at the corner of my mouth and stood back to check out my reflection. Oh man, there was no *way* I was going to be able to go out looking like this. I didn't look like a naughty vampire nurse, I looked like a straight-up hooker who must have bit some poor dude's dick because he shoved it down my throat too far. Ack! No way, I needed to go change. I was sure I had something in my clos-. My thoughts were interrupted by a knock on the door.

"Get out here woman! Luke will be here any time now, and I want to take a few shots before we leave," Macie called from the other side of the door.

Well there goes that plan, I sighed. Tentatively I opened the door and slowly showed myself. I heard her suck in a breath of air before she let out a low whistle. "Holy hot momma, you're going to set *all* the boys' panties on fire tonight."

I rolled my eyes. "Shut up, Mace. I'm not comfortable at all. Can't I change into something that's a little less revealing? I'm sure I have an adult onesie that I can put on. It even has a flap in the back. I could let it hang open and put a sign on the open part that says 'no entrance' or something."

She shook her head and giggled at me. "No way lady. This outfit is smokin'! I don't get why you're so worried. I told you that you looked great, so what's the problem?"

"The problem is my cooter is feeling far too drafty, my boobs are about to pop out, and all this makeup makes me look like a two dollar whore."

She tips her head to the side and deadpans, "I'd totally pay a solid twenty to see your meat curtains."

I cracked a smile. "Really?"

"Absolutely. I bet you have a better roast beef sandwich than any Arby's."

I let a giggle slip out. "This conversation is ridiculous, you know that right?"

"Yep, but if it convinces you to go downstairs and do some Lemon Drops with me, then mission accomplished. Now let's go, or I'm sending Dodger up here to get you."

I paled a little. There was a vast difference between standing in front of your best friend looking like a high-class hooker, *thank God*, than standing in front of a super-hot guy and letting him judge you. She must have seen the indecision on my face because she yelled, "Dodger?"

"What?" he called from downstairs.

I leaned in and grabbed her arm. "Wait, wait, wait…I'll go, just let me get my purse."

"Never mind." She gave me a devilish smile. Little brat always got her way.

As we descended the steps, Macie was walking in front of me looking crazy beautiful, as always. She was wearing a shorts one-piece set that was supposed to look like a fighter pilot. Her long brown hair swayed with each movement she made. A pair of aviators sat atop her head, and she had on tan boots that stopped above her knee. They laced up and looked like combat boots. Where she found those, I didn't know. I admired her confidence. She owned every room she walked into, and people took notice of her. Not because she was the fat girl who looked like she stuffed herself into a sausage tube, but because she has always been this way; gorgeous, stunning, poised.

I was looking down, watching where my feet were and hoping like hell I didn't fall in these killer heels. As my foot hit the bottom step I heard a, "Holy shit," come from Dodger's mouth, and what sounded like an animal growl from Camden. When I was safely off the stairs I looked up. Macie was already in the kitchen pouring the liquid courage, and the two brothers were staring at me open mouthed.

"Jesus Christ, Keegan, have you been hiding *that* under all those clothes this whole time?" Dodger wondrously asked.

As I came toward the both of them, Camden's eyes were following me. The intensity of them lit my insides on fire. I shook my head at Dodger. "I have no idea what you're talking about."

"Your body is fucking banging!" he said appreciatively, but soon after was rubbing the back of his head where Camden had just smacked him.

"Shut your mouth douchebag," he told his brother.

I shyly looked down at the floor and back up through my eyelashes. Camden and I made eye contact and all the air was sucked out of the room. His tongue came out and licked his bottom lip, and I felt my knees go weak. I took a few purposeful steps in his direction and saw his nostrils flare. I felt desire pooling at my core. He was holding me captive with his piercing brown eyes. I was a few feet away from him when Macie broke the trance I was in.

"Get over here Nurse Sexy, it's time to make a toast."

Clearing my throat I went to the counter and picked up a shot glass.

"To new experiences, dancing our asses off, getting laid, and making every cock on campus stand at attention," Mace announced with a raised glass, throwing back her shot. I tipped my head back and swallowed the murky yellow liquid, its bitterness burning my throat. I noticed that Dodger was glaring at her. She leveled a stare at him. I took note of it and would have to remember to ask her what that was all about later. The two of them had been hanging out a lot, and I knew Macie liked him. They'd gone out on a few dates, but apparently Dodger wouldn't give in to Mace and sleep with her. I could tell she was getting upset about it.

I felt someone behind me, and a subtle brush of air across my ear. "Can I talk to you for a minute?" Camden rumbled.

I looked over my shoulder and gave a slight nod. I didn't think Dodger and Macie would even notice my absence. They seemed to be locked in a battle of wills at the moment. Camden put his hand on my lower back, leading me into our small laundry room. When he shut the door behind him, I suddenly felt claustrophobic. Facing him, Camden took up majority of the space. His wide shoulders and tall stance dwarfed me.

"You can't wear that," he said flatly.

My brows drew together. "What? Of course I can."

"Don't test me on this."

"I'm not testing you, but you're not making any sense."

He roughly reached up and yanked on his hair. "Seriously Blue, you can't walk into a frat house where everybody has been drinking looking like that. Every guy in there will get the wrong impression."

"Camden, I'm not wearing anything that's more revealing than Macie, what's the big deal?"

He took a step into me. The warm chocolate of his eyes hard, yet pleading. "You just can't. I'm not going to be there to make sure you stay safe."

"I wasn't aware that you cared so much."

He grunted. "Don't start. You and I both know that isn't true."

"Oh really? Cause I've been going over and over it in my mind the past two days, trying to figure out what exactly this is between us, and I can't seem to figure it out." I had no idea what was making me discuss our mysterious relationship now. Regardless, I let it out and the question was now hanging out there for him to answer.

"Don't be so dense, Keegan," he replied harshly.

I put my hand up to my chest and gasped. "Are you insulting me now?"

"No, I'm stating the facts. You know damn well what's going on with us and yet you come walking downstairs looking like a tramp. Then you say that you are still going with Luke, even after I warned you about him. I'm starting to think you don't know your head from your ass," he reprimanded.

My hand came up on its accord and slapped him across the face as hard as I could. His head swung to the side, absorbing the impact. Ouch, that stung. I was sick and tired of the hatred he spewed, especially after questioning his intentions.

"You're a self-righteous son of a bitch!" I spat. "From the day I walked in here, you've treated me like I was some inconsequential thing that you could speak to and treat however you wanted. You've degraded me with name calling, harassed me, ignored me, and pushed me. Then you all of a sudden find out that I was the poor girl living across the hall without furniture, and now I've become some project. It's like you're testing me to see if you can get me to fall for you. Well fuck you Camden.

I'm not falling for you. In fact I'm jumping off this rollercoaster ride. I'm sick to death of your bullshit, and I call quits. Enjoy your evening, I have somewhere I have to be." I tried to push past him, but he blocked me.

I saw so many emotions warring across his face. If I didn't know any better I would say it looked like sadness, regret, pain. His hands came up to touch my face. I held my breath, knowing that if he did it, I'd melt into him. I needed my resolve to hold strong. If I gave in to him right now, he would never stop this outlandish quest he seemed to be on. There was a knock at the front door, and Camden dropped his arms. Every expression I'd seen only a second before was now wiped clean. The indifference on his handsome face was like a punch to my gut. Stepping aside, he gave me enough space to leave. I guess that was it. I somehow got the last word with him, and I honestly couldn't feel worse about it. He'd always fought me every step of the way, and now he seemed to be giving up. I couldn't afford to let him in right now. Camden would destroy me if I let him. Steeling myself, I squared my shoulders and lifted my head. Hoping like hell that my eyes showed exactly what I felt in that moment, I stared at him. When he tilted his head to the side I knew I needed to get out of here. When I walked past him, my side brushed against his front, and I could have sworn I heard him groan.

Macie was just opening the door for Luke while a very grumpy looking Dodger stood in the kitchen watching her. Apparently I wasn't the only one having issues tonight. When Luke walked in it was like seeing a breath of fresh air. After several days of Camden's intensity, it was going to be nice being around Luke's easygoing demeanor. His tamed blond hair and aqua eyes sought me out. When he found me over by the laundry room door, his eyes grew wide, and the shocked expression was well worth the discomfort of wearing the outfit. We tried to coordinate what we wore, so he was decked out in a pair of scrubs with splatters of blood on the front and had a stethoscope hanging around his neck.

I walked toward him, wanting nothing more than to feel his embrace. He opened his arms to me, and I sank into him, breathing in his clean scent. His mouth came down to the top of my head, and he kissed my hair.

"You look stunning," he complimented.

I tipped my head back and smiled at him. "Thank you. You're not so bad yourself, Doc."

His pointed finger tapped the tip of my nose, and he smirked. "Maybe later we can play doctor. You can be the naughty nurse and assist me with a breast exam."

I threw my head back and laughed. "You're terrible," I said, slapping him on the arm.

His deep chuckling warmed my chest. I stiffened when I heard a door slam behind me. Looking over my shoulder I saw Camden standing with his hands on his hips looking furious. His eyes were trained on mine, and I felt myself sinking into Luke. Those dark brown depths looked lethal, and it made me nervous. Even Dodger and Macie paused what they were doing to look at Cam. The room was silent and nobody moved. Camden's look was meant for me. He was angry, hurt, vulnerable, but there was something else there. He was warning me. I squinted my eyes in confusion and tilted my head to the side. It was barely perceptible but I saw it, he glanced from me to Luke. He was telling me again to be careful. I desperately wanted to know why he felt the way he did when Luke's been nothing but a gentleman to me. Either way, I'd heed his warning. How could I not? No matter how confusing our relationship was, deep down in my gut I knew I could trust Camden. I nodded even more subtly toward him. His mouth thinned into a straight line, and he exhaled loudly. Breaking his stare, he walked over to the corner of the dining room and picked up his gym bag. Slinging it over his shoulder he moved past Luke and me to the front door.

"Where's he going?" I heard Macie whisper to Dodger.

"He has some issues he needs to work out," he replied.

When the front door closed we all visibly relaxed. "What was that about?" Luke asked in my ear.

I shook my head. "I don't know," I lied, not wanting to tell him anything.

When I turned to face him again, he looked down at me skeptically. A slow smile spread across his face, and he brought his lips down to mine. The soft tenderness of his kiss causing me to sigh. It was the briefest of pecks, but it was enough to erase the tension that Camden had caused. However, I couldn't ignore the niggling feeling that there was still so much unsaid between Camden and me. We'd have to talk at some point. Plus I wanted to know what his issue was with Luke.

"You ready to go?" he asked.

"Yep, let me grab my coat."

When I was all set, I shut off the lights, and we headed to the party.

Pulling up to the house, there were cars parked haphazardly all over the place, and the music could be heard all the way down the street. Orange lights were strung up in the trees, and cheesy Halloween decorations adorned the front lawn. There was everything from Styrofoam tombstones to plastic zombies that looked like they were clawing their way out of the ground. Cobwebs were strung all over the front bushes, and black lanterns lit the path to the front door. The house itself was huge. It was a two-story Tudor style that could use a coat of fresh paint and some new trim. Coupled with the Halloween decorations, the place was pretty creepy.

As we approached the front door I hesitated. Not only was I nervous because I never really hung out with the frat types, but it was made worse because of my chosen attire. Silently cursing myself, I wished I'd gone with the onesie. When Luke opened the door, the party was in full swing. People were packed in like sardines; dancing, laughing, kissing, and having a good time. Up against the far left wall was a small DJ booth with speakers planted all over the house. The booming music of Ellie Goulding-Burn was reverberating in my chest. Those who were dancing had their hands in the air feeling the beat. Luke placed his hand on my lower back leading me through the crowd. People were bumping into me left and right, and I lost my balance a few times in these heels. Thankfully Luke was there to steady me. Several couples stopped us as we pushed our way through the crowd, greeting Luke with hellos and eyeing me with curiosity. We made our way into a kitchen that seemed much too small for a house this size. Assorted alcohol littered the counter, along with cups that were half full or tipped on their side. Luke opened one of the cupboards and turned toward me.

"Pick your poison Nurse Rachett." The lazy grin he gave me was infectious.

"Beer from the keg is fine."

"I never pegged you for a beer girl. I would've figured Cosmos and anything with an umbrella was more your speed."

I laughed. "That's Macie's thing. I'm not a high-maintenance girl."

Filling a red cup, he handed it to me and pulled me into him. "No, you're really not," he said with such amusement I wondered if that was what he thought of me this whole time.

BENDER

"Hey, where's my drink?" Macie asked from behind me. She and Dodger came in right behind us but had gotten lost in the crowd. Dodger had been here a few times before, so he knew his way around and I wasn't overly concerned about Macie staying by my side. Luke grabbed another cup and asked her what she'd like. She thought about it for a moment, tapping her black nail polish covered fingernail on her chin. "Do y'all have anything fruity?"

Luke and I both chuckled. I caught his smile and shrugged. "I can come up with something. All the guys in here have to keep their dates happy somehow."

When he handed her the drink she twisted around to face me. "So what are you two going to do?"

"I don't know. All of these people make it hard to move around."

"Well, there's dancing, beer pong out back, there's also some lounge chairs on the deck that we could sit and relax on if you'd like," Luke piped in.

"Relaxing sounds nice. I've never been a big dancer, and I've never played beer pong before in my life."

His boyish grin hadn't left his face since we came in the door. "You don't know what you're missing. I'm the reigning champ in this house. If you change your mind, you would have an undefeated partner."

"Good to know," I said, bringing my cup up to my lips. His eyes were watching my movement, and his pupils dilated.

Turning my back to him, I gave my attention to Macie. "What about you? Where'd Dodger go?"

She bristled and said, "Who knows? He got stopped by some whorish-looking angel before I walked in here."

My eyes softened toward my friend. I grabbed her hand and gave it a squeeze. "Mace, I'm sure he was just being friendly. Besides, does Dodger even know you like him?"

Rolling her eyes she said, "I'm sure. We've gone out a few times, and he's even kissed me. But when I've asked him inside at the end of our dates, he's blown me off each time. I'm starting to wonder if he's gay."

"Jesus Christ, Macie, I'm not fucking gay," an irritated Dodger said from the door.

She spun on her heels, not even remotely embarrassed that she got caught saying that. "Then what's your deal? You'll make out with me, but you won't sleep with me?"

He looked from me to Luke and back to Macie. "We've talked about this, and I'm not discussing it in front of other people."

"Oh come on Dodger, anything you tell me, I'm going to share with Keegan." Gah! Did she really need to bring me into this?

He vehemently shook his head. "No. This isn't the time, nor the place."

"Well aren't you chivalrous," she replied snidely.

Dodger's frustration amplified, and he dragged a hand through his almost black hair. "I swear to God, Mace. I don't know what you want from me."

She flung her arms up in the air in frustration. "I want you to fuck me!"

Dodgers eyes grew wide and then narrowed on her. "You're pushing it. Keep this up and I'm going to drag you out of here and take you home."

"Oh goodie. Then I'm sure you'll just drop me off and leave me there to take care of my own needs. Such a gentleman." Her words were laced with venom, and she wasn't even drunk yet.

I didn't want to be in here for this, and I'm sure Dodger would appreciate it if we left them alone to sort this out. Touching Macie on the shoulder I told her, "We're going out to sit on the patio. Come get me if you need me."

Not breaking her stare, she said, "K."

Luke grabbed my hand and led me back out through the crowd. "What was that all about?" he shouted in my ear.

"Long story," I yelled back.

As we passed groups of girls chatting and laughing, I noticed that a few of them took notice of Luke. Jealousy stirred in my veins. He was mine ladies, eat your hearts out, I thought. I also took note that of all the costumes and how mine was surprisingly tame. There were barely there bikinis and Playboy Bunny bathing suits. A few girls were wearing outfits where the back went up their butt like a thong. I shivered. I'd *never* be caught dead wearing something like that. Not even in the privacy of my own home. The guys, on the other hand, had an array of costumes. From Ace Ventura to Chippendales. A few of them made me giggle with their creativeness. Walking out a set of French doors, we stepped onto a very large deck that spanned the whole back of the house. There were no Halloween decorations out here, but Tiki torches, resting in cylinder holders, lit up the backyard. There were about a dozen lounge chairs scattered across the deck. A group of guys were off to the side loudly talking and having a good time.

"Hey Luke!" a male voice shouted over the crowd. Several heads turned and looked in our direction. Luke smiled, and we went over to where they were sitting.

Luke palmed several of their outstretched hands, and they all greeted each other.

"Keegan, I want you to meet some of my brothers from the house. This is Holden, Brent, and RJ." I gave a shy wave to the three of them. "And the rest of these clowns are pledges." There was a resounding grunting coming from the males standing in front of me. All I could picture was every one of them sitting in front of a television with a beer and their hands down their pants. The thought made me want to laugh.

"Aren't you going to introduce me, Luke?" a sweet female voice said from behind a few of the guys who had stood up, blocking her from my view.

I noticed Luke's jaw working back and forth, and something about his posture said he didn't have any interest in telling me who this chick was.

"Keegan, this is Veronica. Roni, Keegan."

"Ugh, I wish you'd stop calling me that. That nickname is so high school, Luke," she said with slight annoyance. "Please, call me Veronica. Nobody calls me Roni anymore except for him."

"Some things never change," he said under his breath.

Veronica was sitting down on a chair, but I could tell she was tall. Maybe even taller than Macie. Her features were a mix of Asian and Caucasian. She had long black hair that touched the top of her breasts, and a pair of lips that were pouty and full. What was most striking about her were her long full eyelashes that surrounded cat-like eyes. The color was almost a caramel, which I've never seen before. For as beautiful as she was, she also didn't give me the warm and fuzzies. She was eyeing me like I was somehow the enemy stepping into her territory. I had no doubt that a girl like her held every single one of these boys under thumb. That was fine. I wasn't interested in any of them. It would, however, be an issue if she were interested in Luke. We'd only been on a few dates together, but it was enough for me to feel possessive of him. The way she was looking at me made me uneasy.

"So Keegan, what do you do?" the one introduced as Holden asked.

Breaking eye contact with Veronica, I turned to him and said, "I'm a nursing student here at UG, and I work in Medical Records at Dr. Hill's office."

Holden looked like an average guy, brown hair and brown eyes. Nothing really stood out about him. "Sounds cool. What year are you?"

"I'm in the middle of my junior year," I stated proudly.

"You're a junior, and you aren't in the nursing program yet?" Veronica asked, interrupting the conversation. Her voice was suddenly becoming annoying.

"Stop it, Roni," Luke scolded. I hated that he had a nickname for her. I wondered how long they'd known each other.

"What? I'm just asking. Most juniors are already doing clinicals in their third year."

Clearing my throat I felt the need to defend myself. "I would be, but I chose to hold myself back. I don't want to apply without knowing for sure that I am giving myself the best foot forward. The program is highly competitive, and I want to ensure that my grades are up to par. I chose to retake a few science classes. I should be good to go after this semester. I'll submit my application and hopefully I'll know if I got in by the spring."

Luke was smiling down at me, and I noticed Veronica curling her lip. "Oh, well that's good, I guess."

I nodded, unable to say anything else without it coming across as rude. While I was talking I realized that the group of guys who were pledges were glancing at me every now and then, then turning back to their conversation. I ran my tongue across my front teeth, self-conscious that I had something on them. Why did I get the distinct impression that I was being talked about? Luke's hand rubbed across my back, bringing me back to the other four still talking to me. RJ and Brent both had brown hair and green eyes. In fact the longer I looked at them, I realized that they could pass for twins. With their tall stance and wide shoulders, I wondered if they were on the football team. Nothing about those two screamed average. In fact, both were very handsome.

"You okay?" Luke asked, laying his forehead on my temple.

"Mmmhmm."

"Y'all look like you've gotten cozy." I think it was RJ who said that.

Luke once again became rigid. "I suppose we have. Keegan's a sweet girl." I leaned further into him at his compliment.

The smiles that spread across those four faces made something in my stomach turn. "Good to hear, Luke, good to hear," Brent said in an almost sarcastic fashion.

"So how far have you two taken things?" RJ asked.

"Excuse me?" I said.

"Fuck off Brent." Okay, I'd gotten the two guys mixed up.

Holding his hands up, palms out, Brent said, "Hey man, just asking. I didn't know how serious y'all were. Maybe I wanted to ask Keegan out later for myself."

My brows drew together. "That's a bit rude, don't you think?"

If looks could kill, Luke looked like he wanted to throttle Brent. "Maybe," he said with a shrug. "But in case you haven't got the memo, we share around here."

The giggle that came out of Veronica's mouth made me ill. "Well I don't."

"Hey Princess, just stating that you're a *fine* piece. And when Luke's done with you, I'd gladly take a ride." This time it was RJ piping in.

"Enough!" Luke growled.

I was so flabbergasted at the turn this conversation took, I had no response. Needing to take a step back and gather myself, I looked up to Luke and said, "I need to use the restroom."

Gritting his teeth, he nodded. "Down the hall, it's the third door on the right."

Without a backwards glance I rushed into the house and tried to find the bathroom. I needed a little bit of solitude. When I found the correct door, I had to wait for two other girls to go in and do their business. When it was my turn I went inside and locked the door. Sagging against the wood I tried to push away the feeling of panic. In that moment Camden came to mind. If those guys had said all of that in front of him, he would have leveled them to the ground. Luke seemed just as upset over their harshness, but there was something else there that caused him to bite his tongue. I couldn't put my finger on it, but it wasn't right. Having never been to a frat party before, I had to wonder if this was just the way that these guys behaved. Luke had never once treated me like an inconsequential object, but maybe at one point he had acted like them. He was in grad school now, so that must have caused him to do a little growing up and see that women weren't play things. I deserved to be treated with respect. Even though my outfit said trashy, on any other given day, I was very reserved. Steeling myself I decided I wouldn't expect Luke or anybody else to stand up for me. I would demand a certain level of respect from these guys, and they would need to know that I wouldn't tolerate anything less. Washing my hands and checking my ridiculous makeup, I wondered where Macie and Dodger had gone off to, and if they had worked out their issues. No way would they have sat back and listened to the load of crap I'd just heard. Drying my hands I unlocked the door and stepped into the hall. I was greeted by the same cat-like eyes that had been glowering at me outside.

"Are you having fun?" Veronica asked, her tone sounding weird.

"I guess so. All this," I said looking around. "It's not really my thing, but I'm having an okay time."

"It's all been one big joke, you know that right?" she said to me.

"What are you talking about?" I asked, confused.

"Luke dating you, bringing you here to this party."

"I'm not following you."

She sighed in annoyance. "It's what they do. They find a Plain Jane girl to see if she will fall for the guy, and then they bring them to this party for the friends to judge how in deep she is. They do it every year." She casually looked at her finger nails.

I shook my head. "Luke would never do something like that."

"Oh really? So you honestly thought that someone like him would go for someone like *you*? Sorry to burst your bubble sweetheart, but Luke and I are an item. We have been since high school. I let him take on the challenge, because the winner gets a vacation to Cozumel, and I wanted it. He gives me whatever I want." Her full lips contorted into a sadistic looking smile.

My head was spinning, and I felt dizzy. Putting my hand on the wall behind me for support I said, "You're lying."

Her shoulders came up and dropped in a nonchalance attitude. "If you don't believe me, go back out there. The boys are discussing it as we speak."

I darted past her and made my way to the back door. When I reached the handle, I twisted it and hesitantly stepped out onto the deck, trying to keep myself inconspicuous so I didn't tip them off that I'd come back. This was all a big mistake. She was just jealous. Veronica must have had a relationship with Luke at some point, and she wanted him back. It was the only explanation that I could come up with. For one, he's never even mentioned her to me, not that we'd really been together long enough to delve into our past relationships. And two, I couldn't fathom him taking me out, dining me, all of the laughs we've shared, and we'd even slept together, for it all to be just a ploy. Stuff like this didn't happen in real life. This was the shit that you read about in novels. As I neared them, I stayed hidden behind people who were talking, I overheard Luke and the other three with a few of the pledges.

"I'd say it's a done deal. The chick RJ brought could give two shits that she's with him. In fact I just saw her sucking face with some dude from down the street."

"Yeah, well Holden's girl was looking at him with puppy dog eyes, and she looked like she would have gotten on her knees in front of everyone if he'd say he loved her."

There was a round of laughter. "Luke has it in the bag. Maybe after you break the news to her, I'll be the one to pick up the pieces, and she'll let me fuck her sadness away."

"Fuck you dude. Leave her alone, okay?"

I was getting aggravated that I couldn't hear who was saying what, but it didn't matter. My stomach was sitting in my throat. Everything Veronica said was true. This all was for some big game, and I was a pawn for Luke to win.

"Dude, don't tell me you're falling for her. Roni would be pissed."

"I'm not falling for her. But she's a good girl, okay? I've gotten to know her is all," Luke argued.

"Either way assholes, we've got another two hours before we call this thing. Keep your dates happy and their cups full," someone else said.

I was going to throw up. Instead of breaking up their little charade and letting them know I heard everything they said, I rushed back into the house. Looking around frantically, my eyes darted everywhere in search of Macie or Dodger. I weaved in and out of people, bumping into some so hard I thought I'd fall over. I was trying to hold back the bile that was rising up in my throat, but I knew it was only a matter of time before I tossed my cookies. Just then strong arms wrapped around me, and I pushed back against the hold. I thought it was Luke who might have come inside to find me, but I heard Dodger near my ear.

"What's the matter?" His deep voice was like a gentle stroke to my breaking heart. Turning into his arms, I pressed myself into his chest and let him hold me. Tears began to flow freely down my cheeks, and I could tell I was worrying him. Pulling back slightly he tipped my chin up. "Tell me what happened?"

I bit my quivering lip to keep from bursting out bawling. "I can't talk about it right now. Can you just take me home?"

His blue eyes searched mine. "Did Luke do this? I'm going to kick his ass if he hurt you. Did he touch you?"

I shook my head. "No, no it was nothing like that. Please Dodger, I want to go home."

He narrowed his eyes at me and nodded. "Let me see if I can find Macie. Give me just a second."

I slowly made my way to the front door, when I heard Luke calling for me from the back of the house. Turning around I saw him waving and smiling at me, but it faded when he saw my face. He dropped his hand and started coming my way. I didn't want to do this right now. I was too upset, and I wanted nothing more than to get out of these clothes and lay in my bed. If he got to me now, I'd be too tempted to slap him across the face for how he treated me. Dodger came striding up with Macie in tow, concern etched all over both of their faces.

"Hurry, we've got to go," I said, desperate to get out of here and away from the noise of the speakers.

Dodger turned when he heard Luke call my name again. Glancing over my shoulder, regret was plastered all over him. I think he knew that I knew. Shouldn't he be happy? He got what he wanted. He won his stupid contest. Now he could go back to Veronica and leave me alone.

"Keegan wait!" he shouted. Some people stopped what they were doing to watch the scene that was unfolding.

"Take her out to the car. I'll be there in a minute," he instructed Macie.

I grabbed his forearm and was shaking my head back and forth. "No Dodger. Leave it alone, okay? It was no big deal, I just want to go home. Please!" I begged.

Indecision warred on his face. He looked from me to my best friend, finally deciding that he wanted us to go ahead to the car without him. Not knowing what Dodger was going to do made me even sicker. I didn't want him getting into any fights because of me. And sadly I didn't want Luke to get hurt either. Macie took my hand and dragged me outside to the car. When I got to the curb, I bent in half and lost my dinner. Acid was burning my throat, and the taste of regurgitated alcohol made me retch again. Why was this happening to me? This was not how I saw tonight playing out. When my stomach was emptied of everything I'd ingested today, I climbed into the backseat of the car. Macie got in on the other side of me, and she pulled me down into her lap. With my head resting on her legs, I finally felt safe enough to let it go. The sob that tore from my chest was painful. I'd never felt so used before in my life. I held onto Macie like she were my lifeline. She was my safety net. She'd always been here for me, and I couldn't be more grateful that my soft place to fall was here with me tonight.

"Wanna talk about it?" she asked quietly.

I shook my head. The driver's door opened and closed. I lifted my head to see that Dodger had climbed in and was starting the car. His face was set in stone.

"What happened?" Macie asked him.

"Don't worry about it. Let's just get her home." I saw him pick up his cell phone that he'd left in the cup holder, press a few buttons, and set it back down. I briefly wondered who he was texting but didn't think much of it.

The drive home was short but quiet. Macie continued stroking her fingers through my hair, calming my nerves, and silently giving me strength. Neither of them asked any questions, but they knew Luke was the one who upset me. I'd tell them about it later, but right now I was thankful for their reticence. I had no doubt Macie was full of questions, but she knew me well enough to know that I wasn't going to be talking anytime soon. The last time I was this upset was when Mom told me she was pregnant with Sarah. It turned my world upside down, and Macie came over to comfort me. We'd put N'Sync on repeat, and we ate chocolate ice cream well into the night. I didn't really talk then either, I just drew from the strength and company of my best friend. I had needed to process how this was going to change things for me, how my life was going to be different. Right now was much the same. Luke's little operation was hurtful. It had hit me to the core. Much of my life I never felt like I was special, like I deserved anything outstanding. Luke asking me out was the first time I really let my guard down and let myself think that I might actually be good enough for someone like him. Someone who was smart, handsome, charismatic, and fun: the fairy tale man. I was nowhere near falling in love with him. But opening up the box that even allowed that idea to penetrate my shell, the sheer thought that we *could* have had something special, made this hurt all that much worse. I erected walls up around me for a reason.

Pulling into the parking lot of the apartment complex, I sat up and wiped my eyes. Macie gave me a sad but knowing look. I was tired and ready to wash my face and go to sleep. Dodger opened my door and helped me out of the car. I'd slipped my heels off earlier so the ground was rough on my feet. Without even asking, Dodger came up and slid his arms under my knees and around my back, picking me up to carry me. It was a sweet gesture, and one I was grateful for. I rested my cheek on his chest as he climbed the steps and opened my front door. Macie was following behind us carrying my purse, jacket, and shoes. He stood to the side to let Macie in and kicked the door shut behind him. I looked up at him and gave him a tentative smile. It was all I could muster.

A deep scent of sweat and Camden approached from the other side. What on earth? Looking toward the living room, Camden was a few feet away from us and striding toward me. His jaw was set in stone, and I'd never seen him look so angry.

"Tell me *everything*," he demanded.

CHAPTER ELEVEN

I DIDN'T UNDERSTAND MY REACTION to seeing Camden barreling toward me. It was like I had tunnel vision, and he was all I could see. Everything else around me fell away, and I needed him. I needed to hear his voice and be in his presence. Squirming out of Dodger's arms, I heard a quiet 'ooof' before my feet hit the ground. Oops, I must've accidentally elbowed him. I rushed the last few steps to Camden, never taking my eyes off of him. Throwing myself into his arms he caught me and a rush of air blew out of me. I inhaled deeply as I buried my nose in his neck and felt his arms come around me, holding me tightly. He must have just come back from the gym. The musk of his sweat mixed with the laundry detergent we both used permeated off of him. I felt his chest rumbling against my chest, but I blocked everything out. Everything but him. I assumed he was talking to Dodger, but I tuned it all out. I simply went still, letting the warmth of this man seep into my pores, making me feel safe. Why did I need him like this? We had fought only a few hours ago, and I had slapped him across the face. He should be pushing me away and committing me to the loony bin for how I was behaving right now. Except he wasn't. The look of anger that he held when we walked in the door wasn't directed at me, it was at the situation. It was meant for Dodger, demanding that he explain what happened. When I rushed to him, his brown eyes softened. In the few short beats before I hit him like a freight train, his look toward me was forgiveness.

"Hold on, Blue," he murmured in my ear.

I nodded into the crook of his neck and squeezed my arms around him. He picked me up the same way that Dodger did and moved us through the house. I had no idea if Macie and Dodger were still here, and I didn't really care. All that mattered to me was that, with every breath I took in, it was Camden who was surrounding me. Although I knew that Macie was going to have a *load* of questions to fire at me later. Not just about the party incident, but also with my whole Scarlett O'Hare I just pulled with Camden.

I felt the subtle jostling as though we were moving up the steps, and I admired the ease in which Camden carried me, as though I didn't weigh more than a feather. He pushed through a door and walked inside, kicking it shut behind him. Thinking we were in my room, I lifted my head in anticipation that he was going to set me on my bed. But when my eyes adjusted to the dim light filtering through the windows from the street lamp, I noticed we were in Camden's room instead. I'd never been in his room before. I'd never felt comfortable enough to step foot in here. Even before I signed my lease, I'd only given this room the briefest of glances. I stood there taking in my surroundings after he set me down, wanting nothing more than to walk around and look at every single thing that he obviously felt important enough to display. Camden had stepped away from me to get something from his dresser. When he came back, he held out his hand. He was giving me one of his t-shirts.

"Camden," I said, my voice scratchy from crying. "My room is across the hall, I can get one of my own shirts to sleep in."

He shook his head. "Not tonight, Blue. I want you in my clothes and lying in my bed."

Tentatively I took the shirt from him, swallowing hard. "Could you turn around please?"

The sweet smile he gave melted my heart. It wasn't his usual smirk or arrogant grin he showed me on a daily basis. This one was kind and compliant. "I'll actually step out for a minute."

He walked out, shutting the door behind him. I made quick work of getting the uncomfortable outfit off my body. I threw it on the floor, wishing I could take it downstairs and burn it in the sink or something. I made a promise to myself that I'd never be caught dead wearing something so provocative again. All I did was make a fool of myself. I didn't belong in clothes like that. I didn't belong in that frat house like a typical college girl groupie. And I certainly never belonged with a guy like Luke. I chastised myself for thinking that we could have had something. I hated that I made myself believe that he might actually like me. I couldn't get my mind to wrap around the words that were playing over and over in my head. It was all just a game, a stupid competition that they had every year. But Luke was so believable. None of it made sense to me. It couldn't have all just been a game for him. He was so tender, and his words were sincere. Or were they? Had I really been that *stupid*? I sat down on the edge of the bed, my arms resting by my sides, and my hair curtaining my face. My eyes were heavy from crying, and the swirling thoughts were making me dizzy. Every minute that ticked by, I felt more confused and more questions arose. The slight clicking of the door opening and closing alerted me that Camden had reentered the room. I wanted to look up at him, to give him a self-assured smile that reassured him I was okay, but I couldn't muster one. I just sat there with my head down, wallowing in my thoughts. Camden kneeled down in front of me, and I opened my eyes. His fingers gently lifted my chin, and I noticed the washcloth in his hands.

"Let's get some of this makeup off," he said as he gingerly swiped the warm towel across my eyes. I probably looked like a raccoon with all the black.

I chewed on my lip, trying to keep the tears at bay while I let him clean me off. This was a side of Camden I'd never seen before. I was shocked by his compassion. He was always so hard edged, never letting anyone receive this affection from him.

"Why are you being so sweet to me?" I whispered.

He paused and regarded me. His eyes burning into mine. After a few short beats he continued what he was doing. "A girl like you should never cry unless it's tears of happiness."

There was no stopping it. A single tear dripped out of my eye and cascaded down my cheek. Camden reached up and brushed it away. "What did I do to be treated this way?"

I knew he understood what I was referring to. "Some guys just don't understand what they have. And then there's some that never deserved to have what was standing right in front of them. Luke was never worth the ground you walked on."

I sniffled and gave a slight smile. "Thank you."

He tossed the rag into a hamper that was in the corner. "For what?"

"For not saying 'I told you so.'"

He shook his head. Standing up he tipped his head at me. I scooted back and lay down. His bed was so cozy. The silkiness of his sheets and the soft down of his pillows, I could burrow in this spot and not move for days. He sat down next to me and brushed an errant hair away from my forehead.

"I told you so won't fix the wrong that was done to you, Keegan." His eyes were so soft I had to look away.

I nodded. The delicateness of Camden's fingers grazed down my cheek and to my neck. I closed my eyes and let the feeling sink in. He was touching me as if I were breakable. When I opened them again, he was watching me with a deep regard.

"Tell me what happened."

Sighing loudly I attempted to detach myself from the situation. I didn't want to cry about it anymore. Starting from the beginning I told Camden everything. I told him about meeting the three guys, and how they made me feel. I told him about Veronica and how she cornered me outside the bathroom to divulge their little secret. When I'd finally gotten to the part where I stood on the deck and eavesdropped on the conversation about it all being one big competition, I could see every vein in Camden's neck protruding. His nostrils were flaring, and I knew he was doing whatever he could to dial in the anger he seemed to be feeling. My lip started to quiver when I told him about me finding Dodger and begging him to take me home. Camden turned and situated himself on the bed and lifted the top half of my body to drape over his. He kissed the top of my hair and whispered, "I'll fucking kill him," to himself.

"That was pretty much the whole story. I feel pathetic! I should have known better than to believe that I belonged in a place like that and acting like I fit in. That's not who I am."

Camden grunted underneath me, and I lifted my head to look at him. "Who are you?" he asked.

With regret I admitted, "I'm the girl who's always picked last. I'm overweight and act older than my age. I've never attempted to fit in with the popular crowd.

BENDER

Growing up with my mother has forced me to live a life beyond my years. Her actions required me to take on the role of mother with Sarah, and I think it prevented me from doing the normal things that kids my age were doing." I lifted my shoulders and dropped them. "There's nothing extraordinary about me. But I do care about people, and I love helping them. It's pretty much why I choose the nursing field."

He brushed his long fingers through my wavy hair. "You couldn't be more wrong if it hit you between your beautiful blue eyes. You *are* extraordinary."

"How did you know?"

"That you're extraordinary?"

I shook my head. "No, how did you know about Luke? You warned me about him, so how did you know?"

He stiffened. "Back when I was in school, that frat house was known for doing shit like that. I'd heard of stories of them bringing the most unattractive people they could find to those parties, and they would tease them for entertainment. It's why I never went when I was invited."

"But yet you let *me* go to one knowing full well that it might have been a set-up?" I sat up, my body was half turned toward him while I leaned on my arm.

"No, it wasn't like that at all. You aren't anything like what they used to bring in to those parties. You're smart, funny, stubborn, and drop-dead gorgeous, Keegan. How would I have known that they changed the game?"

"How about the simple fact that they even *played* games like that? You should have told me. I wouldn't have gone anywhere near that house had I known."

He clenched his teeth, his jaw was set in stone. "If you want to blame me for how tonight played out, then fine, I'll take the brunt of it. But don't think for one second that I think you deserved what happened to you. I would have fucking thrown you over my shoulder and hauled you out of there if I'd known you were a part of their game. Hell I would have tied you up and locked you in my closet and told everyone you were sick if I'd known beforehand. Like I said, I didn't know that those assholes changed their tactics." He leaned forward and slid his hand underneath my hair to my neck. "It's going to stop."

My pulse picked up at his touch, while confusion settled on my features. "What's going to stop?"

His eyes became hard, and my tough exterior Camden was back. "I'm going to find every single one of the assholes that had the balls to do this to you, and they are going to wish they'd never joined a fraternity. They'll be lucky if they are still walking when I'm done with them."

My eyes widened. "Camden, you can't go beating up everybody who hurts my feelings."

"The fuck I can't. This shit has been going on for years. Maybe someone needs to put the fear of God in them… or rearrange their pretty little faces." The smile that spread across his lips was scary. "They messed with the wrong girl."

"I wish you wouldn't. Fighting doesn't solve anything."

"That's cute, Keegan. You sound like a fucking school counselor." He smirked. "Luke knows what's coming for him. I bet he's shaking in his prissy little boots, and I plan on delivering."

"Seriously Camden. No. Just leave it alone. I want to forget this night ever happened. Okay? Let. It. Go."

"Not gonna happen, Blue."

I laid my head back down on him and shook my head in frustration. Yet another battle I didn't feel like fighting with him. He chuckled at my resignation. I hated that he felt the need to fight for me. I wasn't an advocate for using fists. He was right though, Luke better be shaking in his boots. Not only was Camden very capable of taking him on, I was pretty sure *I* was going to flip my shit if I saw him again. Sighing deep into Camden I buried myself into his side and inhaled his scent again. His need to stand up for me was sweet, but misguided. He'd eventually figure out that there wasn't much to me but a plain girl who could offer a nice friendship. It pained my heart that I thought so little of myself, but it was what I felt was true. I wanted Camden. I wanted him more than my next breath, but at what expense? Sadness seeped back into me as my eyelids grew so heavy I could no longer keep them open. While I drifted off to sleep, I had the scary thought that I was becoming attached to this man. With all of the passionate fighting and sometimes gentler moments, he had become a source of comfort. The apartment didn't just feel like home to me, Camden did.

Opening my eyes, I saw that it was still dark outside. Looking at the clock on the bedside table, it was two in the morning. I closed my eyes and stretched my still muscles. The feel of the bed was foreign. Where was I? It dawned on me that I wasn't in my room. Grabbing the sheet I pulled it up to my chin. The scent of Camden washing over me, I moaned in contentment. I was in his bed, and I'd fallen asleep on him. Except, I glanced around and he wasn't in the room. Where did he go? Maybe he moved to sleep in my room to give me space. I wouldn't blame him. First I flung myself at him and bawled my eyes out, then he felt obligated to take care of me. I was the quintessential needy girl. I bet this was why Luke chose me. The events that happened only a few hours ago plowed into me like a Mack truck. The game, their words, Veronica, Luke… it was real. He must have sensed my loneliness and zeroed in on me. It was like I was a standing target who was flashing a bright red sign screaming 'pick me, I'll be your next victim.' Tears welled in my eyes, and the sorrow I felt came down around me like a heavy weight. Why me? What did I do in this life to deserve this? I was a decent daughter growing up, and I took care of my little sister like she was my own. I showed up at my job on time and did what was required of me. And academically I was an overachiever. It was like the world was playing a cruel joke on me. Was I so desperate for attention that I missed any warning signs from Luke? At any point did he do anything to indicate that it was all pretend? I wracked my brain to the point of pain. A deep ache was settling in just over my eyes and made me feel queasy. I gave myself to him in every way that I could. I felt so stupid.

So where did Camden fit in to all of this? I was definitely frustrated with him for not telling me about the frat's history. If he'd known about it, he should have said something, not just warn me away from Luke. I'd thought his only reason for doing that was because he was jealous. What a ridiculous thought. Camden couldn't be jealous... could he? I knew we had *something* going on between us, but was it what I thought it was? Clearly my track record with figuring out men wasn't very on point. But Camden had kissed me, he had pushed me to the brink of orgasm, and touched me like he wanted me just as bad. I couldn't be that far off base.

Sliding out of bed, I picked up my clothes and padded to the door. It wasn't closed all the way, and I noticed that the shower water was running. Why on earth was he showering at two in the morning? *Well I take that back.* He had just gotten back from the gym when I went running into him, so he probably didn't have a chance to get cleaned up before he was picking me up off the floor. I walked out into the hallway and tossed the nurse costume that I hated so much through my open bedroom door. I made a mental note to throw that sucker away the first chance I had. Turning and looking at the bathroom door I took a few steps toward it, noticing that the door was cracked open. The shower that we shared wasn't one that had a curtain hanging on a rod. This one had a glass door. Peeking in, the whole bathroom was fogged up. The glass that he stood behind was steamed over, but I was able to make out his figure on the other side. Swallowing hard, I felt like my heart was in my throat. What was I doing? Since when had I become a Peeping Tom? I knew I should go back into my room like I'd planned, but something was holding me here. I watched as his muscled arms came up and brushed several times through his hair, the white foam from the shampoo cascading down his body. I was riveted. Lust and desire were burning hot through my veins. I was drawn to him. An ache deep down was pushing me forward. Placing my hand on the door, I inched it open and took a step inside. My thoughts were going nuts, screaming at me to get the hell out of there, and pretend like I didn't just walk in there like a little pervert. But I couldn't. I needed something, and it was propelling me to keep moving. I watched in fascination as if every move of his body was the most incredible thing I'd seen. Seeing his hands move over his chest and down to his abdomen… lathering areas I wished I could run my tongue over. Just as the thought passed through my head, his eyes snapped up like he had sensed me. I braced myself, thinking he was going to yell at me or kick me out. Instead he tilted his head to the side. His large hand came up and wiped the glass so he could see me better. Connecting with his brown eyes, I was hit with the innermost need for him to touch me…to hold me. Whether he understood what I couldn't say out loud or not, he opened the glass door, never breaking eye contact.

Then he stood in front of me, completely nude and looking like an Adonis. You never really know just how sexy a man can look until you've gotten them completely wet and dripping with water. Nothing on earth like it! At least not in Camden's case. My heart's rhythm stuttered, trying to find its new beat. Oh God, what was I doing? I felt the pooling of tears in my eyes, and Camden took notice of my sudden change.

Holding out his hand to me he said, "Come here." It came out deep and raspy.

I stepped forward and placed my hand in his. Giving me a light tug, he moved me till I was standing in the shower facing him. The air was thick and humid making it hard to take a full breath. Or maybe I was just choking on my own words. He was blocking most of the water from spraying me, but little droplets were landing on my skin. I was only wearing his t-shirt and a pair of underwear, but the vapor in the air kept me warm. Or maybe being in his presence was overheating me. I had yet to let my eyes roam over the rest of his body that was on display. I'd already come barging in here, like some deviant teenage girl trying to see the goods. I didn't think I should take advantage of the situation. As I stood in front of him I couldn't gather the courage to look up at him. I didn't know what this was, what I was feeling, how I *should* be feeling. Embarrassment was overshadowing all other emotions that had previously been coursing through me. Sucking in as much air as I could I was about to tell him 'sorry' and leave when he put his fingers under my chin and forced my eyes up to meet his.

"What's going on in that beautiful mind of yours?"

His words pierced my heart. My lip quivered. "Anything…everything."

"Want to talk about it?" There he goes again with his sweet caring words. I didn't know how to deal with this side of Camden. When he fought with me, warred with me, irritated me, I could handle him. I simply fought back. This was foreign.

All at once my emotions bubbled to the surface and came crashing out. Tears were pouring out of my eyes as my shoulders shook with heavy sobs. I covered my face with my hands and tried to turn away from him. "I'm sorry, I'm sorry," I hiccupped.

"Hey, hey, what's this?" he asked, his arms coming around me, holding me to his chest.

Confusion and hurt wracked my body like a tidal wave. It came slamming into me when I wasn't prepared. Nothing felt right, and yet in his arms *everything* felt right. It was like my jumbled up mind was a contradiction in terms. How did I explain to him that I was sickened by what was done to me tonight? How did I express that I felt so degraded and used that I didn't want to step foot outside of the house again? I was so ashamed for falling into that trap. That I slept with a guy who did nothing but use me. How did I tell him that I felt like maybe I deserved it? That maybe it was my penance. I shook even harder, and his arms squeezed me tighter. How did I tell Camden that I wanted him more than I'd ever wanted anything in my life? That when he fought with me, he didn't just make me angry, he made me delirious with need. Even now, I craved to feel his skin on my skin. To know what it was like to have the slickness of the water glide my aching nipples across his chest. I wanted to feel his fingers brushing along my clit and bring me to the brink of orgasm. My tormented body couldn't decide what it wanted to do, so I cried some more.

I had no clue how long I stood there in his arms and wept, but as my tears slowed I was able to take deeper breaths. I became acutely aware of Camden's hold on me. I was pressed tightly to his warmth, and I couldn't help but noticed the very obvious erection that was digging into my stomach. I wiggled a bit to readjust my footing. He hissed at the sensation. My eyes shot up to his, and he knew that I knew. I watched as his look changed from gentle and caring to dark and toxic in a matter of seconds. The brown of his eyes were completely swallowed by his black pupils. His Adam's apple bobbed. Ghosting his hands down my arms, his fingertips drifted across the hem of his shirt, brushing the tops of my thighs. I sucked in a breath. His eyes narrowed at me, and I knew in that moment that I wouldn't be able to stop this. I didn't want to. He lifted the shirt a few inches, gauging my reaction. He waited for me to tell him that this was okay, that this was what I wanted. I gave a slight nod, giving him permission to continue. As he raised up the fabric, I had a fleeting thought that I wasn't wearing a bra. Camden was about to see a whole lot of me. I should have been worried about whether I had on my pretty lace panties, but I was more concerned with my body. I remembered the last few girls he'd brought home and how they looked. I still wasn't at my goal weight, and I hated that I was scared that he might think I was too big or unattractive. He sensed my apprehension when he got the shirt as high as my belly button. Leaning forward he placed his forehead on mine.

"Clear your head Keegan. You're going to be perfect."

"I don't look like the other girls, Camden."

"I know. That's what makes you perfect."

And just like that, he melted me. I raised my arms up over my head. Like moving in slow motion, the fabric came up over my stomach, breasts, head, and then my arms. Each one tingling as the damp air hit them. When he dropped the shirt on the floor I let my arms come back down to my sides. I watched as his russet eyes traveled from my face to my breasts. Every single one of my nerve endings were alight with fire. My nipples pebbled under his watchful gaze. I had the urge to reach up and cover myself, but I refrained.

"Take off your underwear." He spoke so deeply it was like a low rumble in his chest.

My face reddened, and I was feeling shy. "You…you wa-want everything off?" I stuttered.

"I want to see all of you. I want nothing in my way when I touch you. Underwear Keegan, now," he demanded.

My hands trembled with a nervousness I'd never known before, but I complied. Hooking my fingers in my black silk panties, I slid them down my thighs and let them pool at my feet. I lifted one foot at a time and stepped out of them. I was completely bared to Camden, and he was to me. He reached up and touched my no longer covered hip with the subtlest of brushes. While he looked over my very naked body, I finally gave myself permission to see all that was Camden. My mouth parted at the view. He was quite a bit more endowed than I originally assumed. It was multiple inches of velvety skin with a smooth crown stood at attention. I'd felt his cock against me before, but I couldn't tell just how big he really was.

"Enjoying the view, Blue?"

Ack! He caught me staring. "No! I was just noticing this little freckle on your side."

"So you don't like what you see?" he teased.

"Yes! No! Wait…what was the question?"

Camden chuckled. "It's okay to look," he said, trying to lighten the tense atmosphere.

"In that case, I looked but didn't see anything special." I shrugged with indifference.

He gave a full bellied laugh. "You know, this just wouldn't be right if that little attitude of yours didn't come out to play."

"What attitude? I showed you mine, you showed me yours, I said wasn't impressed. Now I'm ready for bed." I knew full well I was poking a sleeping bear, but Camden was my bear, and I was ready for the chase.

His strong hand shot out and wrapped around my bicep. Yanking my back to him, my body was flush with his. His cock pushed against the crack of my ass, and my skin was engulfed in goosebumps. Growling in my ear he said, "We'll talk later about how impressed you were when I make you scream my name. But in the meantime let's get one thing straight. There's no going back." The hand that wasn't holding my arm came around to splay across my stomach. "When I touch you, you will be begging for more. You'll be panting for me to take you every way that is humanly possible." Hard calloused fingers moved down to cup my sex. I moaned loudly, wishing like hell that he would spread me open and touch me where I wanted it. Nipping at my ear he breathed, "And when I fuck you, you'll know no one else owns this pussy but me." My whole body shook with desire. One deft finger slid between my folds and circled my clit over and over until my knees threatened to give out. When the room around me started to fade away he suddenly stopped, and I whimpered at the loss. I felt his lips form a smile, he knew he had me. "This…all of this." He pressed his cock between my cheeks, and he reached up to tweak my nipple. "This won't happen unless you tell me one thing."

I was breathing so hard, and my mind was so lost to him I didn't know how I answered, "What?"

"That you're mine."

He pinched my nipple again, this time harder, and it sent a jolt of pleasure straight to my core. I ground my ass back against Camden. He groaned and brought his hand down on my cheek with a slap. It startled me but intensified my need.

Chuckling he said, "Naughty girl. Give me what I want first. You're mine, Keegan. I won't share you with anybody else. Say it."

"Yes," I said breathlessly.

"Yes what?"

God! Why was he teasing me? "Jesus Christ Camden…please! I need you."

"Give me what I want."

I turned my face toward him and glared. "Stubborn ass."

"Keegan." He said my name in warning.

I fought him because I knew he liked it, and he knew I liked it. It was what we did. We both knew I'd cave, but I enjoyed taunting him.

"Yes, I'm yours. Only yours."

The brilliant smile he gave me made all of this worth it. "Good, now it's time to have fun." He said, shutting off the shower and leading me out of the bathroom and to his room.

CHAPTER TWELVE

My body had been literally shaking with desire. Except, when he led me back into his bedroom with his hand on my lower back, my nerves kicked in high gear. My heart started palpitating for a totally different reason, I was nervous. I was about to cross a line with him that would change the course of our strange and tumultuous relationship. Feeling his lips brush across my bare shoulder, there was no reservations. I wanted this. He wanted this. But the little voice in the back of my head was telling me that this could go horribly south. As I reached the foot of his bed I stopped, waiting for him to indicate what I should do next. I never minded being the aggressor when I got comfortable with someone in the bedroom, but that wasn't the case here. Camden was the dominant one. I could tell that he was going to be the instructor, and I'd be his student. I quivered knowing that I was about to be schooled in a whole new art of passion.

Large hands moved from my elbows to my shoulders. Slowly I turned in his arms. Camden's eyes were smoldering, and that look alone made me weak. His immense size blocked out the room behind him. I loved that everything about him made me feel small. He brought his mouth down to mine, pausing a breath away from my lips. Somehow I instinctively knew that he was coaxing me forward. He wanted me to close the final half inch to him, showing him that this was my decision and not something that he was seducing me into. There was no hesitation. I wanted him. I needed him now. I wanted him surrounding me. I wanted him to hold me, to rock inside of me, and bring me greater pleasure than I'd ever known before. Moving onto the tip of my toes, I pressed my lips to his. His resounding groan of approval told me that I gave him what he was asking for. His fingers dived into my hair, grasping the back of my head. It felt so possessive. I parted my lips slightly and felt him flick my lower lip with his tongue. Wrapping my arms around him, I molded myself to his body. I could feel every ridge of muscle on my bare skin. His erection was pressed up between us. When he pushed further into my mouth, I slanted my head to give him better access. Camden nipped and sucked on my lips and tongue, making me incredibly wet. When his hips nudged forward, my already shaking knees gave out. His arm came around my back in support, a smile cresting his lips

"If you're already this responsive, Blue, it looks like *I* might be the one who's in for a treat."

"You have no idea," I breathed against his mouth.

He pulled back slightly and showed me his brilliant grin. He was so handsomely beautiful. It was the kind of beautiful that took my breath away with just one look. The type that was so intense that I could lose myself in his brown depths for the rest of my life. They were expressive and understanding. I was drowning in everything that was Camden. He reached down and grasped the back of my legs, lifting me so that I was wrapped around him. With my legs spread open and gripping him around the waist, my folds parted, and his cock was pressed up against my center. The smile that was on him dissipated, morphing into a straight line. The contact of his silky hard skin against my clit was more than I could handle and I moaned, my head falling back in pleasure. His fingers were digging into my ass, holding me tightly to him, as I rubbed on him harder.

I felt us moving. He was climbing up onto the bed with me clinging to him, and he laid me down when we reached the top of the bed. The soft plush pillows under me were a contradiction to the firmness of the man above me. Camden's mouth came back down to mine in a bruising kiss that made my body quiver. His tongue dove in and out in a rhythm that matched how I wanted him to move inside me. When he broke away from the kiss, his lips traveled down to my jaw and to that spot behind my ear. His breath blowing against my oversensitive skin lit a brighter fire to my need, and I knew I was soaking wet.

"Camden, God...please touch me," I rasped.

The bass of his voice was low. "Is right here not good enough?" His questioning lick to my earlobe made my nipples pebble.

"Huh-uh."

"How about here?" He dragged his nose down to my collarbone and nipped at my flesh.

"Lower," I whispered.

He descended down my body with his torturous lips. One finger came up and circled my nipple, then pinched lightly. His mouth went to the other, and he pulled me into his wet warmth. My body bowed, as I tried to get more. Tentatively he released me, his teeth grazing the peak. "Would you like me to stay here, or should I keep going?"

My hands moved to grab his and hold him there. I wanted his palms on my breasts. His almost black eyes flashed up to mine. Slipping his hands out of my hold easily, he brought both of my wrists together and held them in one of his large fists. Raising my arms above my head he came back up to being eye level with me.

"You want something, you ask for it," he said, lifting one of his brows. "You have no control here Keegan. You're mine, and in here, in my bed, I top you." I whimpered at his threat. He brought his forehead down to mine. The hand that wasn't holding my wrists came to trace tiny infinity circles on my stomach. It tickled, making me suck in. "Now I'll ask again, lower?"

"Yes," I hissed.

I kept everything bare below my waist. There was no hair to block the feeling of his fingers cresting over my sex. His middle finger slid between my folds and gave one long brush to my swollen clit.

"Christ you're wet," he growled down at me.

The keening noise that came from my back of my throat was one I couldn't swallow. Using the other two fingers to spread me open he used his calloused fingertip to flick up and down the sensitive nerves. His cock was pressing into my leg, and I could feel him grinding himself against me to get some relief. My head turned toward his. The motions of Camden's very skilled hand were becoming overwhelming. It wasn't until he slid one long digit inside of me that I lost all sense of control. I was spiraling, and there wasn't anything I wouldn't do to take what I needed from him. My impending orgasm was already so close that my hips started bucking forward. He released my hands and pushed down on my hips to hold me in place. I'd never been worked so senseless before. Orgasm for me was always a gentle build. This was slamming into me, and I was ready to fall off the cliff. Pushing another finger inside, I felt Camden bend them. He slid them in and out as each stroke was brushing up against the spot inside of me that made me see stars. My nails dug into his shoulder blades as I held onto him.

"Oh shit I'm…I need…I." I panted the words, but nothing sounded coherent.

"You're almost there, baby, just let go."

His words were my undoing. A burning low in my stomach exploded into an array of feeling. I cried out as he continued thrusting into me. The tremors wracking my body were uncontrollable. My legs were scissoring, and my head thrashed on the pillow. I bit down on my lip so hard I could taste the metallic of blood. I could feel my inner walls pulsing and gripping him as each wave washed over me. Coming down from the high, little shocks still shook me, causing me to shiver. His fingers were still inside of me, and he moved them infinitesimally. I reached down and encircled his wrist to hold him still.

"St-stop," I stuttered, my body trying regain some control.

He chuckled a please sound. "That was one of the most incredible things I've seen." He gave a little wiggle.

I moaned loudly. Popping my eyes back open I glared at him. I squeezed his wrist harder to try and make a point. I attempted to pull him out of me, but I knew it would just send me back into convulsions. "Don't move. Sweet Jesus, please don't move. Not yet, I need a minute."

The look of wonder in his eyes was something to behold. It wasn't that he was seeing me for the first time, but it was more like he was seeing me in a new light. Kissing me on the tip of my nose, he moved down and licked the nipple that was closest to him. Oh shit, what was this man doing to me? My tense muscles were just loosening, and his simple movements were building me back up.

"Ready for more?" he asked, as he sucked the tight bud into his mouth.

"Fuck, don't stop." My back arched toward him.

BENDER

He lifted himself up to come over the top of me, his fingers still in place. Camden gently slid them out, and I flinched with the small wave of pleasure it sent through me. Glancing down I watched as he stroked his cock once, twice, a third time before looking up at me through his dark lashes. I swallowed hard. He brushed the smooth head up and down over my clit, coating himself in my fluid.

"You're fucking glistening, Keegan. I wish you could see what I see right now. Your hair all over my pillow. Your bright blue eyes looking up at me with such an innocence that makes me want to shatter the little world you've been living in. And fuck…this fucking amazing body that I can't seem to get enough of." He pushed the tip of himself into me and stopped. "Hold on."

Hold on to what? When I noticed that his control was slipping, I reached up and held on to the headboard. With one sudden drive forward, he slammed into me. I screamed his name as pleasure and pain tore through me. Camden's body came down and he held himself up, hovering with his hands braced on either side of my head. He withdrew himself slightly before he rammed forward again. The steady rhythm was something that took no time for my body to adjust to as he did this over and over. I could already feel the climax building low in my stomach. Rocking my hips I brought them up, trying to match him thrust for thrust. The sheer size of him had me feeling so full and stretched, that if he were any bigger, he wouldn't fit. I already felt tight around him. Each rocking motion of our bodies brought him in deeper. My mind was completely lost. There was no room, no bed, and no covers, no anything. It was just Camden. I was unequivocally enraptured by him. If he stopped now, I was certain I would die. He was in my every breath, my blood pulsing through my veins, the sweat dripping off my skin. I was consumed.

My whole being was reeling, ready to float away from another impending orgasm, when he sat back on his knees and lifted my hips in the air. My lower back was off the bed while the top half of me still rested where it was. Camden had a sheen of sweat across his brow that glinted off the moonlight coming through the window. I watched as a drip of perspiration traveled down his magnificent chest to his navel. If I wasn't stuck like this, I'd lean forward and lick it off his incredible abs. His rough fingers dug into my hips. Somehow, with this new angle, he was able to get deeper than before. His relentless movements brought me right back to the brink of explosion. His crown was rubbing so aggressively against my g-spot that dark specks were forming in my eyes. My ears were ringing, and I felt like he was fucking me senseless.

He groaned deep in his chest. "Your pussy is so tight. Fucking made for me. You're mine. Tell me you're mine."

He wants to talk? Like right now? I couldn't even form a full thought, let alone have enough air to breathe out a sentence. My fingernails clung to the sheets and the swinging of my breasts with his thrusting was almost my undoing. I was about to fall over the edge when he stopped. I was panting hard. If he hadn't been holding me down, I was certain I'd take a swing at him for pulling back.

Gritting his teeth he said, "You know what I want to hear, Keegan."

I twisted my head back refusing to look in his intense eyes. Maybe if I just reached down and used my own fingers with him still inside me I could give myself a decent orgasm. I was right there anyway, wouldn't take much work. I started to do just that when he snagged my hand and paused my movement.

"No fuckin' way Blue. You get your pleasure only from me. Now say it." I couldn't help the giggle that bubbled up my throat. The action caused my pussy to clench around him because he let go of my hip, my butt resting on his legs, and he fell forward with a groan. He said a string of curse words, and I smiled.

"I'm sorry, what was that?" I cupped my ear.

His head snapped up and the vicious look he gave me made me shut my mouth. Oh, he was on the verge of coming just like I was, but he was torturing both of us. Bastard.

"I'm not fuckin' around Keegan."

He reared back till he almost fell out of me, and I swore I'd cry if he left me like this. Being that I was so close to what would likely be the most mind blowing orgasm of my life, I figured I'd pick this fight another time.

I brought my free hand up to his cheek and brush my fingers across his warm skin. "I'm yours Camden. Just yours."

His eyes never strayed from mine. He rocked forward and seated himself back inside me. I sighed with relief. I continued to watch him as he slid in and out in a punishing pattern. We were both so worked up before his movement had subsided that it didn't take long for me to get back to the moment of ecstasy. A few more pushes. When my vision clouded over and my body arched, my orgasm hit me with brutal force. My legs locked up and I shook, screaming out Camden's name. I felt him stuttering above me, and he shouted out in satisfaction shortly after I did. He came down on top of me, his heat almost too much. He filled me to the point of overflowing, and I could feel his wetness dripping down the crack of my ass. Aftershocks wracked us both, as we came back from the euphoria.

Camden was still inside me when he lifted his head from being buried in my hair. He looked completely sated and sleepy. It was yet another new face that I'd never seen from him. It warmed me to know that I put him in the exhausted state. He gave me a lopsided grin that made him appear boyish and young. He brushed a few strands of hair that were sticking to my forehead away and tucked it behind my ear.

"How are you doing?" he asked, his voice tired and raspy.

"Fine," I answered, unsure of what else to say.

As the high of what we'd just done started to fade, worry worked itself in. Were things going to be awkward between us? Did he regret it? What did he think of it, of me? I wasn't fooling myself into believing that I was good in bed, but Camden was experienced. Ranking low on the totem pole would have been a blow to my ego. At best I hoped fit somewhere in the middle.

Tilting his head to the side he looked at me curiously. "It's like all of your emotions are written on your face right now. Breathe Keegan, whatever questions and worries you have, let them go. Feel the moment and just be in the now."

"Since when did you become a mind reader and so philosophical?"

He smiled at me. "I'm not a mind reader, just a Keegan reader. I've watched you enough to know when you can't let yourself relax. Like this." He tugged on my lip, releasing it from my teeth. "Or this." He used his thumb to smooth out the crease that was likely between my brows. "And there's always your eyes."

"What about my eyes?" I asked.

"I'm right here. You look over my shoulder, never at me when you're nervous and lost in your head. I like eye contact, I know you're with me when I can see those baby blues looking at mine."

His words were sweet and laced with so much sentiment. I didn't know he paid enough attention to me to pick up on certain habits. I felt a blush creep up to my cheeks, and I stared into the warm chocolate color that was reflecting just how I was feeling.

"I'm going to get something to clean up with. I'll be right back."

Despite the sex we'd just had, he still had a semi-hard erection that slid out of me when he lifted himself up. Cool air hit my bare skin on my chest, and my body shivered. Camden stood up and pulled the covers over the top of me in a very tender and sweet gesture. When he turned, I got a full view of the ass that I've been admiring through clothing for the past several months. It certainly didn't disappoint. I made note to get a good feel of it the next time we were together.

Whoa wait…next time we're together? Would we do this again?

I guessed I never made it that far in my thoughts as to whether this was a one-time deal just to get it out of our systems, or if he actually wanted me. I was clear on one thing, and that was the way that I felt about it. Every preconceived notion I'd had of Camden prior to tonight went straight out the window. I liked him. Like *like* liked him. I shouldn't because of how he'd treated me in the past, but none of that really mattered.

My thoughts were cut short when Camden came back in the room with a washcloth in one hand and a folded t-shirt in the other. He approached the bed, and I noticed he put on a pair of black briefs that were snug. I lifted the blanket. He handed me the cloth, and I tried to discreetly clean myself. He either noticed my discomfort, or was being respectful because he sat on the edge of the bed, keeping his back to me. When I finished I tossed the cloth over his shoulder. He chuckled. Climbing back in beside me, he pulled me in close to him so that my back was to his front. I sank into him, loving the way that his biceps pillowed my head and supported me. He was completely curled around me, making me feel safe.

"Are you sore?" he rumbled in my ear.

I wiggled a bit just to check. Unfortunately it also caused my ass to grind back into him, so he poked me in my side with his fingers. I laughed and squirmed some more. "Maybe a little, but it's a good sore."

Camden grunted, and I felt him rearranging himself. "Good. Now let's get some sleep. It's been a really long night. I'll make you breakfast in the morning."

I sighed deeply, feeling my muscles loosen and becoming limp. "Mmm… sounds good," I said, closing my eyes.

"Moan like that again, and neither of us will be sleeping," he threatened.

I shut my mouth and smirked. "Good to know Camden, good to know."

He barked a laugh and squeezed me tight. That was the end of the talking before we both passed out from exhaustion.

CHAPTER THIRTEEN

THE MORNING SUNLIGHT SHONE IN through the cracks of the blinds. Peeling my eyes open, I squinted. My cheek was currently plastered to Camden's firm chest. I breathed in deep and smelled everything that was him. I lifted the corner of my mouth in a smile. His soapy scent was still clinging to his skin. I was tempted to lick him, just to see if he tasted as good as he smelled. It was a mouthwatering essence. If this was what waking up in Camden's arms was like every day, sign me up. He had a hand resting on my hip, and one of my legs slung over his. I lay there, feeling his heart beating under my palm. He breathing was deep. I tried not to move, but carefully raised my head and glanced up at him. I took my time and let my eyes roam over his features. His strong jaw didn't appear to be as harsh in the light and from the angle that I was laying. He had high cheek bones that gave him a chiseled look. Long, dark lashes fanned his eyelids, and his hair was sticking up haphazardly. He had a very subtle boyish appearance in his sleep. It was almost approachable and not so intimidating. I turned to rest my cheek back in the same little nook of his shoulder. It felt like a place that was meant just for me. Tentatively I let my fingers trace the pattern of his defined abs and carved chest. He was exactly the type of man girls like me admired from afar but could never attempt to have.

"I'll have you know, that tickles." His groggy sleepy voice sounded under my cheek.

I smiled, knowing that he could feel it. "Just looking at everything that's Camden."

He shifted slightly, giving me a lovely view of the V down his waist. "And what do we think of everything that is *me*?" he asked in amusement.

I spelled my name with my finger over and over on his golden skin, trying to think of the right words. "Well...." I paused. Might as well get this all out in the open. Camden and I *did* cross a barrier last night, and it might be time to define what we are. "I think that you are arrogant, stubborn, full of yourself, and can be a complete asshole."

He scoffed, "Tell me how you really feel." I could feel his stomach bouncing up and down with light laughter.

I lifted my head to glare at him. "I wasn't finished. Now shhh..." He put his hands up in a sign to continue. I put my head back in its special spot. "You're all of those things, Camden. But you're also kindhearted, warm, caring, protective, genuine, and funny. It's like all of your negative qualities are overshadowed by your good ones. And even then, your bad ones can be spun into something positive. Like your stubbornness. Most guys wouldn't put up with my sarcasm. They find it offensive and off-putting. But you somehow play off of it and turn it into this weird flirting thing that I don't think I get, but am strangely attracted to."

"Hmmm...I'm intrigued. Go on."

"Well, last night you were sorta...here for me. I'm assuming that Dodger gave you a heads-up that we were coming home, but when we walked in the door, you had this look about you like you wanted to pound somebody's face in."

"That's because I did."

I nodded. "I know. That's the side of you that confuses me."

He brushed his fingers through my long waves. "What do you mean?"

"Camden, since I moved in here, things didn't get off on the right foot. You were cruel with your words, and you acted like you wished I never walked into your apartment. Nobody has ever made me feel like the mere sight of me disgusted them."

"Keegan, that's not how it happened," he argued.

"That's how it happened to *me*. You said some very hurtful things to me, and they cut pretty deep. My weight seemed to be an issue for you, but yet your words now say the opposite. Do you see how I could be feeling like a yo-yo in my head?"

"Yes, but I'd like to have a chance to explain all of it."

I shook my head. "Not yet. I need to get this out." He sighed in resignation. "I like you Camden. Despite how the last couple of months have played out between us, there has been one constant. You've always been the protector. I don't know why you took on that role, but you did. From the night I brought my little sister back home, to bossing me around and telling me what I could and couldn't do at the gym, and then warning me about Luke. For some reason, regardless of how you came across to me in the beginning, you've always been there. You wedged yourself into my life when I wasn't asking for it, and when I least expected it. As much as you piss me off, and I've secretly plotted how to murder you in your sleep, you've grown on me."

I could feel the vibrations of his chest as he laughed at what I said. "Boy this conversation keeps getting better and better." I reached up and tweaked his nipple. "Ouch!"

He grabbed my wrist and flipped me on to my back, pinning my arms on either side of my head. "Careful. If you're wanting to play, I'll play."

I narrowed my eyes. "Then quit laughing at me."

"Quit saying funny shit," he retorted.

"Gah you frustrate me! I wasn't trying to be funny, I was telling you how you make me feel."

He maneuvered himself between my legs and rolled his hips till he rubbed against parts of me that were still sensitive from the night before. "So then tell me how I make you feel."

My eyelids fluttered shut, and I bit my lip to hide my moan. "Stop distracting me," I whined.

"Look at me Keegan. Let me see your eyes." I opened them and gave him my full attention. "Good girl, now tell me how I make you feel. I won't distract you."

"Yeah right, you're one big distraction," I mumbled under my breath, and he chuckled. I sighed before continuing, "Look, somewhere along the line, something between us shifted. You went from just being my roommate, to the person that I look forward to seeing when I come home. If you're not around, I'm wondering what you're doing. When I go to the gym, I catch myself searching for you. There's even been times when I can *feel* you come into a room, and I know your eyes are on me. It gives me butterflies, and I don't know what to do about it. It's been a lot of confusing emotions that I don't know how to express because you have to be one of the hardest people to figure out that I've ever met."

His brown eyes seemed to sparkle down at me. "Is it my turn to talk yet?"

I nodded.

"You sure are a contradiction in terms. But you're not alone in how you feel. It all started when I saw you sitting in my apartment about to sign the lease and I thought, what the fuck is Dodger doing now? But then you looked up at me, and it was like my whole world shifted. All I saw were your bright innocent blue eyes and that was it." He sat back on his heels and rubbed the palm of his hand down his face. "I was so fucked."

"How so?" I asked.

The corner of his mouth lifted. "Because with that one look, I knew you were the girl who could ruin me." Camden shook his head as though he were clearing his thoughts. "I shouldn't have said the shit that I did, and for that I'm very sorry. I didn't know how to take you. Here was this little tiny blonde who came storming into my space, needing a place to stay, and all I wanted to do was push you right back out the door. Ever since then you've been a tornado, uprooting all aspects of my life. I live by my routines, always have. Except now I find myself coming home early, because I know you're here. I'll come home to eat lunch just so I can hear you tell me about your day. Anything just to be around you. This is new territory for me, Keegan."

"I accept your apology, but Camden, your words about my weight or referring to me being 'easy' were a hard pill to swallow. My self-esteem isn't the highest when it comes to my body. My confidence is lagging."

His jaw worked back and forth. Not in an angry sort of way, but more of a 'how can I fix this'. "I was an idiot okay. I mean, I fucking work in a gym. I know how self-conscious people can be, and I'm never one to judge. I don't know how else to tell you that I never meant what I said. I was trying to get you to leave. You throw me off my game, Keegan. I've always been with girls that are tall and thin. You're thin, but you have these graceful, plush curves that make my mouth water." He ended his sentence by licking his lips.

I looked down and felt a blush creeping up my cheeks. "Thank you."

"You're welcome. I want you to be comfortable in front of me." He tugged on the sheet. "I don't want you hiding your body when I want to see everything."

I shivered at his brazenness. Things were starting to fall into place where there were holes before. I hadn't expected him to be so straightforward with his feelings. Still unsure and unsettled, I asked the question that had been looming in my head for days. "So where does all of this leave us? What is this happening between you and me?"

Camden grabbed my arms and pulled me up in a sitting position. I made sure to take the sheet with me and cover my naked breasts. He noticed and gave me a devilish grin. "Well, I can tell you where it *doesn't* leave you and Luke. Or you and anybody else for that matter. I meant what I said last night. You're mine. I won't share you."

I quirked my brow and took in his serious expression. The mention of Luke's name grated on my nerves. "Am I supposed to share *you*? Cause I can't Camden. It was already hard enough to watch you parade women in and out of here with no regard to my feelings. But if you're claiming me in some weird caveman sort of way, then I expect the same from you. I'm not saying we have to put a label on this," I motioned between us with my hand. "I just need to know that if I'm exclusive, you will be too."

He tipped my chin up to meet his eyes as he descended dangerously close to my mouth. "I think I can handle that."

Camden moved in to kiss me but I pulled back an inch. "I mean it Brooks. I'm a sensitive girl. You fuck around on me, and Macie will have your ass."

He barked a laugh that sounded so carefree and relaxed that it melted my heart. "Macie huh, and what about you, killer?"

I smiled. "I have my ways to make you pay."

"Pretty sure you're well acquainted with a bat."

I slide my hand up his chest and clasped it around his neck. "You bet your ass I am," I said as I pulled him down to me in a kiss that could have lit fireworks.

Camden and I stayed in bed the rest of the morning and part of the afternoon. We only got up to use the bathroom or when he went downstairs to make breakfast and sandwiches for lunch. I would have given anything to still be there snuggled up against his warmth right now, but I had to meet Macie for dinner, and I needed to go pick up Sarah because we hadn't really spent much time together in the past three days. I missed her. Being away from Sarah for longer than a day was hard. I saw her every day when I lived at home, but now it seemed that the time between our visits was growing, and I didn't like it. Sitting in my car on the way to my mom's I made a vow to make a better effort to bring her over or take her out places.

I made quick work of grabbing Sarah from Mom's so I didn't have to deal with the twenty questions about when I'd bring her back home and where we were going. The less she knew the better. She only wanted to know because it would be her excuse to leave the house and go do all of the irresponsible shit she normally did. I'd rather not give her the satisfaction. Mom and I still weren't on the best of terms. I noticed that Sarah was being pretty quiet on the ride to the restaurant, which was completely out of the norm for my chatty sister. I glanced back at her in concern.

"Hey, how've you been?"

She shrugged. "Alright."

"How's school going? Are you still getting good grades?"

"It's alright. Math is getting harder. The teacher is making us do fractions, and I hate them. When am I ever going to use them?" she said in an irritated tone.

"How about when you help me cook? You have to know the measurements so I know how much to pour or scoop," I replied.

She brought her eyes up to mine in the mirror. "Yeah, but we don't cook together anymore."

I sucked in some air. Apparently my absence from her has been noticed not just by me, but her as well. I felt terrible. "Listen Sarah, I'm sorry I haven't been around much lately. I've had a lot of things on my plate, and it's taken me some time to get it all situated. I don't mean to ignore you. Okay?"

Tears glistened in her little eyes, and she nodded. "I miss you. We used to be together every day. Now it's just me and Mom, and she doesn't even play with me."

I swallowed the lump that was in my throat. "I miss you too. How come Mom doesn't play with you?"

She brought her shoulders up and dropped them. "She says she's busy and can't. And some days she isn't even home, and I have to take care of myself. I get bored when no one is there."

This little bit of information was complete news to me. "What do you mean she's not home? How often does she leave you by yourself?"

"A couple times a week."

"Why didn't you say something to me?"

"Because every time we're together you are too busy. You don't play with me like you used to either."

I shook my head. "Sarah, if Mom leaves you at home alone again, I want you to call me. You aren't old enough to stay in the house without an adult with you. When she leaves, is she gone for a long time or just a few minutes?"

"Both. Yesterday she was gone until after dark. I had to make my own dinner."

Oh my God. My mom was leaving my eight-year-old little sister at home to fend for herself? This was not acceptable! We didn't live in the ghetto or anything, but it was not like we knew many of our neighbors either. Anything could happen to Sarah while she was gone. I flashed back to being her age and having to take care of myself. I liked to believe that I had a little bit more responsibility and knowledge than Sarah did by then because I'd been doing it for a while. I had no one else there to make my meals or take me to the park. She wasn't as self-sufficient. I've tried to teach my baby sister what to do in case of an emergency, and to not talk to strangers, but I wasn't sure that if something happened, she'd really know what to do. I was going to have a long talk with my mom about this. At what point did her social life become more important than her own flesh and blood? If she was incapable of taking care of her kids, maybe she shouldn't have had any in the first place.

Meeting her eyes in the mirror I made sure Sarah was hearing what I was about to say. "I'm going to talk to Mom. I can't have you staying alone by yourself. It's just not right. I mean it when I say you *will* call me and let me know if she is gone so I can come pick you up. Okay? And I'll be around more often. Nobody is more important to me than you. I love you, Sarah."

Her lip quivered. "I love you too."

We pulled up to the restaurant about five minutes later. My mind was muddled with thoughts of how I was going to approach this with my mom. I hated talking to her like I was the parent and she was the child. But Sarah needed someone in her corner. I'd take one for the team if it meant keeping my little sister safe and happy. Macie's car was already here, so Sarah and I went inside and found her sitting in our usual booth toward the back. She smiled and waved at us when we walked in.

"Hey kid, how's it going?" Macie asked Sarah.

"Good. Can I have dessert before dinner?"

I rolled my eyes. "What do you think the answer to that is going to be?"

"Aww, come on *Mom*," Macie teased. "A little splurge never hurt anyone."

"Seriously Mace? I'm trying to instill good behaviors here. You're like the little devil sitting on her shoulder chanting, 'walk on the wild side… eat cake.'"

She picked up her glass of water and sipped it. "Who doesn't like cake for dinner?"

"Please, please, please…" Sarah begged.

I put my face on my palms. "Why do I bother?" I lifted my head in time to see Macie wink at Sarah, and Sarah grinning like an idiot. I totally lost this battle.

"*Yesssss!*" Sarah hissed.

"Hey." Macie pointed her finger at her. "You're giving me a bite of that cake, kid."

Sarah laughed and agreed.

After we put in our orders, conversation was slow. I was waiting till my little sister was knee deep in a game on my phone so I could ask Macie what was going on between her and Dodger.

"Are we going to talk about it?" I asked casually.

One perfectly plucked brow lifted in question. "I don't know, are we? If you're wanting me to dish, you're going to have to spill some secrets too. Like what in the hell happened last night? *And* hello… Camden? You ran into his arms Keegan. What haven't you been telling me?"

"Huh uh, you first. You're going to need a few drinks in you before I tell you everything."

"That sounds promising," she said sarcastically.

"Whatever, now go. Tell me what the blow up was about between you and Dodger. So he still hasn't *you know* with you?" I glanced over at Sarah to indicate that we needed to keep this a PG chat. I so wasn't ready to have the talk with her.

She let out a dramatic whimper. "No! He's being stingy with the sausage."

I grinned. "Do you think that maybe he's just not ready for it yet? Not every guy out there likes to move fast."

"Uh, I know all about Dodger's history and just how fast he likes to move. My freaking Chemistry partner said her best friend hooked up with him at a party last year. Apparently it was mind blowing. Speaking of which, there's not been any of that going on either!"

I couldn't help the giggle that slipped out. "So there's be no fooling around *at all*?"

"None. My poor love tunnel needs some TLC."

"What's a love tunnel?" Sarah asked, still looking at my phone.

My mouth dropped, but Macie answered without missing a beat. "It's the river that runs through the Venetian hotel in Vegas. It's pretty cool."

"So why do they call it a love tunnel? And why does it need TLR?"

"It's TLC, which stands for tender loving care. TLR is that stuff that cleans pipes? Wait…that could totally work too in my situation," Mace said with a twinkle in her eye.

I kicked her under the table. "Focus!"

"Right, anyway it's a love tunnel, because it's supposed to be like a romantic gondola ride that they do in Italy."

We paused, waiting for Sarah to response, but turns out she was into her game and didn't hear a word. Thank God. I shook my head at Macie and mouthed 'careful' to her.

"So are you going to give him some time then, or are you going to move on?"

She shrugged. "I don't know. I really like him Keegan. He's not like the other guys I've been with. It's like he really wants to know me, the real me."

I reached across the table and took her hand. "It scares you doesn't it?" Macie nodded. "Thought so. Maybe it's time for you to allow someone in. Dodger's not going to hurt you. At least not intentionally. Give him a chance."

She bit her lip and gave my hand a squeeze. "K." There was a moment of silence before she said, "Okay, enough about me. I want to know everything."

Our waitress was just passing by so I got her attention and said, "We're going to need a few drinks." She took the order, and I started talking.

Two drinks, dinner, and forty minutes later, I finally finished telling her every last little detail about the party, and what happened between Camden and me. She sat back in her seat with a dumbfounded look on her face. "Holy shit. You did it before I did."

I blinked at her. "That's what you took away from all of that?"

"No not entirely, but I totally feel like I should give you a congratulatory hug or something."

"Macie… it's not a big deal."

"The hell it's not. We're talking about *Camden Brooks* here. Have you seen what he looks like?" her voice squeaked.

I laughed. "Oh yeah, I saw plenty of him." We both giggled. "That's not what meant though. Camden and I aren't going to give what we are a name, but we are definitely exclusive. I want to know about the Luke situation."

She narrowed her eyes. "He'd truly be better off if Camden or Dodger got a hold of him. If I see him, there will be no mercy. Nobody does that to somebody I love and walks away with all their body parts intact."

I'd find what she said funny, except I knew that she really wasn't kidding. Macie could be quite the scary little thing when she wanted to be. "Just leave it alone. I'll deal with him by myself."

"I get that you want to, but the jerk needs to pay for what he did. I can't believe that happened, and I was freaking *there!*"

I nodded in agreement. "It's not your fault. But I'll take care of Luke. I just need a couple of days to think about what needs to be said to him about all of it."

"Alright, I'll give you some time. But if I see him around campus, I can't promise that he will be in one piece when you *do* say something. I'm already plotting his very tragic accident."

I laughed. "I can handle that."

We stood up from the table and made our way out to our cars. There were brief hugs all around, and I loaded Sarah up and took her back home. On my ride to the apartment, I got butterflies knowing that I was going to see Camden. For the first time in a long time, I felt like the possibilities were endless. I was truly happy, and I liked having something to look forward to.

CHAPTER FOURTEEN

CAMDEN AND I HAD FOUND OURSELVES a new routine over the past week. Which was probably a good thing, because he liked routines. He woke up before I did and would go for a run. By the time I rolled out of bed, he would already be downstairs making me breakfast. We'd eat together then I'd head off to my classes. The day always seemed to drag by, because I was anxious to see him. Between school and work, they took up too much time. Being able to see Camden at the end of a long ten hours was like my own little special reward. That was not to say that we haven't had a few minor hiccups. Living with Camden and being in a relationship with him were two very separate entities. He could be very pushy. Like, which room we were sleeping in. He grumbled about buying me a new bed and needing to break it in. And we really did almost break it the other night, but I liked his bed. It smelled like him, and it was cozy. Then we had an issue over him paying for things when we went out. I liked to pay my own way when we went places, but Camden said I wasn't letting him be the man in the relationship. He said it made him feel good to know that he was taking care of me. I understood the words behind what he was saying, but convincing me that he needed to take care of me, when I've always taken care of myself, was a whole other issue. And apparently arguing in front of the movie theater about such a thing was grounds for a good spanking in the bedroom. I didn't mind. Yep, Camden was quite the man to adjust to. I really liked everything about him, but he was an extremely dominant man in every aspect of his life. Control was the name of the game with him. He thrived on knowing that he could get me to submit. I was more than okay with it, but I certainly put up a good fight before I gave in. The more I fought, the harder he gave it to me. It became an interesting give and take.

 I was just getting off work after a particularly hellish day of filing and was heading to the gym. It was something that had become part of the routine. Listening to music in the car perked me up and by the time I pulled into the parking lot, I was feeling particularly feisty. Camden had sent me some text messages earlier in the day about what he wanted to do to me when I got home, when he knew damn well I'd be sitting in my office blushing. An idea hit me, and I decided I was going to get back at him. Grinning in my car, I knew I'd totally pay for it, but it was going to be epic nonetheless. Grabbing my iPod I got out of the car and walked into the gym. The girl that usually sat in the front was already gone for the day, but Camden was just coming out of a back room when he saw me walk in.

 I loved the smile that spread across his face before he said, "Hey Blue."

 He came around the counter and put his arms under mine, lifting me up and bringing his mouth down in a crushing kiss. My legs were dangling so I wrapped them around his waist. Oh God a girl could get used to this. "Hey back," I said, pulling my mouth away.

His hands were gripping me under my butt. His kiss alone was enough to turn me on, but when he held me like this, like I weighed nothing, I felt like I was floating on cloud nine. People were walking around us, but we continued on as if we were the only two in the gym. Camden asked me a few questions about my day, then set me down. I was wearing a white button-down blouse, and black dress pants with heels, so I still needed to change. I was scheming how I would get behind the front desk and do what I needed to, I just crossed my fingers he wouldn't pick up on it.

"I'm going to go change real quick. Be right back." I got up on my tip toes and kissed him lightly on the mouth. "Ouch." I reached out for his arm.

His eyebrows came down in concern. "What's the matter? Are you hurt?"

I lifted one of my heels up. "No, not really. These shoes are giving me a blister, and it's rubbing the back of my heel. Do you have a first aid kit back here that I could get a Band-Aid from?"

He helped me over to the chair behind the desk and pulled open a drawer. "Yeah, help yourself. I need to go check on my client real quick. See you in a few minutes."

Camden walked over to some machine where an older gentleman was pulling on a cord while standing. I still had no idea what those things were called. Didn't matter. I needed to focus, I was on a mission. Reaching into my pocket I pulled out my iPod and connected it to the stereo that played throughout the gym. I had to wait until the song that was currently playing was over before I could hit play on my own playlist otherwise Camden would be on to me. I got it all set up, and the first song started playing. I looked around to see if anybody noticed the difference in music but fortunately they were none the wiser. I smiled to myself. Oh man I was going to be in so much trouble. Getting up from the chair I went to the locker room and made quick work of changing out of my work clothes and into a pair of capri black stretch pants and a tank top with a built-in sports bra. I came back out into the main part of the gym, and Camden had shifted to the free weights, spotting his client. He looked over at me and smiled. I enjoyed seeing this side of Camden. Although I still loved 'brooding Camden' as well.

Smiling back, I went over to the mats and stretched out my legs. Every time the song changed my heart rate would spike. I had no idea when the song was going to play. Eventually I got up and moved to a treadmill. I figured I'd do a little cardio and get my body warmed up, and then hopefully Camden would be done with his session and could help me on the weights. Stepping on, I set my pace. I was going at a slow speed, gradually increasing at every minute interval. I was almost done with my warm-up when it happened. The sound of a flute floated through the gym, and a very familiar tune began to play. There was a collective round of groans from the ten or so people who were working out, and a few of them said, "What the fuck are we listening to?" I bit the inside of my cheek and tried to maintain my composure. It was quite the change to go from a "Woe Is Me" song to "My Heart Will Go On" by Celine Dion. I kept my pace on the treadmill refusing to make eye contact with the one person who I *knew* was glaring at me.

"Hey Brooks, I think your stereo's broken," one of the regular weight lifters called from across the gym.

Several people chuckled, but the song continued to play. I could feel the heat creeping up my cheeks, and I decided to grow a pair and meet Camden's stare. My treadmill was directly in front of a set of mirrors that allowed me to view the entire gym behind me. My dark brooding man was standing in the same spot that he had been in when I started my warm-up. His eyes were almost black and narrowed into slits. His stance was rigid, and his chest was moving up and down. I knew smiling right now *probably* wasn't in my best interest, but what the hell…I liked to live crazy. Looking directly at him I lifted my shoulders in a very casual shrug as if to say, 'what'? Which I followed up with a sly smirk. He gave me the slightest head shake. Oh he was mad. My heart was in my throat, but I continued to act like I hadn't just announced to the whole gym that Camden was a closet Celine fan. I pried my eyes away from his and kept trucking along on the treadmill, knowing that something big was coming my way. A couple of minutes passed, and I could see that he was still in the same spot in my peripheral vision. Crap! Maybe I went too far. He couldn't actually be mad at me for this. I might have played the song, but we were the only ones that knew *why*. Maybe I should go apologize to him. Just as I thought that, I noticed Camden going from person to person saying something. One by one, everybody gathered their things and made their way out of the gym. What was he doing? Was he kicking everyone out? As the last person left, I watched in the mirror as he followed them and locked the door behind them. Then he went to the stereo and shut it off. The only sound was my feet pounding down. When he turned, his face was unreadable. Holy shit, he kicked everyone out, and I was about to get bitched out. Why, oh why, did I have to be an idiot sometimes?

    Camden stalked toward me as I bumped up the speed on the treadmill. I wondered if maybe he'd just go away if I ignored him. I went from walking to jogging to running in a very short period. My freaking thighs were on fire before, but now they were screaming at me. Camden came to stand beside me while I stared straight ahead and refused to look at him.

    "Keegan."
    "Yeah?"
    "Keegan."

"Uh huh?"

"You know you're in trouble right?"

"I'm sorry, what's that?" I tried to play dumb. Pushing my luck a little bit more I started humming the song, picking it up where it left off.

The grin I saw spreading across his face out of the corner of my eye gave me the chills. "You. Are. In. Trouble," he emphasized each word.

I held my hand up to my ear. "I can't hear you. Maybe you should wait till I'm off of here then we can talk." For starters I was so out of breath I thought I would pass out. Second I'd like to believe that I could wait him out, but at this rate, I'd be in v-fib, and he'd have to shock my heart back into a normal rhythm.

I saw his arm move out in front of me, and he pulled the red cord that was attached to the emergency stop. The belt below me came to an abrupt halt, and my forward momentum almost made me fall. Camden reached out to steady me. Helping me off, I bent over at the waist and put my hands on my knees, trying to slow my breathing. A bottle of water was placed in front of my face, and I took it. Tipping my head back, I chugged as much as I could, then dumped the rest of it over my head. It was too damn hot in here. I wiped my eyes and noticed that Camden was watching me with a lust I had yet to see from him before.

Leaning against the mirror he crossed his arms over his chest in a casual stance. When he did that it made him look huge. "Can you breathe?"

"Yes." My chest was still rising and falling in a heavy pattern.

"Are we still playing that you can't hear what I'm saying?"

"I wasn't playing."

He smirked. "Hmmm… can you hear me now?"

I rolled my eyes. "Of course I can hear you."

The smirk that was there abruptly went away. It was replaced by a darkened expression. "Good, now let's talk. You're playing a very dangerous game Keegan. And I'm assuming that you probably knew that." His russet-colored eyes never left mine. "You're a smart girl. Which also means that that little stunt you pulled, you did it with intention. Were you testing me to see what sort of punishment I'd dole out?"

He hit the nail on the head, but I couldn't let him know that. Everything about him screamed sex right now, and my body was quivering in anticipation. His posture, the way that his eyes sparkled with possibility, his clenching jaw; these were all signs that Camden was revving himself up for something big. I had to clear my head. *Put on your poker face Keegan.* "No of course not. It was just a silly little prank."

The corner of his mouth tipped up. "My, my, you've been a naughty girl."

I put my hands on my hips, showing a display of indifference. "Oh cut it out Camden. You could laugh you know. It was a joke, it was funny. You know, ha, ha funny?"

"Am I laughing?"

"No, but you're always a hard ass."

When his smile spread, his teeth gleamed from the lights. He looked positively vicious. The hard edge of him that seemed to tip the scales of mean and dominant. It was everything that I loved about this side of him. My sex clenched, knowing that I was just making it worse for myself by egging him on.

"Oh you have no idea how hard I can be, Blue."

"I'm shaking in my sneakers Camden."

I dropped my arms and started to turn to walk away. He stepped in real close causing me to halt my next movement. His breath blew across my now cooling skin. "I'm going to tell you what you're going to do to make this right, and I suggest you don't make me repeat myself. My control is quickly fading Keegan. Don't speak, but nod that you understand."

His voice was low and threatening. All of the anticipation and build led me to this moment. He really was close to snapping, and I knew better than to push him again. I did what he asked.

"Good girl. Now I want you to go to that little machine over there in the corner, and I want you to take everything off. There had better not be a single scrap of clothing left on your gorgeous body by the time that I get over there or I'll bend you over and spank you till you ass is flaming red. Nod if you understand."

I swallowed hard and shook my head in understanding. Camden walked away from me, going into one of the rooms where they hold classes, disappearing behind the door. I turned and walked to where he said he wanted me. The machine he sent me to was called a leg adductor. It was one in which you sit down, and set your legs into two different leg rests. You could add or subtract weight according to what your tolerance was, but it was meant for you to be able to squeeze your thighs together and the weights would pull them back open. *Holy shit, he wants me on this thing completely naked and spread eagle?* But I would be totally open and exposed. Every part of my being was shaking with anticipation but, could I be this brazen in front of him and let him see me this way? Did I even have a choice? Of course I knew the answer to that question. If I didn't comply, Camden would come up with something else that would be even worse. Despite my nerves kicking in, I was also curious about what he wanted to do with me. This machine had a lot of possibilities. With shaking hands I began to strip. I took off my tank top, shoes, and yoga pants. I was standing there in nothing but a pair of blue boy cut underwear. I covered my breasts with my arm. Looking up, Camden had stepped out of the room with something dangling from his hand. He had dimmed the lights while he was in the back so I couldn't make out what he was holding. He paused when he looked over at me. He looked positively carnal.

"Everything Keegan. Do not hide yourself from me."

Bravely I dropped my arms from my breasts but thankfully my hair was flowing over my shoulders and covered most of me. His eyes narrowed. Hooking my fingers in my underwear I turned around, giving him my back, and slowly slipped my panties over my hips, letting them fall in a pool at my feet. I heard a low rumble across the space.

"Happy?" I said in a seductive voice.

"Very. Now not another word. Do you understand?"

I glanced at him over my shoulder, licking my lips. "Yes."

I stood completely still, waiting for him to come to me. I watched him move behind the desk and turn the music back on. Instead of the heavy beat of hard rock, it was the alluring sound of the bass. It was a sound that drew you in and made you want to sway your hips from side to side in a tantalizing dance. One that had I still be wearing clothes, I would have gladly removed them once more. Awolnation's "Sail" carried through the speakers, and Camden started walking toward me. His dark brown eyes were feral. Every beat of the music that brought him closer to me, my heart kicked up another notch. He chose this song on purpose. He knew it would affect me in every possible way. The sound reverberated through my already high-strung body. He stalked toward me in slow motion. Like a wild animal sneaking up on its prey, and I was his next meal. My legs quivered, ready to give out. And they would, when he touched me, I wouldn't be able to hold myself up a second longer. He was only a few feet away now. He glanced down my body. Everywhere his eyes touched was like a fire licking at my skin. I was already soaking wet with need, but him being just out of reach was unbearable. My need was too great. The sigh that came from my parted lips was more like a moan. His eyes shot up to mine. He shook his head so subtly I wouldn't have seen it had I not been staring at him.

When he finally spoke, his voice was a full octave lower than normal. "You're going to sit down and put your legs in the rests. I want your hands on the handles by your side and don't even think about moving, or I'll make this worse for you."

"Worse?" My voice shook, giving away my anticipation.

He raised his eyebrow. "What did I say about talking?"

Gulping, I took a step toward the machine and sat down. Reluctance was kicking in in full force. If the music wasn't so loud, I was certain he'd be able to hear my heart. My bare butt touched the cool plastic of the chair but quickly warmed. I put my hands where he instructed then hesitated. I felt like I needed to give myself a pep talk to do this. Camden didn't say anything. He saw the indecision on my face, but stood there, allowing me to work through my discomfort on my own. I appreciated him doing that. It assured me that despite being on the edge, this wasn't just about him. He wanted me to feel good too. He cared. I brought my eyes up to his when I felt that I was ready and watched him when I put my left leg up first. I wasn't entirely uncomfortable just yet, but when I lifted my right leg and placed it in the holder, I felt like all the air had been sucked out of the room. I knew what I looked like right now. My pussy was completely exposed to him, and he could see every inch of me down there. I was slick with desire, and no doubt it was showing. Camden's eyes left mine, and he looked down. I gripped the handles tightly, wanting desperately to cover up, but I wouldn't do it. I wanted to be confident with Camden. I wanted to know that the mere sight of me brought him to his knees. I wanted to be the girl who could open herself up and feel like I owned him.

"Fucking perfect," he whispered.

I broke eye contact and looked at the object that Camden had carried over. He was holding two resistance bands. They were each about three foot long, and my curiosity sparked. What was he planning on doing with those? I didn't have to think about it too long. He took a step toward me, and squatted by my right side. Being this close to him, I could smell the underlying scent of his soap. It was mouthwatering. Camden started making short work of tying a knot around my wrist and securing it to the handle that I was holding. The rubber against my skin wasn't exactly uncomfortable, but it wasn't the softest material either. When he felt like it was tight enough, he went to my other side and did the same thing. I'd never been tied down to anything before, let alone a piece of workout equipment. My blood was scorching, and I could feel it thrumming through my veins. I didn't like the idea of not being able to move. Other than being able to squeeze my legs shut, I had no mobility. I was trapped and unable to do anything to hide or protect myself if things went further than what I was okay with. I was about to tell Camden that I didn't think I could do this when he looked up at me. Underneath the ferocity of his stare was something that I didn't expect to see. There was understanding and gentleness. He was pleased that I was letting him take me this far. Bringing his hand up, his palm cupped my cheek. I leaned into his touch. With a subtle nod, I knew the tenderness was over.

He stood up over the top of me in a very domineering fashion. I could see the clear outline of his cock through his gym shorts. Camden was rock hard, and all I wanted to do was take him in my mouth. I had no idea what he was going to do, but the not knowing was part of the fun. Apparently he wasn't done restraining me. I thought I'd be able to keep some mobility of my legs, except he leaned over and added enough weight to the machine that bringing my legs together was no longer an option. I glared at him.

"That's right Blue, get pissed at me. But don't worry, you're going to enjoy this just as much as I am."

Using one of his hands he reached up and pinched one of my nipples hard enough to make me cry out. Leaning down he took the sensitive peak into his mouth and soothed it with his warm tongue, rolling it between his teeth. The pain then pleasure sent a bolt of pleasure to my center. Camden was switching back and forth between pinching and sucking. He did this over and over, and my eyes rolled back. When he felt that he'd given my breasts enough attention he stood back up and looked down at me. Gripping his cock he rearranged himself. Was he trying to drive me crazy? Why wasn't he getting naked too? I wanted to see him in all his magnificent glory. Camden had one of the most incredible bodies I'd seen on a man. I'd been around him plenty of times walking around the house, or here in the gym with nothing but a pair of shorts on. The tight corded muscle of his arms and back were solid. His abs had defined ridges that were made for a woman's fingers to smooth over. And his V... it taunted me. Everything about Camden was a tease. I wanted my hands on him all the time. His tanned skin was smooth and flawless. He screamed sex.

"I'm going to taste every inch of your body with my tongue. And in case that's not enough, I think I'll fuck you until your pussy is red, throbbing, and dripping with my cum."

Holy shit, he'd never spoken to me like this before. I wanted to respond so badly, but I knew it wasn't allowed. Biting my lip, I waited for his next move. Dropping down to his knees, Camden brought his face up close and personal to my open flesh. I closed my eyes trying to hide the embarrassment I felt creeping in. I'd never let a man do this before, and Camden and I hadn't crossed this boundary until now. It was mortifying. Using one of his fingers, he dragged it around the lips of my vulva, but never once touched me where I wanted him the most. He did several passes, causing the build within me to boil over. I shifted my hips, and he brought his forearm down to hold me in place.

"Do you want to taste yourself?"

I shook my head. Doing something like that had never seemed appealing, not even out of curiosity. When Camden flicked his finger over my swollen clit, I shouted out. The tension in my body was palpable, and I shook hard. He swirled his fingertip over the tender nerves several more times, and I felt like I was ready to explode.

"I'm done asking. You're going to lick all of the juices off, and I want you to describe to me how you taste. Then I'm going to lap up every last drop when you come in my mouth."

He made me heady with need. I didn't want to refuse him. Giving me his pointer finger, Camden brought it up to my lips, and I parted them enough to let him slip it in. Drawing in his finger with my tongue, I licked off what he was offering me. It was nothing like I expected it to be. I enjoyed watching his eyes grow wide with my boldness. When he withdrew he gave me an expectant look.

"I taste salty and sweet all at the same time. Sort of like a salted caramel apple."

He grinned in approval. "One of my favorite desserts."

His mouth went down on me, and I felt like a caged animal wanting to break free. The sensation sent me into overload. He lapped at my open folds over and over until I was mewling and begging for more. I had no idea that this was just the start. When he latched onto my clit, stars shot across my vision, and I screamed out in pleasure. The music that was floating in through the air disappeared. I had tunnel vision, and the only thing I could comprehend was what Camden was doing to me, and that I needed more *now*. I tried lifting my hands to grab his hair and hold him to me, to tell him that I didn't want him to stop, but there was no movement. I'd forgotten that I was tied down. My fingers curled into fists, and my nails bit into my palms.

"Untie me Camden, I want to touch you. I *need* to touch you," I ground out through my teeth. He chuckled, sending vibrations straight through my core.

He looked up at me, his brown eyes dancing with mischief. "In your dreams Blue. I said I'd make you feel good, but I never promised to make it easy."

"You son of a bitch!" He nipped at my clit, and I sunk down in the chair. "Fuck! I fucking hate you. Untie me, or so help me Camden…"

I watched him in rapt attention as his tongue shot out, and he made one long stroke from my entrance to the top of my lips. I shook so violently I thought I was going to pass out. "You're a tough girl, I know you can handle it. You taste fucking amazing." Oh my God his taunting was going to send me to the looney bin. I didn't know whether I wanted to beg him for more, or wring his neck.

I felt the tip of his fingers circling at my entrance. If he kept up this pace with his mouth, and he started finger fucking me, I'd be lost. Camden coated his fingers, making sure that they were wet with my juices. Ever so slowly he slid two fingers inside of me. Making a steady rhythm of pressing in and pulling out, I couldn't hold on any longer.

"Oh God oh God…I'm going to come!"

With a slight curling of his fingers, he sucked my bundle of nerves so hard that I exploded. Pleasure washed over me in blinding waves, and my body quaked. The grips where my hands were digging into were sure to have permanent dents from my nails. Camden's free arm had come up from under the chair and wrapped around my waist. His hand was splayed out across my hip holding me down as I came back down from the incredible feeling. My ears were ringing, my lower lip felt swollen from biting it, and my body was covered in sweat.

"That was your reward for being brave enough to let me do this to you. But now it's time for your punishment," he said as he got up from his knees. "Your mouth and my dick are about to get friendly."

I almost laughed, but nothing was working quite right just yet. My synapses weren't firing off normally, and I was pretty sure everything was tilting to the left. Camden's palm cupped my cheek for the second time tonight. I could smell my arousal on his fingers. He lifted my head. Oh...there we go, it's all straight now. Blinking a few times I saw the smirk that was plastered on his face.

"You're going to need to be carried out of here when I'm done with you, I can already tell." He chuckled.

"Shut up," I said groggily.

"Time to do something about that mouth of yours."

He took a step toward me. Hooking his fingers in his waistband, he pulled them down, and his heavy erection came out. The sheer sight of him perked me back up. I couldn't wait to feel the velvety soft skin in my mouth. Camden fisted his dick and pumped his hand up and down several times. Every time I saw him this way, he took my breath away. Every part of him was perfection. And of course I still questioned how he ever fit inside of me. I'd been with other guys, but none were built quite like he was. I looked up at him through my eyelashes and licked my lips in anticipation.

"Hungry are you?" A sly grin spread across his face.

"Very, but I'd like the use of my hands for this."

BENDER

"No," he stated firmly. "You need a reminder of who's in charge and who tops you Keegan. That would be me. You don't get to use your hands unless I say so, and you will take what I give you."

"Do you think I'm actually going to behave while your dick is in my mouth?" I raised my brow. "Careful who you're bossing Camden, I've got teeth."

He narrowed his eyes at me and bent at the waist to come face to face with me. "You wanna try it…be my guest." He shrugged. "But you won't be able to sit down for a week."

He spoke so matter-of-fact, I knew he wasn't kidding. We stared at each other for several long moments before he stood back up and brought himself up to my mouth. I might have played my cards wrong, because I wanted nothing more than to feel him coming in my mouth. I wanted to taste the salty liquid pooling in the back of my throat. He knew it, and I knew it. He held himself at the base as the smooth head of him rubbed my lips. The tip of my tongue came out, and I licked up the drop of pre-cum. It was exactly how I expected him to taste. I moaned and opened my mouth for more. Guiding himself in, I closed my lips around him, and flattening my tongue against the bottom of his shaft.

"Oh fuck," he groaned.

His hips tilted forward, and he fed me a few inches before he withdrew. Each time I swirled my tongue around the rim of his cock and sucked a little harder. Camden's head dropped back, and he grabbed my head. He was controlling every move we both made. I desperately wanted my hands to be free so I could dig my fingers into his ass and hold him to me, but that wasn't going to happen. At least not this time. Leaning my head forward I took him further into my mouth than he was expecting. His cock touched the back of my throat, and I made a swallowing motion. He jerked forward in surprise, clearly enjoying the sensation. Camden's fingers wound into my hair, and he pulled me back. He made my head tilt so that I was looking up at him.

"You want me to fuck your mouth? I was trying to take it easy and let you adjust, but it seems that my eager girl wants more. I'll give you more. Is that what you want?" he growled, frustration plastered on his face.

"Give me all you've got."

"Little girl, you've just stepped into the big leagues." His fist tightened in my hair, and the pulling was slightly painful. Camden wasn't kidding when he said he was taking it easy. This was downright brutal. Nothing prepared me for how fast he began to piston himself in and out of my mouth. He had a death grip on my head, and with every thrust he hit the back of my throat. I barely had enough time to swallow before he was shoving back in. Saliva was pooling in my mouth, and my gag reflex was kicking in. When I tried to cough, Camden abruptly pulled himself out and laughed a cruel laugh.

"Like I said, maybe next time you'll behave and let me do things my way. I've had enough fucking around. I need to be inside you, *now*."

I choked down the spit that was in my mouth. I felt a little angry that he was being so brutal, but then again I knew what I was in for when I poked my sleeping bear. Either that or I was angry that he still wasn't letting me touch him. I mean, enough was enough. I didn't like him being out of my reach. I hated it. Just as I was about to tell him I was done for the night, Camden loosened the bands around my wrists. I wiggled my hands back and forth trying to help the circulation return to normal.

"Decided to let me go?" I asked, rubbing a sore spot on my arm.

"Blue, you make me laugh. No, we're just relocating."

"Relocating? Where?" Honestly I was tired and ready for sleep, but Camden hadn't finished yet, and if he didn't come, he was going to have a serious case of blue balls. I wasn't a guy, but I was pretty sure it was not the greatest feeling.

When I tried to lift my legs out of the rests, they were stiff. My knees were locked, and I struggled to make them move. I managed to get one of them up and out, but when I winced in pain, Camden took notice and picked me up. He cradled me to his chest, and I sank into his warmth.

We walked over to a desk that was in the opposite corner, and he sat me down. Back here, people couldn't see into the gym if they looked through the front door. Gently Camden massaged my legs. "How're you holding up?"

"Just dandy."

I loved the sweet smile that he gave me. It was one that he reserved just for me. "I think we'll stick to the desk seeing as how you're legs aren't functioning right now."

I bent them over the edge and let the soreness settle in. "I'm not sure I want to know where else you had in mind. That little stunt you pulled over there was enough to drive me batty."

He chuckled. "We need to build up your endurance and stamina."

"Spoken like a true personal trainer," I teased.

He leaned in giving me the softest of pecks on my lips, then the tip of my nose. "Hmmm…you're cute. And you're making it incredibly hard for me to want to continue your punishment."

I batted my eyes and held my hand to my chest. "Are you saying you're quitting? I never pegged you for a quitter."

He playfully reached up and pinched my nipples causing them to stiffen. "Are you trying to get me riled up again? Because Keegan, you can't handle it right now if I did what I really wanted to."

"Try me."

He dragged his hands through his brown hair that was spiking up every which way. He was so damn sexy with he did that. Giving me a pointed look he said, "I can't be gentle right now, I'm still too worked up. But no way am I going to do what I had planned. We'll save it for another night." He winked and my skin shivered in goosebumps. "Lie down on your stomach, I want to see that gorgeous ass bent over and up in the air."

I blanched. "Camden I've never done *that* before."

"And what exactly do you think I'm planning on doing?"

I gulped. "Ummm… well, I mean it's not that back door entrance doesn't appeal to me, but, I don't think that I'm ready for-"

He cut me off when he barked out a laugh. "Relax Blue, we aren't doing *that*. At least not tonight, but someday I plan on taking your ass and having you every way possible." His expression darkened.

I was speechless. Nodding, I decided that I was done talking. Sliding off the desk, I turned around and bent over the wooden frame. I heard him suck in before I felt his hand grasp my hips.

"Jesus I don't think you've ever looked so good. Grab on to the edge and hold on."

I did what he instructed, and that was when I felt him behind me. He ran the head of his cock up and down through my slit, and in one quick movement, he pushed in all the way to the hilt. I cried out at the sudden feeling of fullness. I was very wet and more than ready for him, but there wasn't any preamble to his intrusion. Camden's forehead came down on my back, and he let out a string of curse words. Giving me a moment to adjust to his size, he pulled back till he was almost out then he came forward again. He did this several times, sliding in and out more easily. My body was being worked up and I was able to feel him much deeper this way. Every time his hips slammed into mine a slapping sound echoed in my ears. Camden was holding my hips so roughly that I was certain I'd have bruises when this was over. I didn't care. I wanted him to mark me. A tight coiling began low in my stomach, and I knew I was getting close. Rearing back I tried moving myself back into him.

"Harder," I grunted.

"No," he growled back at me, bringing his hand down with a loud *whack* against my ass cheek. "I set the pace Keegan, not you."

The stinging only heightened my arousal. "Spank me Camden. God I want your hands all over me."

He obliged my one request, and his hand slapped the other cheek. I shook with pleasure. Gathering all of my hair in his fist, he pulled my head back, and he licked the top of my spine. My body was arched at a seductively awkward angle, my breast protruding out, and my hand reached back to dig into his hips.

When he felt the bite of my nails on his skin he released me, and I fell forward. My sweat was slick on the wood. He bowed over my body, encasing me in his arms. Nipping at my shoulder with his teeth he whispered, "Naughty girl. God your pussy is so tight. You're close aren't you? Does my girl want to come?"

I was on the verge of tears because the sensations rolling through me were more than I could bear. "Please…please…Jesus, I can't. Camden it's too much. Oh God."

I felt him expanding inside of me and based on his tempo, he was getting close as well. Wrapping his arms around me, one across my breasts, and the other at the apex of my thighs, Camden tweaked my clit. I screamed, and my legs gave out. He had me standing up and he pounded into the back of me at an impossibly fast rate. The tip of his cock was hitting my cervix, and the pain shot me over the edge.

"Come, now Keegan!" he demanded in my ear.

My whole body exploded with a violence I'd never known before. I felt like I was being ripped apart from the inside, and there was no way I'd be put back together. Ringing in my ears was caused by Camden's loud roar of pleasure. I was going to have teeth marks on my shoulder from him biting down on me. My vision went completely black, and I think I was holding my breath. I was being held in a tight embrace as he slowed his motion, but continued to rock into me. He had filled me so full that with each subtle thrust, more semen trickled down my leg. My body was quaking with aftershocks that made me feel like I had no control over any of my limbs. I was totally languid. When I finally opened my eyes I realized that we had sunk down to the floor, and Camden was holding me to his chest. I was engulfed by his large arms, and I'd never felt so secure. Hair was sticking to my sweat-covered forehead.

He spoke against my temple. "There you are. Thought I lost you for a minute."

I took a deep breath and exhaled. "I think I passed out."

"Hmmm… you did. Has that ever happened to you before?"

I shook my head. "Nope. Definitely a first."

"I'm going to have to go easier on you next time."

I tucked my head under his chin. "No way. It was totally perfect."

He pulled back and lifted my chin with his finger. "I don't want to break you Keegan."

"I'm not made of glass, Camden. I won't always want it that rough, but that was probably the single most incredible sexual experience of my life. It was like you were everywhere, and I couldn't get enough."

His pursed his lips, thinking about something that he wanted to say but didn't. "Thanks for the compliment." His eyes softened. "Do you think you can stand, or do I need to help you get dressed?"

I wiggled my toes and tried to move my legs. "Definitely going to need help. I'm running on empty here."

Camden smiled. "Alright pretty girl, up you go." He stood with me in his arms. How he wasn't wiped out I had no clue. Note to self: need to build up my endurance. We both got dressed together, giving each other knowing looks. I'd give him a shy smile, and he'd wink at me making me blush. Hard to believe that after what I just let him do to me, I'd feel embarrassed about anything. But he had that effect on me.

He laced his fingers through mine, and he gave me a slow easy kiss. "Let's go home, I'll grill us some burgers."

My stomach rumbled. "Good, I'm starving."

As we reached the door, Camden's cell phone went off, and he dug it out of his bag. I'd caught a quick glance of the name that appeared on the screen. It was a text message from someone named Bree. He read whatever she sent and quickly put his phone back. He looked down at me as he held the door open, and I could see something in his mood had shifted. My stomach dropped, and I wondered who she was. He didn't respond to her, but my curiosity was peaked. Was Camden still seeing someone else? I didn't know what I'd do if he was. I was falling hard for him, and the idea of him with anybody but me made me feel sick. He gave me a tight lipped smile as we got into our vehicles. I drove the rest of the way home in silence. My mind went every possible direction and I wanted to ask him, but that would make me seem like I didn't trust him. I wouldn't start our relationship off with doubt and questions. Before I got to the apartment, I decided I'd let it go. I was sure it wasn't a big deal. I prayed like hell I was right.

CHAPTER FIFTEEN

I WAS JUST WALKING OUT of my A&P classes feeling extra stressed due to prepping for finals when I was greeted by a mouth-watering sight. Camden was leaning against a pole outside the door in all his hot male glory. A well-worn pair of jeans that I'd only seen him in a handful of times were hanging low on his narrow hips, and he had on a plaid button-down shirt with the cuffs rolled up to his forearms. He topped off the outfit with a pair of black Nikes. Seeing him after the morning I'd had was like taking a breath of fresh air. Without hesitation, I walked to him and tipped my head back. He bent and kissed the tip of my nose, then my forehead. His arms came around me and held me to his chest as I rested my cheek against him.

"Rough day?" he asked.

"Very. These finals are going to kill me."

Reaching around me, he slid my bag from my shoulder and placed it on his own. He did little gestures like that for me now all the time. "Better not, I have some new things I'd like to try with you before you bite the dust."

I slapped his arm. "Shut it, Brooks."

Chuckling, he grabbed my hand and started walking me through campus to the parking lot. We talked about the human body, and surprisingly, because of Camden's job, he knew quite a bit of how things worked physiologically speaking. If we were talking about anything else, well…he was also pretty well versed in those subjects. Looks like I'd be hitting him up as a study partner later this week. We were almost to my car when I heard someone calling my name from a distance. Stopping, I turned around to see who it was. I brought my free hand up and shielded the sun from my eyes to try and get a better look. No way. Of all the people…was he serious right now? Luke was jogging across the field to where Camden and I had stopped. I risked a glance up at Camden and checked to see if he looked as furious as I was feeling. All I saw was indifference. *What the hell?*

As Luke drew nearer, he appeared exactly the same way that he always did. I don't know why I would have assumed he looked any different. It had only been a few weeks since the Halloween party.

"Keegan, can we talk?" he asked, as he halted in front of me.

I frowned. "No, I don't think so. I have nothing to say to you."

He looked from me to Camden, then down to our joined hands. Camden still seemed calm and collected. "Wait, are you two an item now?"

"Not that it's any of your business, but yes, we are," I answered.

Luke shook his head. "Unbelievable. You went from me to Brooks, in let me guess, no time at all."

I was quickly unraveling. I had hoped I'd never have to see him again, but apparently the universe was feeling extra cruel today. Every word out of his mouth was serving to fuel the fire within me to throttle this asshole across campus. "For starters, it doesn't matter *how* long it was until Camden and I began our relationship. And another thing, I'm pretty sure you lost any say when you decided to play me in your fucking little fraternity games."

He sighed a frustrated breath. Dragging his hands through his hair he said, "See, that's why I wanted to talk to you. I need to apologize for what happened—"

I held my hand up. "Save it. I don't want to hear your shit excuses. You knew what you were doing from the start. It was like 'oh let's pick the vulnerable girl and see if I can make her fall for me' wasn't it?" When he didn't answer, I shouted, "Wasn't it!?"

He looked down at the ground. "When I first spoke to you, yes." He brought his familiar blue eyes up to mine. "But then I got to know you, Keegan. You weren't at all what I was expecting, and I started falling for you."

I think I was possessed. I released Camden's hand and brought it behind me in a swing so hard that when it connected with Luke's face I felt the reverberations up my arm. Tears were forming in my eyes from the rage I was feeling. His head twisted from the blow, and he looked genuinely shocked.

"No you weren't, Luke. You were afraid of your little bitch of a girlfriend dumping you because you couldn't win a bet. This was never about me, and frankly you could've cared less who you trampled on in the process. So fuck you, and fuck those assholes that you live with. People's lives aren't a game. Grow up." I turned to walk away, completely blinded by the white hot anger rippling through me. Luke's hand shot out and tried to grab my upper arm when Camden finally stepped in.

Taking a hold of Luke's wrist, Camden bent it at an awkward angle causing Luke to shout in pain. "Alright asshole, you've stated your peace, and now I'm going to state mine. That girl you chose to fuck around with and hurt," he pointed to me. "She's mine now. You so much as look at her, blink at her, breath the same air that she breathes, or attempt to contact her again, I will break you. There will be nothing that she says that will stop me from putting you in the ground. You feel me?" Camden leaned in close causing more tension on Luke's arm. "And for the record, she was never yours. Whatever feelings you think you may have had...they're gone now. You didn't know a good thing when you had it, so run along to your little buddies and tell them that this goes for them too. This shit is done. If I ever hear of another party like this, none of you will survive it." He released him and Luke cradled his wrist. "Oh and just so we're clear, your gym membership...it's been revoked."

Camden turned around and took several strides in my direction. Without so much as a backwards glance to see if Luke was still standing there, he cupped my cheek tenderly. I leaned in to his touch as his thumb swiped away a stray tear. I sniffled. "Sorry."

"Huh uh. Nothing to be sorry about, Blue. But this will be the last time I want to see you crying over him. He doesn't deserve your tears."

"I'm not crying *over* him, I'm crying because of how I let myself feel. It doesn't matter though, he means nothing to me. I have you, and I'm happy." I tried to give him a reassuring smile.

Grabbing my hand, I winced. "You gave him one hell of a slap. Do I need to get you some ice?" He smirked.

I bit my lip trying not to smile at his playfulness. "Quiet, you. Just take me home."

"You got it." He walked me the rest of the way to my car, officially closing the chapter that was Luke.

Thanksgiving break was coming up in two days. Macie and Dodger were just at the apartment talking about our plans for the short break. Naturally I'd be spending it with Sarah at home, but I wasn't looking forward to seeing my mom. I'd considered bringing her here so that I could just not deal with the added stress of being around my mom, but I knew she'd be upset if I didn't come to the house. Macie and Dodger were going to his family's house for Thanksgiving dinner since her parents were going to be vacationing in Cabo like they do every year. Mace usually tags along but after her and I talked, she was trying to give the relationship with Dodger a chance. Camden and I hadn't talked about the holidays but, I figured we'd do our own thing and maybe I could talk him into doing some Black Friday shopping with me bright and early in the morning.

Speaking of Camden, he just walked through the door and set his gym bag down. Coming straight toward me I felt like a deer caught in the headlights. How did I get so lucky again? His gym clothes were sweaty and clinging to his muscled body, his brown hair was spiked as if he'd ran his fingers through it a few times. But his eyes, those russet eyes that I loved so much, were looking at me like I was the piece of chocolate cake that he'd been craving all day and could finally eat. Oh yes, I enjoyed being his reward after a long day apart from each other. I had been standing in the kitchen washing some dishes from earlier when he plowed through the kitchen and lifted me up into his arms. Camden's soft lips came crashing down onto mine, effectively stealing my breath away. Sighing I parted my lips and felt his tongue slip into my mouth. I let him lick and nip at me before I pulled away. He gave me the cutest pout.

"Sorry, Sarah is over there in case you missed that."

He turned both of us since he was still holding onto me. He saw my little sister watching TV and doing her homework on the coffee table. "Shit, I didn't see her," he whispered to me.

"It's okay. You didn't get too carried away." I gave him smile. He set me on my feet, and I leaned against the counter. "You just missed your brother and Macie."

Camden unloaded some of his shaker bottles and rinsed them out in the sink. "Oh yeah, what were they up too?"

"They wanted to know what everyone's plans were for Thanksgiving. Macie is going to your parents' place instead of her usual vacationing in some exotic location." I fanned myself dramatically.

He smirked at me. "And what are our plans?"

"I figured I'd go to my mom's and cook dinner, that way it keeps things semi-normal for Sarah, and you would spend time with your family."

He set his cups down and turned toward me. "You don't want to spend the holiday together?"

"Of course I'd love to, but I just assumed that you wanted to be with your family, and I can't be away from my sister right now. My mom's been in and out so much lately that I can't trust that she won't leave her alone to fend for herself."

"Would she really do that?"

I tilted my head to the side and gave him an 'are you kidding me' look. "My mom has shown me time and time again that her social life is more important than spending it with her kids."

"Okay, then why don't you two come to my parents' house for Thanksgiving? They'd love to meet you, and my mom always makes more than enough food."

I giggled. "I'm sure she does. There *are* four of you boys aren't there?"

"Including my dad, there's five."

I shook my head. "Your mom's gotta be a saint."

He gave a heartfelt smile. "She's amazing. You'll love her."

Sighing I said, "Camden I can't leave my mom alone. She's already dealing with me moving out, and with all of these changes, I think our relationship is really feeling the strain."

My little sister came bounding into the kitchen, and she hugged Camden's hip.

"Hey kid, what's shakin'?"

"Stupid homework…stupid boys," she said nonchalantly as she reached for a cookie on the counter.

"Boys *are* stupid," he said, teasing one of her curls.

"Dodger's not stupid though." There was a pink tinge to her cheeks, and she looked down at her feet.

My eyes shot up to Camden's and his shoulders were shaking from trying to contain his laughter. How did I miss that my sister had a crush on Dodger? Well, couldn't say I didn't blame her, he was pretty cute. "No Dodger's not stupid."

"Psh…."

"Camden!" I stomped my foot at him and shook my head. Let's not burst her bubble. He winked at me.

"Alright back to what we were talking about. I think you and Sarah should just plan on coming to the house. We eat around noon, and you don't have to make anything. After we eat and play ball I can drop you both off at your mom's, and you can bring her food from my house."

"Play ball?"

"Yeah, we sort of have a tradition that after every family dinner we go out to the field and play baseball. Since you two and Macie will be there, we'll have a good little team going," Camden answered simply.

Sarah beamed at him, "That sounds like fun. Can we go Keegan?"

"There's no way my mom will be okay with me taking Sarah for the holiday," I said.

"Yeah she would," Sarah's little voice chimed in.

"Why do you say that?" I asked.

"Because." She shrugged. "Mom was talking to someone on the phone yesterday, and I heard her say that she was going to her boyfriend's house, but that she was trying to think of what to do with me. I think she was going to ask you if I could come over."

I gaped at her. "Mom said she was going to her boyfriend's house for Thanksgiving?"

"Yep!"

This couldn't be put off any longer. I'd talk to her when I dropped Sarah off. I was so fed up with her blowing us off. And during the holidays? It was not okay. I looked up at Camden, and he bent down to whisper something in her ear. She nodded her head and went back into the living room to watch TV. Coming over to me, he pulled me into his arms and rested his chin on top of my head.

"My house?" he asked.

I took a deep breath, feeling more upset than I should be. I've always known how my mom was. Age normally matured people, but in her case, she seemed to be digressing. I wanted to shake her by her shoulders and say, "Wake up Mom, you're a grown woman. You got dealt a shitty hand in life but that doesn't make Sarah and me objects who got in your way of living a good life." I loved her. I loved her unconditionally, but sometimes I really didn't like the choices that she made.

Tipping my head back I looked up at his soft brown eyes. They were full of understanding, and I swallowed the lump in my throat. "Okay, your house. *But* I plan on contributing in some way. I can't show up empty-handed. So could you call your mom and ask her what I could bring?"

He kissed the tip of my nose. It was quickly becoming one of my favorite things that he did. "Yeah I'll go call her right now and give her a heads-up that we have two more coming." He swatted me on the butt and grabbed his phone before he walked over to the dining room.

Oh boy, now was not the time to panic about meeting Camden's family for the first time. I was sure that his parents were lovely. It didn't take a rocket scientist to know that they had raised two great boys. The other two had to be just as wonderful. Holy crap two more Brooks brothers. I didn't know if I was in for a treat, or if I should be worried. Camden and Dodger couldn't be any more different from one another. One brother was serious and a hard ass, but with a sweet side he didn't show often. The other was charismatic, funny, and easygoing. Both were drop-dead gorgeous. I was curious what their parents looked like. It had to have come from somewhere. Sighing, I went back to washing the dishes and tried to decide what I was going to say to my mom later this evening.

"Blue, you got the pies?" Camden called from upstairs. I was loading the desserts I'd made the night before into the car.

"Yeah, come on!" I shouted up to him. He was leaning over the railing and looking as delicious as ever. Who needed dessert when I had him?

Locking up he came downstairs and we all got in the car. Sarah stayed the night last night since we were leaving kind of early. Turns out she was right about my mom wanting to duck out of the holiday festivities. We got into a pretty monumental fight over her leaving my sister at home by herself. She started crying and telling me that I was accusing her of being a bad parent. Maybe I was. But I hadn't had the first clue how I could make her wake up and see just how destructive she was being.

 On the drive to his parents' house, my nerves began to kick in. The only comfort I had going in to this was that Macie was going to be there too. Camden knew I was getting antsy because every few minutes he'd give my hand a squeeze. Looking over at him, he was ridiculously handsome. He was wearing dark jeans and a black thermal henley that molded to every curvature of his arms and chest. He styled his hair in a spiky mess, and he had on a cologne that was a deep woodsy scent. Between how he looked and smelled, he was a lethal combination. I wanted him. I felt like I wasn't up to par with him, and I fidgeted with the hem of my shirt. I had on a pair of white skinny jeans, tan flats, and a loose fitted peach chevron design top. I'd put something in my hair that helped make the waves stand out more than normal and it hung down my back. Camden's face when he saw me this morning was all the approval that I needed. I just hoped I wasn't underdressed for his family.

 We'd been on the road for almost thirty minutes when we turned off into a nice subdivision on the other side of Athens. The homes weren't necessarily brand new, but it was the type of neighborhood that had beautiful large trees, and well-manicured lawns. The further we drove, the bigger the houses got. My palms were sweating, but Camden never said anything about it. When he pulled into the driveway of a stately looking home, I looked up. It was a two-story colonial that could have been plucked right out of a *Southern Living* magazine. White columns adorned the front and the green shutters made the anterior of the home pop. Poppies, daffodils, lilies, and hedges were laid out around the front of the house and around a tree in the middle of the yard. This was certainly not what I imagined when I pictured Camden's childhood home. Parking the car, he got out and came around to open my door. I saw Macie's vehicle, along with a few others, and I felt a little relieved that she was already here.

Sarah had already jumped out, and she was racing up the path to the front door. "Don't touch *anything*!" I shouted to her.

Camden put his arm around me and kissed my cheek. "It's not a museum Keegan. My parents are cool, promise."

Just as he spoke, someone opened the front door. I was looking at a younger version of Dodger; black hair and bright caramel colored eyes. He was tall but leaner than both Dodger and Camden. He came walking down the steps with a broad grin on his face. He approached Camden, and they clapped hands and pulled each other into an embracing hug.

"Hey little bro, good to see you."

"You too." They both stood back and beamed. When those eyes shifted to me, I got a quick once over. "Nice arm candy, dude. You going to introduce me?"

Camden rolled his eyes and shoved his shoulder. "She's not arm candy asshole. Wrig, this is Keegan. Keegan, this is my youngest brother Wrigley."

I held out my hand, which he took. "So nice to meet you."

"The pleasure is definitely all mine." He smirked and wagged his eyebrows.

"Give it a rest little man. She ain't interested."

"Says who? Seems good looks run in your family. Where's the oldest brother, I need to see my options," I retorted.

Camden narrowed his eyes at me. "Keegan," he said in warning.

"Well, I'm just saying… who says you're the brother for me? Macie may have one of you but that leaves me with three—" I was cut off. Camden hoisted me over his shoulder and slapped my ass. I squealed, "Put me down! I can't meet your mother like this."

"Sure you can, she'll love you."

"But I'm upside-down. Come on Camden, my hair is going to be a mess."

"You're still beautiful." He strode toward the door. I heard Wrigley chuckling behind us.

"Camden Mason Brooks, what are you doing to that poor girl?" a lovely sing-song voice chimed.

"Oh hey Mom. I'm just trying to teach a lesson."

I was going to kill him. "Do you really have to be such a caveman? I swear you're more like your father every day."

"That's not a bad thing." He seemed pleased with himself. "Mom, I want you to meet my friend and roommate, Keegan." He spun me around so when I pushed up with my hands against his back I could look up at her.

She nearly took my breath away. I was looking at a flawless porcelain doll. The boy's mom was more petite that I would have imagined. Definitely shorter than my five-foot-three stature. She had long brown hair that she curled at the ends, deep brown eyes that matched Camden's, and the softest features I think I've ever seen. Although it was kind of hard to tell from this angle. She gave me a welcoming smile that eased some of my discomfort.

Holding out her hand she said, "Hi, I'm Donna. So nice to finally meet you."

At least she seemed amused at her son's playfulness. I shook it and returned the greeting. It wasn't lost on me that two things have been said that made me take pause. For starters Camden introduced me as his *friend*. I realized that we hadn't put a label on whatever this was, but I assumed we'd surpassed the friend category. And second, what has he told her about me? Her use of the word 'finally' rang in my ears, so he must have told her something regarding me. None of this sounded promising.

"Cam put her down, and come give me a hug." She patted his arm.

He set me down, and I tried to comb my hair back in place with my fingers. *Seriously? Great first impression, Keegan, just wonderful.* The hug that he gave his mother was reverent and loving. I could tell in the tenderness that he showed her that he loved his mom very much. I liked that. Boys who loved and respected their mothers always scored points in my book. When she let him go, she smiled back at me and gestured toward the house.

"Please, come in. Your friend Macie is in the game room with my husband Paul."

"Oh God, is Dad showing her his dirt collection?"

I looked at him strangely. "Dirt collection?"

Donna took my arm and started leading me into the house. I glanced back at Camden who was now walking beside his brother, and he shrugged. "Cam has told you about all of my boys being named after baseball fields right?" I nodded. "Okay, well we are a baseball loving family, and we try to go to as many games as we possibly can all over the nation. My husband likes to be a rebel and climb down over the wall when a game is over, after most people have left, and collect dirt from the field."

"Has he ever gotten in trouble for doing something like that?"

I heard snickering behind me. "Dad's not as limber as he used to be," Wrigley responded. "There was a game where the Cubs were playing the Cardinals, and he couldn't get himself back over the wall. Mom was screaming at us to help him up before security caught him."

I giggled. "Oh I could have killed him," Donna said in an irritated voice.

Stepping inside the house was like walking inside a country chic store. Everywhere I looked were little touches of rustic wood, faded paint on furniture, and antiques. It certainly wasn't like a museum at all. It smelled of cooking turkey, baked apple pie, and cinnamon. It was inviting, like a home should be. Camden stepped forward and placed his hand on my lower back to show me which way to go. Donna took the pies from him and went to the kitchen to keep cooking. I'd offered to help, but she shooed me away.

The living room was open with exposed beams that ran the length of the ceiling, and worn looking couches sat in the middle of the room. Dodger and Macie were standing in a corner looking at some sort of photo album and hadn't seen us yet. An older gentleman was sitting down talking to someone who looked strikingly like Camden. I didn't think it was possible for anybody to beat him in the size category, but this guy did. He was monstrous! When both men saw us coming in the room, they stood up. The older man held a look of pride in his eyes. His eyes resembled Dodger and the other man's piercing blue ones. The boys all clearly got their build from their father. He was tall with broad shoulders and a wide stance. If I had to guess his age, I'd say he was in his mid-forties, and it was obvious that he took care of himself.

No words were exchanged between both men when they greeted each other, Camden and his dad hugged each other tightly. After a few claps on the back, his dad pulled back and held on to his son's shoulders.

"You're lookin' good son. Real good."

"Thanks Pop." Just the look on Camden's face told me how much his father's words meant to him. "Oh, I have someone I want you to meet. Keegan, this is my dad, Paul."

I was going to shake his hand but when he took a hold of it, he pulled me into a bear hug. "Sorry kiddo, I'm a hugger. And it's very nice to meet you."

A lump was forming in my throat. This was what a dad was supposed to be like; supportive, loving, caring. Not missing from your life for the past twenty years, never caring that you were alive. I hugged him back tightly, almost wishing that I could stay this way a little longer, regardless of just meeting him. I could feel the warmth radiating off of him.

"Nice to meet you too," I said, stepping back into Camden and enjoying that he possessively put his hand on my hip.

"You going to introduce me, little man, or are you afraid I'll steal this beautiful creature from you?" Camden's almost identical twin said, approaching me.

"What is it with my brothers trying to take my girl?"

"Well if you were giving her what she needs, then it wouldn't be an issue, now would it?" He looked at me. I was immediately drawn to his blue eyes. His compliment caught me off guard, and I blushed a deep shade of red. I didn't know if this was normal banter between the two of them or not. Both of their faces were serious, but slowly a grin slipped onto Camden's face.

"Asshole," Camden growled. "Keegan, this is my older brother Turner. Turner, this is *mine*," he stated possessively.

Their dad chuckled. "Nice to meet you Turner." I tipped my head at him, thinking better of shaking his hand like I had with the rest of the family.

He noticed and smiled. I gulped loudly. The resemblance was uncanny minus their eye color.

I felt a presence sidle up to me on my other side, and I looked up to see Dodger. He flung his arm over my shoulder, and he tipped me over to kiss the top of my head. I loved that he felt so comfortable with me. "Lookin' good beautiful. Where's Sarah?"

Oh crap, in my moment of distraction, I'd forgotten where my sister was. "She's in the kitchen with Mom. I think she's having her help make sweet tea," Camden answered for me. I let out a sigh of relief.

Macie had sat down on one of the couches and was thumbing through a magazine when she lifted her eyes and smirked at me. I bet she could sense how awkward I was feeling. I rolled my eyes at her and leaned my head onto Camden's shoulder. If we weren't in front of his family, I would kiss him so hard right now. I loved that Turner pushed him to stake his claim on me. And I love that he did it in front of the people that meant the most to him. Hello warm and fuzzies.

"Well." Paul rubbed his hands together. "Hopefully your mom is almost done cooking 'cause I'm starving! Cam, why don't you take Keegan and show her around the house. We can catch up when we sit down to eat."

"Wanna see the house?" he asked softly.

"Sure I'd love to."

I gave a small wave to everyone in the room, because they were watching me intently. I briefly wondered if I was the first girl Camden had brought home before. They sure seemed to be intrigued by me. Camden had taken my hand and started leading me through the house. He showed me everything downstairs from the dining room that was set up for dinner, his parents' master bedroom that made me drool with their beach theme and four-poster bed, to the laundry room that could make washing clothes seem like fun. When we started going up the stairs, Camden's mom called him to come help her with something real quick. He left me standing there so I took advantage of the alone time to look at all the photographs hanging on the wall. There were family pictures from vacations they had taken, school pictures, and ones of the boys playing sports. They all looked so happy. I had a pang of jealousy run through me. I wished I could give Sarah something like this, but I knew it wasn't going to happen. Pushing it aside, I continued up the steps one by one reveling in each smile and action shot. They seemed like the picture perfect family. Almost at the top of the steps, one photograph caught my eye. It was of Camden during his high school graduation. He was wearing his cap and gown, and the smile that was on his face took my breath away. But what had caught my attention the most was the girl he was standing next to. She had dark hair and sea-blue green eyes. Her tanned skin almost matched the color of Camden's. She was strikingly beautiful. What threw me was the hold he had on her. She was looking at the camera, while he beamed down at her. It seemed so intimate. Who was she? He's never told me about an old girlfriend, but we've also never discussed our pasts. Something about it wasn't sitting right. I'd seen who he'd brought in and out of our apartment before; this girl was different, this one was special.

Only a few minutes went by and Camden came up the stairs taking two at a time. When he reached me he kissed my nose in typical Camden fashion, melting my heart and making me forget my worries. I was sure whoever she was it wasn't a big deal. And if she was, well maybe he'd share at some point when he felt like it. We continued on through the rest of the tour. His parents still kept each of the boys' rooms exactly the same since the day they left. Granted, Wrigley still lived at home, because he was still in high school. But he'd be graduating this year and going off to college. I loved seeing each of their individual styles. Turner was only a year older than Camden, so he was twenty-six, and his room was decorated in plaid bedding and collegiate posters. Camden had weights, trophies, and an overall sense of a typical guy's space. Dodger's room had a couple of guitars and some pictures of girls in bikinis. Wrigley's space was trashed. He had clothes laying all over the place, it smelled like a high school boy's room, and the walls were riddled with baseball things. Yep, pretty typical boy's room. Out in the hallway I pushed Camden up against a wall. He looked down at me in amused surprise.

"Thinking about getting frisky, Blue?" he teased.

"Nah." I playfully rubbed up against him.

Chuckling he said, "Okay, then what did I do to deserve the rough treatment."

I brought one of my hands up and touched his lower lip. He parted them, and his pupils dilated. "I wanted to say thank you."

He licked his lips and his tongue touched the pad of my thumb. "For what?"

"For saying what you did downstairs. You called me your *friend* to your mom, and it was a sucker punch, but I get it, we don't have labels. Except, when Turner pushed, you staked your claim. Not only that, but you did it in front of your brother and dad. So thank you. It made me feel wanted."

"You *are* wanted, Keegan. More than I think you know. And I'm sorry about my mom. I wasn't sure what your comfort level was, so I didn't want to push the issue. If you are wanting to define us, then we can do that."

I shook my head. "No I don't want to force you into something you might not want to do."

He furrowed his brows. "What the hell are you talking about? Am I with you right now?"

"Yes."

"Then what about that says you're forcing me? Nobody *forces* me to do anything. You should know that more than anyone."

Sighing I looked down. "You're right, I'm sorry. I didn't mean to start a fight."

"Are we fighting? Pretty sure if we were, you'd fucking know it." He tipped my chin up with his finger. "But, if we are, I'm ready for the make-up sex. It's my favorite kind."

Now I was the amused one. "I thought gym sex was your favorite."

"That too."

"Mhmm…"

He brought his lips down to mine and kissed me so softly it felt like a feather's touch. The delicate sensation of this kiss gave me butterflies; it made me feel like I was floating, it made me wonder how deep my feelings were for Camden. What began as a slow caressing of our mouths shifted into something more. I leaned into him, pressing my full weight into his chest and stomach. His tongue glided along the seam of my lips wanting access to more of me. I could feel his arousal against my front, and I let myself forget where I was and who was downstairs. Camden made me lose myself whenever he kissed me like this. He consumed me.

"Turkey's ready!" Sarah yelled from the bottom of the steps.

My sweet brooding man tenderly pecked my mouth once more and smiled down at me. I pouted at the interruption. The look in his eyes seemed different. More loving and open. I knew every wall I had was crumbling down, and I felt my heart pick up its pace. I was falling for Camden Brooks, and the "L" word was trying to sneak itself into my vocabulary. He made me very happy, happier than I think I've ever been. I needed to slow myself down though. There was no way, despite how it seemed like he was seeing me right now, that he could be feeling anything but like. Camden didn't do love, and least of all, not with me. I'd have to be more careful with my emotions around him so that I didn't slip and say something that could make him walk away. The "L" word would ruin everything.

"Come on, let's go eat. I swear I could hoover a whole cow right now," he said, breaking up my thoughts.

"You mean turkey," I corrected.

He laughed. "You've never seen one of my mom's Thanksgiving spreads. I meant cow. Come, I'll show you."

He tugged my hand, and we went downstairs to join the family at the table.

CHAPTER SIXTEEN

"OH MY GOSH SOMEONE IS GOING to need to wheelbarrow me out to the field," Paul said, rubbing his distended belly. "The turkey was delicious dear, you outdid yourself again."

She beamed at him.

"Yeah, I feel like a stuffed bird. Get it? Stuffed....bird?" Wrigley joked, trying to be sarcastic.

A napkin was chunked at his face, and there was a round of grumbles. In the short period of time that I'd been at Camden's house, I'd learned that Wrigley liked to tell the cheesiest jokes. What made them even funnier was how he delivered them. Being the baby of the family, he got the most flack but could get away with anything. Turner, the oldest, was the practical one. He'd gone off to college at LSU on a baseball scholarship, then was picked up by a major league team. However, he chose to come back home and work on a doctorate degree. Their parents were very proud of him despite loving the idea of one of their boys joining the big leagues. I think they were actually holding out hope for Wrigley. Scouts had their eye on him, and it was his last year in school. Camden was the serious brother, the one that took on the role of family protector. During dinner I listened to him grill his brothers on the things going on in their lives, letting them know that he'd be there if they needed it. Always my broody man. Dodger's personality was easygoing. He was the most passive of the four of them, but I knew from the Halloween party that he had a strong side that didn't take shit. He was like the quiet storm that brewed out at sea. I could easily see how someone like Dodger was good for Macie. He let her get away with things when necessary, but reeled her in when she needed to be caught. I loved all of their individual personalities, and yet they somehow were all the same, because they were the product of their parents. Parents who looked on with pride while we ate. This was a family who was close and supported each other no matter the battles. I envied them.

"Ready to get your asses whooped?" Dodger stood up from the table and pulled out Macie's chair.

I had been slightly shocked that their parents weren't offended by some of the things that their boys talked about, but I realized that not a lot really bothered them.

Turner barked a boisterous laugh. "In your dreams Wild Thing."

I leaned into Camden who was grinning from ear to ear. "Wild Thing?"

"Yeah, Dodger here, thinks that he has the best pitch in the family. Except he can't get it over home plate for shit. He started calling himself Wild Thing after Charlie Sheen's character in the movie, *Major League*. He even has some of those black frame glasses around here somewhere," he replied.

"My pitch is awesome, you fuckers. Keegan, you can be on my team, that way you know what *winning* feels like."

Camden shook his head. "She goes to bed with *me* every night, so I'm pretty sure she already knows what winning feels like."

"Camden!" I scolded. Could he embarrass me any more today?

Paul chuckled when Camden shrugged. "No worries honey, we all know Cam's all bark."

Oh boy they had no idea there was certainly more than a bite that went along with his bark. He looked down at me, confirming that he was reading my mind. Winking at me, he got up as well. "We'll divide the teams when we get to the field. Let's go."

I started picking up my plate to take it into the kitchen when Donna put her hand on my forearm and said, "Don't worry about that, we always clean up after we play."

I smiled at her and set it back down. Out in their garage were two golf carts and a couple bat bags sitting next to them. We all loaded up, Paul driving one cart, and Turner driving the other. Sarah sat on Dodger's lap since there wasn't enough room for all nine of us to ride over there. I was sure she was thrilled. We went about two blocks over and stopped at a baseball field that was well maintained but looked like it wasn't used often.

Camden spoke into my ear. "My parents bought this acreage when I was a kid because they wanted a place that they could take us to practice and not worry about us slamming any balls into the neighbor's windows. They made it into a baseball field and opened it up to anybody that wanted to come use it. We still come out here after every family dinner and play. It's been our tradition for over fifteen years now."

Unloading, we all stood near the fence that ran along the catcher's position. "Alright time to choose teams." Turner was taking charge. "I've got Mom, Dad, Keegan, and Macie. So Cam that leaves you with Wrigley, Dodger, and Sarah."

"Sounds fair." He nodded.

"Y'all can bat first. Macie, how's your arm?"

"Honestly, I kind of suck at throwing balls."

He smirked. "I'm sure you're better playing with them."

She laughed, but I heard Dodger growl. "Watch it asshole, or Wild Thing might peg you in the face with a fastball."

"Alright, play nice boys, and Turner cut it out with the wisecracks," Donna chided.

"Sorry Mom," he said. "Okay since Macie can't pitch, how about you Keegan, can you toss a ball? You don't have to do anything crazy, just underhanded softball pitching."

I had no idea whether I could or not, but I shrugged and said, "Sure, I can try."

"Good girl," he praised, which made me think about Camden saying the same thing to me in the bedroom. My face reddened, but thankfully nobody noticed. "Macie you go stand between second and third base. I'll take the spot between first and second. Mom, you and Dad go in the outfield. Everyone good?"

We all nodded and went to our prospective positions. Everyone else was off to the side waiting for their turn to bat, while Sarah was up first. Dodger helped place her feet the correct way and put her hands on the bat where they should be. He nodded at me when she was ready. I stepped in a little closer to go easy on her. First toss, she swung and missed. We all clapped and told her to keep trying and to keep her eye on the ball. Her second swing she clipped the ball, but it was a strike. The next one I threw was way off its mark. She laughed at me, and it warmed me that she was having such a good time. Dodger stayed close to her and was coaching her when to swing. My fourth pitch, she swung and hit the ball. It went rolling on the ground, and Macie took off after it. Sarah ran to first base, and we all slowed down to let her get to the base. Dodger whooped and cheered for her. I didn't think I'd ever seen a bigger smile on her face. Next up was Wrigley. He wound his arm around while holding the bat, warming up his arm.

"Don't worry pretty girl, I won't hit it too hard," he taunted.

"I'm sure you don't," I dished. I heard Donna laughing in the outfield, and I saw Camden shaking his head.

"Just hit the fucking ball asshole," Camden yelled.

I tossed my first pitch, and he swung and missed. Granted it wasn't the best throw, but I think Wrigley had planned on swinging at everything I threw his way. The second ball, he hit, and it went sailing past my head and out toward Turner. Sarah took off running at Dodger's command, and she made it to third base before she stopped. Wrigley made it to first base, and he looked all too pleased with himself.

Camden was up next. When he walked up to the plate, his baseball cap shadowed his eyes, and I took my time to shake my shoulders out. When he brought his face up, and our eyes connected, I swallowed hard. *Holy shit… keep it together Keegan, he's trying to intimidate you.* He nodded at me, letting me know that he was ready. Why did I love his serious face so much? I brought my arm back and underhanded the first pitch. It went wide, and Camden let his bat fall to his side as he went to get the ball. Tossing it back to me he smirked. He knew exactly what he was doing to me. Fine, two can play at this game. Everyone else was chanting, "Here batter, batter," over and over, not paying attention to the tension that Camden and I had going on between the two of us. I kicked my feet back and forth on the dirt and held the ball up to my face. I licked my lips, knowing that he could see it, and gave my hips a little wiggle. His eyes narrowed at the movement. Throwing the second ball, he swung and missed.

"Come on Cam!" Wrigley yelled. "This isn't fuckin' tee-ball, let's go."

Camden flipped him the bird and repositioned himself. "One more time, Blue. Give it to me good."

Oh I'll give it to you. He already had two strikes, and I was pretty confident I could get him to swing and miss a third time. His deep chocolate eyes were silently challenging me, testing me to see if I'd waver. I gave him another pitch. If a ball could move in slow motion, I swear this one did. I watched as it went straight toward home plate, Camden was focused as he brought the bat around and took a swing. The ball never connected with the wood, and I let out a "whoop."

"You just let a girl strike you out hot shot, good going," Dodger grumbled.

He said nothing in return. He simply looked at me and grinned. Why did that grin tell me that I was going to pay for that? Either way it made my heart flutter.

"Better luck next time, hot shot." I picked at him.

He barked a laugh. "Yeah, we'll see Blue."

The game continued on, and we played four innings. We all were having a blast, and I didn't think I've had so much fun in a long time. That was until we paused because Camden's phone was ringing. He ran over to the fence where all of our stuff was, and his smiled faded when he looked at the screen. His eyebrows came down and he brought his finger up to tell us all to hold on. He walked off the field and out toward the street, seeming tense. What was going on? I glanced at Macie, and she shrugged her shoulders. Everyone else started talking to each other as we waited for him to finish his phone call. Something about his demeanor wasn't right. Never taking my eyes off of him, I wondered who could possibly be calling him on Thanksgiving when all of his family was out here with him. Or who could get him upset like this. When he hung up, he looked defeated. I wanted to go to him and ask what was the matter, but I could tell he was closed off. Whatever it was about, he wasn't going to tell me. Camden had come back on the field and went directly to Dodger. He was the brother who he was closest to, and I knew they shared everything. Dodger was nodding as he listened, and I could tell that whatever this was he didn't like either. As we started the game back up, I knew he was ignoring my questioning looks. If he thought I was going to shrug it off and act like he was bothered by something, he was sorely mistaken. The rest of the game everyone was having a good time except for myself and Camden. His mood was affecting my mood, and I was anxious to get him alone so we could talk. Thankfully nobody else seemed to notice.

After the game, everyone packed up and loaded up on the golf carts. Camden was still holding a bat and ball when he told them, "You guys go ahead. Keegan and I will walk back."

Paul and Donna gave each other knowing looks, while Macie and Dodger both said, "Uh-huh," in unison. When they all left, Camden directed his attention back to me.

Holding the bat out, handle first he said, "Step up to the plate Keegan."

I didn't know whether it was his tone, or how his eyes were drilling into my own, but I gladly obliged. Taking the bat I went to home plate and waited for his next command. He walked out to the pitcher's mound and stood with his body to the side. I almost gaped at the view. I loved the line of his back that led to his well fitted jeans. I'd never tired of his perfect body. It was a treat to look at with clothes off *and* on. It was getting cooler outside in the evening with the fall weather. Chills ran across my exposed skin.

"Let's see how you can hit when *I'm* pitching."

"I'm pretty sure I can hit it out of the park if you're throwing."

Delight danced across his features. "You think so?"

"Oh I know so. Throw the ball Brooks, I've got this," I taunted. Putting the bat up by my shoulders, I place my elbows out and my feet wide.

He tossed the first ball, and it went a little faster than I'd been expecting. Then again he threw it overhand, which was a switch up from earlier. It went past my bat, and I swung at the air.

Quirking an eye brow he bemused, "You sure about that pretty girl?"

"Shut up and give me another one," I ground out, steadying myself.

He got back into a pitcher's pose and held the ball near his face. When he threw it, the ball went too far to the left, and I couldn't have hit it if I'd tried.

"You talked a big game earlier, and now look who can't hit the ball?" He was trying to piss me off, and for some reason I took the bait.

"It would help if you threw it over the plate."

"You could have it hit that and you know it." I nearly growled. Biting my tongue I got back in position but pointed my bat out to the field. He caught my meaning and chuckled. "Okay Babe Ruth, let's see if I can strike you out, or if you can knock it out of the park."

Rolling his shoulders he looked at me, his intense stare building my confidence with a drive to beat him. When he threw the pitch, I kept my eye on the ball, ignoring everything else around me. Bringing the bat down and extending my arms, the wood connected sending a stinging vibration through my hands as I followed through on my swing. The ball went sailing high up in the air and traveled to the far end of right field. A smile spread across my face, and I dropped the bat. Taking off running, I went to first base, my foot touching the corner of the padding, then second, then rounding to third. Camden was laughing at me as I slowed and skipped my way back to home, enjoying my happiness. Hopping on the dirt covered diamond I lifted my arms up in the air and let out a loud 'woo'! Have you ever seen a football player do a celebration dance when he scores a touchdown? I thought the moment called for it. I did a little shimmy and shake humming along to the beat of my own drum. I could hear my brooding man's laughter getting louder. He was coming toward me. Instead of letting him reach me, I wanted the chase, I *needed* the chase. Picking up my feet, I took off running, making my way toward the outfield.

He was hot on my heels when he said, "I'm going to catch you, Keegan. I always do."

I giggled and ran a little faster. I heard the sound of his feet hitting the ground behind me, causing my heart to beat harder than it already was. I darted to the side, looking over my shoulder at him. I knew that if he wanted, Camden could catch me, he was easily faster that I was. My short stride didn't take me near as far as his longer one did. Thinking I was being smart, I slowed myself down and waited for him to get close enough. At the last second, I switched directions and moved just out of his grasp. I was about to take off again in a sprint, but he did some crazy spin and was able to wrap his arms around me. He picked me up so that my back was to his front, and he lifted me off the ground. I was laughing so hard that my stomach hurt.

"Gotcha!" he stated proudly.

Between fits of laughter I said, "I totally knocked your ball out of the park."

Maneuvering me in the air, he flipped me over and for the second time today I was dangling over his shoulder. "Gloating is usually not a very attractive quality, but for some reason it's cute on you so I'll let it slide."

I slide my hand down the back of his pants and reveled in the feel of his firm ass cheek. "Mmm...I know something that's cuter."

He slapped my butt, and I yelped. Smoothing his hand over the burn he said, "How about you not start something you can't finish."

"Who said I wouldn't finish?"

I heard him rumble something under his breath before he set me down on my feet. My back was now up against the fence where our belongings had been, and Camden hovered over the top of me. "Never pegged you for the public indecency types, but I'm willing to go along with it."

I shoved his shoulder. "Shut up. You know I'd never."

He brought his face down to mine, causing me to tip my head back and look at him. His mouth brushed mine, and his lips feathered across face. His tongue came out and grazed my bottom lip, causing a sigh to escape my throat. His hands came up, his fingers lacing through the wire, caging me in. My eyes were still open as were his, and I felt like I was drowning in a pool of decadent chocolate. His chest rubbed against my already aching nipples each time he inhaled. Desire was pooling at my center, and everything around me revolved around this man. When Camden drew his leg between mine and pushed up against me, I closed my eyes and moaned. How bad would it be if I just rubbed myself on him until I got the relief he was building up in me?

"Keegan look at me," he demanded.

I blinked them open, not realizing how lost I was. He was smiling in victory. "What?"

"You were saying? *No* public fornication?"

I rolled my eyes. "What are you doing to me Camden?"

"What do you mean?"

"I mean, how is it possible that I lose myself in you so easily? It's kind of scary, it's never happened to me before."

"It's not scary, it's a good thing."

"I suppose so, but what's going to happen when this is all over?"

He tilted his head to the side. "Who says this is going to end? We just started Keegan."

"Yes but we don't even know what we are. You could choose to walk away at any moment, and I'm the poor pitiful girl who is left reeling from the ridiculously hot guy who took a chance and treated her right." God, even I sounded whiny to my own ears.

"Are you wanting to put a label on us?"

"No. Maybe?" I sighed. "I don't know."

That got a soft smile to grace his mouth. "What's causing this sudden insecurity?"

I jerked my head back. "This is sudden? Camden, you're in a totally different league than me. I've been insecure from the start."

He clenched his jaw, the muscle ticking. "This isn't high school Keegan. There are no leagues, groups, cliques, whatever the fuck you want to call them. There's you and me, that's it. And that's all that I care about."

I looked down, knowing that I needed to ask him something but unsure of how to word it without sounding like I didn't trust him. "I'm sorry. I'm ruining the fun we were just having."

"No you're not. Your body, and feeling your subtle curves up against mine, is always fun." He paused waiting for my reaction. "See? That made you smile." And it did. "Blue, I'm with you. I'm not concerning myself with anybody else. If defining what we have here is what will make you happy, then I'm fine with that. The word 'girlfriend' doesn't scare me. I've already been thinking of you that way since this started."

"You have?" I looked up at him again.

"Yes. You were the one who mentioned not using labels, so I didn't."

He kissed the tip of my nose, and I relaxed a little. Time to go in for the kill. "Camden who was it that called you earlier?"

I watched his reaction like a hawk, waiting to see any changes that would indicate a lie when he spoke to me. His eyes darkened, narrowing at me and making me feel like *I* was the one being scrutinized. I saw his biceps bulging through his long sleeves so I knew he was gripping the fence harder than he needed to. "It was nobody. There was an issue at the gym and the receptionist didn't know how to handle it, that's all." He paused. "Are we going to have trust issues?"

The gym was open on Thanksgiving? I shook my head. "No, I just noticed that you seemed upset about something, and you wouldn't look at me when you got off the phone. I know that you have a past Camden, and I am not so blind to not think that past might want to come back around." I was trying to give him a push to open up to me about any exes that might want him back. Particularly someone named Bree. "This isn't about trust, but it *is* about you confiding in me. You can tell me things, I'm not going to judge."

There were a few seconds between when I spoke and when he did. "There's nobody coming back in my life like that. There's also no reason for you to feel insecure. I know that I don't say a lot or maybe open up, but I know that you are here. And I appreciate that."

I swallowed the lump in my throat. He was hiding something. Every fiber of my being told me I was right. But I couldn't call him out on it without getting into a huge fight right now. I'd just have to cross my fingers that at some point he'd want to tell me what was really going on and who it was that called him and had been texting him. In the meantime I nodded and gave a weak smile.

"Okay," I said.

Placing his forehead on mine he repeated me. "Okay." Giving me a quick peck on the lips, he took my hand and pulled me away from the fence. "Let's get back to the house *girlfriend*, my brothers have probably already tore into the pumpkin pie, and if it's all gone, I think I might murder someone."

I grinned at his now silly demeanor and followed him back to his parents.

CHAPTER SEVENTEEN

To say that I've had a bad week would be the understatement of the century! First it started at work with going from a paper system to an electronic one. Scanning and inputting a couple hundred patients' records was not only time consuming, it was tedious. And don't even get me started with having to file the paperwork that was still coming in so it could all be switched over. Then I had a pop quiz in A&P that I wasn't even close to being ready for. We had gone over the different types of cells in the body the day before and I hadn't had a chance to look at my notes. Sarah had called me to say that Mom had left, and she was home alone. So I had to go get her and bring her to the apartment then take her back when my mom got home. I would have just let her stay if she didn't have school in the morning. It has been one thing after another, and I was exhausted; mentally and physically exhausted! Not only that but Camden had been working later than normal so I'd barely seen him over the past few days, and it was making me crabby. I also noticed that when he was home with me, he was distracted. It didn't' sit right, and I wondered what was going on. But after our talk at the baseball field, I knew that I needed to trust him.

It was Thursday morning, and I was leaving the café with Macie. She knew about my talk with Camden and what was said. She told me that there was probably nothing to it, and it was more than likely something that he wanted to handle on his own. I agreed and decided I needed to let it go. I was stressing myself out over nothing, and I had no reason not to believe what he told to me. When we parted I decided to head home to take a nap before I went to work. When I got in I noticed Camden's car was here. He hadn't come home all week for lunch and seeing him was a nice surprise.

"Hey you, how was class?" he asked, getting up from the couch to greet me.

"Good I guess. Did you know that there are two hundred and six bones in the body…and that I need to know every single one of them and how they function? Ugh! Kill me now!" I practically collapsed in his arms.

Chuckling he said, "Yes, I'm aware of the number of bones, but unfortunately I can't help you with all of them. Are you tired?"

"Mmm…hmm," was the only response I could give him.

"How about we both go get a little sleep? I have a client in two hours so I have a little time to rest."

"I'd love some sleep. I swear this is like the week that never ends," I grumbled.

"Hmmm, and I thought it was just me. Alright Blue, hold on." He lifted my arms around his neck, and he picked me up, cradling my too his body. Carrying me up the stairs we went into his room, and he laid me on the bed. He pulled off his gym shorts and crawled under the covers behind me, spooning me. "I'll wake you up before you need to leave," he said, kissing my temple.

"K. Thank you." I yawned. His body was like a big blanket, and it comforted me in so many ways. It only took a few minutes for sleep to drag me under.

Beep, beep, beep. What the hell was that noise? Opening one eye I looked at the clock feeling completely discombobulated and stiff. Did the alarm just go off? Rolling on to my back I stretched my limbs and glanced at Camden's side of the bed. It was empty, but I heard the shower running in the distance. Man I must have been really out, because I didn't even feel him get up. I had a little over thirty minutes to get ready for work.

A second little *beep, beep, beep* went off.

Sitting up, I rubbed my tired eyes and looked on Camden's night stand. His phone was sitting there and the screen was lit. I tried not to look at it, I really did, but curiosity got the best of me. I didn't know why all the trust conversations that I'd had with Camden and Macie went out the window in that moment, but I needed to look. Something was drawing me to see who it was. Reaching for his phone, I pushed the bottom button on his to light the screen up, and I saw two text messages from Bree. Instantly I felt sick. Why was she texting him? I was able to see partial messages, but I'd never be able to look at them without him knowing that I read them. I looked up at the door and listened for the shower. It was still running so I had a little bit of time. With shaky hands I picked up the phone and lit up the screen again.

Bree: Hey I'm in town. Need 2 talk….

Bree: Meet me @ Fastfreddys @….

That was all that I could see of the messages without actually opening them up. Bile was rising in my throat, and I had to swallow it back down. I put the phone back exactly how it was before and sat on the bed in a shocked state. Why was she texting him? Would he actually go meet her? The bigger question would be would he tell me about it? None of this was sitting well with me. I wasn't a jealous person, at least I didn't think I was, but I'd also never dated someone who made me feel jealousy. I always knew without a shadow of a doubt that I was with them, and they were with me. So now brings the question of whether I ask him what it was about, or did I even bother telling him that I saw the texts? I wanted to so bad, but I thought I'd wait to see if he mentioned it.

I heard the water cut off, and Camden came back in the room a few minutes later. He had a towel wrapped around his waist and droplets of water still clung to his skin. He saw me looking at him and a little ghost of a smile appeared on his perfect lips.

"Sleep good?" he asked.

I wanted him. Despite how I had been feeling only a few short seconds ago, I wanted him. I didn't think I'd ever not want him. "Yeah, I needed a nap. I don't think I've been getting enough sleep at night."

"I don't think you have either. You've been tossing and turning quite a bit, and you've been mumbling."

"I have? What have I been saying?"

"Yes. But none of it is coherent. You're just making little noises."

"Oh. Hmmm…sorry if it's been keeping you awake."

He went to the closet and pulled out some clothes. When he dropped the towel, he was faced away from me, and I couldn't remove my eyes from his toned ass and how the muscles in his back moved. I think I was salivating.

"You aren't. You settle down a little when I tuck you back into me."

My heart melted. "You cuddle me closer?"

"Mhmm." He tugged his gym shorts up over his hips, and I pouted not being able to see all of him any longer.

I covered my mouth to stifle a yawn, and he smiled at me. Walking toward the bed, he bent down and kissed me tenderly on the lips. I wanted to yank him down and have my way with him, but both of us needed to get going. The unease was still flowing through me as I watched him grab his phone from the night stand and check it. I tried to tell if there were any differences in his demeanor or if he'd come out and tell me what was up, but he held it in. There were no changes in his expression, nor did he mention the texts. I felt myself pull away slightly, not wanting to give away that it was killing me not knowing.

"I'm going to head downstairs to get my bag ready, do you want me to make you something before you have to leave?" he offered.

I shook my head. I definitely wasn't feeling hungry with this pit sitting in my stomach, and I wanted to scream at him to tell me what was going on.

"Nah, I'm good. I think I'll brush my hair and teeth and take off."

He looked at me a little funny, but nodded. "Okay."

He turned and went downstairs. Getting up, I made myself presentable and followed after him to say bye. Everything about our movements was completely normal... until he told me he was going to be working late. Alarms started ringing in my head and I was reeling. I needed to get out of here and get away so I could try and clear my head. Words wouldn't even form on my lips and I simply nodded at him and made my way to the door. Before I walked out, I looked back at him and saw him staring at me strangely. He said bye, and I had no response, there was nothing. Walking out the front door, I half expected him to follow after me, to question what my problem was, but he didn't. I think I found that more disturbing that he didn't. Now who was the one acting differently?

Once I was at work, I couldn't concentrate. My mind kept playing over and over the text that I'd seen, and this Bree girl who wanted to meet my boyfriend at FastEddy's. I was only thirty minutes into my shift, and I couldn't deal with it any longer. Have you ever tried to concentrate on the job when every single thought was being consumed by something else? Not really feeling like I was lying, I went to my boss and said I was sick and needed to go home. She looked at my sympathetically and told me she hoped I felt better. As I walked out of the office, one thought occurred to me. I needed to see for myself. I had no idea what time she told Camden to meet her, but I did know where. There was another small hole in the wall restaurant across the street from FastEddy's where I could sit inside and not be seen. My mind made up, I made the short drive and parked my car around the corner. I'd only hoped that the person serving me wouldn't mind that I planned on staying there until I was certain Camden wouldn't show up at the other diner.

I'd been seated for only ten minutes, and I was sipping my water when it hit me what I was doing. Had I lost that much faith in my relationship with Camden that I felt the need to resort to spying, or had I not had faith in the first place? He'd never given me a reason not to trust him. And at what point did I become this crazy person? I wanted to leave, to prove to myself that I didn't need to be here and I could put aside my doubts. No scratch that, I *needed* to leave. Except every time I was going to call the waiter over to me to pay my tab, I stopped myself. My stupid head was spinning in circles and every minute that ticked by I was getting angrier with myself.

Just over an hour into my stalking, I looked across street at the outdoor patio of FastEddy's and watched as a familiar looking dark-haired girl was seated. How did I know her? I was going through faces in my memory trying to peg exactly where I've seen her but nothing was ringing a bell. Hmmm… maybe I knew her from class or something. I was going to shrug it off but then Camden's car came pulling up to my side of the road and parallel parked. I ducked in my seat as if he could see me, when in actuality the windows were too dark for him to see in. My heart went into my throat, and I was holding my breath as he got out of the car and looked across the street. The girl gave a small wave and that was when it hit me. Holy shit it was the girl from the photograph. The one that was hanging in his parents' hallway. No, no, no, this wasn't happening! I felt like my eyes were deceiving me. Dizzily looking from her to him, then him to her. I was going to puke. Camden turned in my direction but was looking at the other side of his vehicle. The passenger side door opened and Dodger stepped out. What the hell was he doing here too? They both made their way across the street and through the restaurant until they stepped out on the patio. The women stood up, and I looked on as she hugged Dodger and kissed his cheek. Oh Macie would have a field day with his balls right about now had she seen him do that. When Camden greeted her, she smiled big, as if she were happier to see him. She went into his open arms, and he held her tightly. He was speaking into her ear, and she nodded as he spoke. When he broke away, she held his hand as they sat down.

  He'd been lying to me. He came to meet up with a girl, and he never told me about it, and for whatever reason Dodger was in on it. Mindlessly I sat and watched as they conversed and shared some laughs. I didn't know why I stayed there letting every ounce of respect for Camden dissolve into nothing, but I did. Call it torture, call it affliction, call it whatever you want, I was planted in my chair as it all unfolded. Every emotion one could

BENDER

feel— disgust, hurt, pain, anger— were rolling through me like a raging storm.

I snapped.

Pulling out my wallet I threw some money on the table and stood up. Fury was fueling me to move forward. Once outside I went to Camden's car and looked over the hood at the three of them. All I kept saying to myself was, 'he told me he was working late'. When I heard the chime of her laughter float across the air, I think that was when I broke. Tears welled in my eyes clouding my vision, but not enough to do what I did next. I slung my purse at his passenger side door as hard as I possibly could. The sound of the beating amped me up to do it again, over and over. A few people stopped and watched what I was doing, but nobody said anything to me. Well, maybe they did, but I didn't hear them. I was in my own little bubble. I'd hoped that it would give me some relief, some sort of reprieve from the need to go over there and hurt him. I never said anything about what I was doing was right, but all sense of reason had left my body. When it wasn't enough, I dropped my bag and started using my feet. As my destruction continued I had looked up in time to see Camden reach across the table and place his palm on the woman's cheek. Have you ever been so angry that you saw red? His gesture repulsed me. I kicked everything that I could lay my eyes on; the bumper, the door, the hood. I was running around it like a mad woman. A small crowd was forming around me, murmuring about calling the police. I wanted to say, 'yes, call the police, because if he comes over here I am going to be charged with murder'. When my feet were no longer enough I started using my fists, pounding on the windows attempting to break the glass. It was like Camden was the car, and I was kicking the shit out it like I wanted to do him.

Arms suddenly closed in around me and I was lifted in the air away from the object of my focus. I screamed, "No! Put me down!"

Camden came to stand in front of me, his chest heaving. "Keegan? What the fuck are you doing?"

"I hate you. I HATE YOU!" I spat. "Who is she you son of a bitch? You lied to me."

I didn't realize who was holding me from behind until I heard Dodger's voice in my ear. "Keegan, settle down. Jesus Christ, would you relax."

"Fuck you, Dodger! I can't believe you've known about him being with someone else, and you didn't say anything." I grunted.

I kicked against him trying to break free. "Shit!" I hit him in the shin. The girl that they were sitting with had made her way through the crowd and saw me. Her mouth dropped open in shock, but then a funny thing happened, she looked at me... in approval? What the hell?

Camden took two steps toward me and grasped my upper arms, pulling me away from Dodger. "Seriously Keegan, would you calm down, you're going to hurt yourself more if you don't stop."

I tried to use my arms to bring them up and around to break his hold, but I should have known better. Camden was built like a brick house, and I didn't stand a chance. He brought me in, locking me in a bear hug, and his face came down to mine. His eyes were deadly serious, and all I saw the black of his pupils. "Enough!" he commanded.

"Oh screw you! How long have you been cheating on me, huh? How long Camden? Or should I ask your little whore over there?"

I was still squirming, and I kicked him hard in the knee. He grunted but didn't waver in his hold. Instead, he pushed me up against his car and wrapped one of his legs around me, preventing me from any further movement of my limbs.

"I said, enough," he said through gritted teeth. "If you'd stop for one second and let me explain, you'd know that I'm not cheating. In fact it's not even close."

I was just starting to feel some pain in my hand, but I ignored it. "What in the hell are you talking about? I saw you! I saw you kiss her on the cheek, I saw you holding her hand."

"Keegan, look at her." I was glaring at him. "Look…at...her." My eyes shifted to where she was standing in the crowd. "See her. Does anything about her look familiar?"

Of course she was familiar. She was the girl from the photograph, she was my worst nightmare come to life. I hated her. I hated her so severely that just seeing her made me want to bend at the waist and throw up. But for some reason Camden wouldn't let me move until I gave him what he wanted. I eyed the girl, taking in her beautiful features. The black hair, and striking sea green eyes. She was watching me as though she were willing me to make a connection, to see something that was right in front of my face. And then it happened. The face, the chiseled cheeks made more feminine because she was a female, the hair… I glanced back at Camden in confusion.

"Do you see it now?" he asked, his tone softening.

I shook my head. "Who- who is she?"

I saw her step forward out of the corner of my eye, and she came to stand beside me. "Keegan this is my half-sister, Breslin." He told me in a way of introduction.

"Half-sister," I said as a statement, rolling the words around on my tongue, tasting it and letting it sink in.

"Yes."

"But you don't have a sister," I nearly whispered.

"I do. And I swear I'll explain everything to you, but can I trust that you won't go beating the shit out of something else if I let you go?"

Wait, what? Of course I wouldn't hit anything, I didn't do that. Okay, well actually it seemed that I did, but this wasn't normal behavior. My adrenaline was fading, and my emotions were sweeping through me.

"Okay." I told him even though it didn't really answer his question. I was staring at Breslin, and my brain was trying to make the connection. "Sister," I repeated like it would make more sense if I said it again.

"Do you think she's in shock?" I heard Dodger ask.

"I don't know, but we should go somewhere where we aren't being stared at," Camden replied.

"Right," Dodger responded. "Let's go."

And just like that we were on our way back to the apartment. I barely remember the car ride, or how I got in the vehicle. I just know that I never once took my eyes off of *her*, the one who made my heart feel fractured.

CHAPTER EIGHTEEN

"Keegan I'm sorry that you were misled into believing that I was someone else," Bree told me. "Seriously Cam? You didn't bother telling your girlfriend?"

He glared at her. Jesus their features were similar. "You told me not to talk to anyone about it. What the hell did you want me to do?"

"Oh I don't know, maybe let her in on it so shit like this could have been avoided?" she replied sarcastically.

I sat on the couch still somewhat confused as Camden was cleaning my knuckles of blood and dirt. I'd apparently done a number on them, and they were swollen and split open.

He was squatting in front of me as he glanced up at her and said, "Bree, you didn't want me to tell anybody about your situation, not even Dodge. Except now you're telling me I was supposed to explain to someone that didn't even know you existed, 'hey, my sister that you didn't know about called me in a panic because she got knocked up by some random guy and I need to help her out of that mess'."

She threw her hands up in the air. "Argh! You're impossible you know that?"

Bree walked into the kitchen to talk to Dodger who was currently icing his shin. Hmmm…I didn't think I kicked him that hard.

I was looking down at what Camden was doing, my eyes refusing to meet his even though I knew he was watching me. "So a sister? Care to tell me how that happened?"

He shrugged. "My dad had a long-time girlfriend throughout high school and college. His junior year she got pregnant. At first she wasn't going to keep it, but my dad's really against abortion, and he felt like he should have a say in keeping it. Before they split up, she told him she'd have the baby but she didn't want any responsibilities. Of course as she went through her pregnancy she ended up changing her mind and wanted to keep her. My dad was able to get partial custody of Bree, and then two years after she was born, Dad met my mom."

Wow! That wasn't the story that I was expecting. "So why the secrecy then? Are you two close?"

"Sort of. Out of all my brothers, it's me who she comes to. Bree has always struggled with where she fits in with my family. My dad has always been there for her, and he took part in raising her. My mom treated her like she was her own daughter. And of course, we all grew up with her during the summer months and some holidays, but for whatever reason, Bree stopped coming around. She knows that we do family dinners, and that she is always going to be a part of that. I just think she's trying to find where her place is. Her mother isn't always there. As far as the secrecy goes, well I was going to try and handle this without anybody knowing, but Dodger somehow figured it out and demanded that he come with me so Bree knew we were here for her."

It made sense, it really did, but I was dumbfounded as to why he never even mentioned Bree before now.

Why I had to find out about her like this, instead of me acting like a psycho in the middle of Athens and making a scene.

I flexed my hand, pain running up my arm. "You should have told me."

"I know."

"No, I don't think you do. *You should have told me.*" I tried my hardest to emphasize that statement.

"Keegan," He tipped my chin up. "I know," he said looking me straight in the eyes.

My vision clouded over and tears welled up. His face softened, and he could see that I was about to break down. Instead of me doing it in front of Bree and Dodger, he gently picked me up and carried me upstairs. Taking me into the bathroom he set me down on the counter and went to the faucet to start the shower. Coming back over to me, he lifted the hem of my shirt, raising it over my head and tossing it aside. He tugged off my shoes and socks and gasped when he saw my swollen ankle. His eyes shifted to mine, and I simply shrugged.

Shaking his head he said, "When you kick ass you don't just beat up what's in front of you, you do a number on yourself too. Jesus, look at your toes, they're red."

Sniffling I told him, "I was imagining it was your face."

He smirked. "Nice, but seriously, I'm going to have to teach you how to throw a punch. You could have broken your hand hitting the way that you were. And so you know, we're going to have to talk about my car too. I'm not going to just forget about it or sweep it under the rug."

Sighing I told him, "Whatever. I'll give you money to fix it when you find out how much it costs."

Camden mashed his teeth together. "No, you won't. But that's not what I'm concerned about. Blue, I've never seen you so worked up over something, and I'm not sure how I feel that you went haywire on my vehicle instead of approaching me at the restaurant."

I closed my mouth, refusing to give him an answer when I didn't even have one myself. Helping me down from the counter, he quickly stripped his clothes off, and we climbed into the shower. The heat on my skin made me hiss. The pain was overwhelming and my head wouldn't let go of the fact that he hid something that was important from me.

"I looked at your phone," I announced.

"What?"

I met the brown of his eyes. "Earlier, I saw the texts while you were in the shower. That's how I knew where you'd be."

He regarded me for a moment before he said, "I'd like to say I'm upset about that but, I'm not."

"You should be."

"Why?"

"Because Camden, it was an invasion of your privacy, and I had no right going through your things. If I had a question, I should have come to you, and talked to you about it."

"I'm not saying I appreciate you doing it, but I'm not angry with you for it. I should have told you about Bree right from the start."

"Yes, you should have, but stop giving me the easy out, it's pissing me off!"

He ran his hands through his damp hair causing it to stick up every which way. "What do you what me to do, huh? Yell at you, scream at you, tell you that you obviously don't trust me? Because I'm not going to do that. Keegan, what was your gut telling you?" I looked down. "No, you don't get to close up on me. What did your gut tell you?"

My breathing had picked up, and I clenched my fists despite the pain. "It told me that you were hiding something, okay? That's why I looked."

"And is that something that you normally would've done?"

"No."

"Then I'm not mad at you for it."

"Argh!" I threw my hands up in the air. "That's partially why this is all so fucked up." I turned away from him and faced the showerhead. The spray was beating down on me, and I closed my eyes while I let the water wash over my body. He remained quiet, letting me work out whatever was in my head on my own. "I lost it today, completely lost it. I've never felt so out of control before in my life. Do you know what that feels like?" My words came out as barely a whisper.

I heard him breathing behind me. "Yes."

"I don't even know how to make sense of what's going on in my head. Camden, until today, I didn't realize how much you have come to mean to me, how much I *really* care for you."

"Keegan, believe me I know."

I shook my head again, turning around to face him and wiped away the water that was mixing with my tears. "No, I don't think you do. Until today I'd pushed aside any feelings that were more than just 'like'. I thought that if I didn't allow myself to feel how I really do, it wouldn't affect me. Ignorance is bliss, right? But then I saw you. I thought I was seeing you with another girl, and it broke me. I couldn't stomach the idea of it but that's when it happened."

His eyebrows etched together and he was solely focused on me. "What happened?"

Swallowing hard and threw my cards on the table. "I realized that I am head over heels in love with you, Camden. I know I shouldn't be. And that you're not the type to have a serious relationship like that. To tell you truthfully, I don't even know how long I've actually been feeling like this, but now I'm aware, and I don't think I can ignore it. I've let you put yourself in every little crevice of my heart, and I couldn't stop this even if I tried."

So many emotions flitted across his face, and I attempted to read every one of them. "Why would you?" His voice sounded timid, which was completely out of the norm for him.

"Because I'm spinning toward the ground and I'm twenty thousand feet up with no safety net. This is not the kind of control that I'm willing to let go of. Today showed me something that's been blaring in my face for weeks now and just when I'm finally seeing it, I can't process it. I need a little bit of time."

"Blue, what do you mean by time?" He reached up and cupped my cheek. I placed my hand over his and felt his compassion seeping into me. Why did he look like I was about to crush *him*?

Tears were streaming down my face, and I let out a small sob. "You kept something important from me Camden. Honesty could have prevented this whole thing from happening. Not just what you did, but what I did too. I love you, and there's nothing I can do about it. But I need to take some time to figure out how this makes me feel, how all of this can even work."

He leaned forward and put his forehead on mine. "We can talk this out, time isn't necessary."

"It is." I had nothing else to say. Stepping away from him, his hand dropped from my face, and I opened the shower door. Getting out I wrapped myself in a towel and walked to my room, retreating into my own space.

Camden didn't follow me that night. He left me alone to wallow in my thoughts and resolve what a jumbled mess my head had become. I never even let him respond to my news breaking revelation. I hadn't a clue if the feelings were even mutual, but I doubted it. It was like over the last few weeks I'd compartmentalized the feelings I'd established for Camden and tucked them away because I felt that he wasn't ready for it. I wasn't ready for it. Then the issue with Bree? I would have been understanding, I really would have. There was no reason for him to hide it from me. But obviously he didn't feel that we were close enough that he could share something like that. That was the part the stung the most.

This morning at school I'd run into Dodger, and he apologized profusely for not telling me about Bree, but because he'd just found out himself I forgave him. I asked him some questions about her, which he gladly answered. I think he feared any negative repercussions from Macie. He confirmed that she has always taken to Camden more than the other three brothers, but mostly because he was the protective one, and he figured Camden made her feel safe. Apparently when you tell him something, that secret was on lockdown and he wouldn't say a word. Yeah... no kidding! When I asked about the pregnancy, he didn't seem to know much more than I did, except that she apparently had a one night stand with a bartender in the town that she lived and now she didn't know what to do. I could understand why she'd be waffling about it. Not knowing if this guy was going to stick around when you hadn't planned on a long term relationship with him, and then the sheer fact that her own mother had considered aborting her; she has quite a bit on her plate right now. I liked Breslin and the little bit that I knew of her now. And it turned out that she was thoroughly amused with my ass kicking of Camden's car and had approved of me right then and there. She said if I dealt with Camden's shit like that every time, I'd survive in this family. It made me smile for the first time in twenty-four hours.

I had just gotten home from work and plopped down on the couch. I thought I'd order a pizza and pop in a movie until Camden got home then we could talk. My phone was sitting next to me when it went off. ***MOM*** appeared on the screen.

"Hello?"

"Keegan! Oh God Keegan, I can't find her."

"Can't find who, slow down Mom. Where's Sarah?" My heart started beating in my chest.

She sounded frantic. "Sarah. She's not here. I picked her up from school, and I thought she went upstairs to her room, but when I called her down for dinner she didn't answer. Oh my God I can't find her anywhere!"

I abruptly stood up and looked around my living room. *Okay, okay… don't panic.* Where did I put my goddamn keys? "Have you checked outside?"

"Yes!"

"Did you look across the street at the park? Sometimes she likes to hide under the slide."

"Yes, yes…Keegan oh God she was mad at me."

I found my keys on the counter by my purse, and I took off for my car. "Did you two get into a fight?"

"I told her I was going to have your uncle pick her up from school tomorrow, because I had to work late, and she got upset. She told me that I'm never home anymore, so I said that she was being overdramatic." Her voice quivered.

"Mom! You aren't ever home! She misses you. She was trying to talk to you about it, and you blew her off." I was fuming mad and terrified that something bad had happened to my little sister.

"Don't yell at me, you're not helping."

"Shut up Mom, just shut up! I'm on my way. I swear if something has happened to her, I'm never going to forgive you!" I hung up not wanting to hear anything else she had to say. I called Macie on my way and told her what was happening. She tried to calm me down, but I was too worked up. She said she would meet me at the house and make some phone calls to places around town to ask if they'd seen her, then she'd let Dodger know. I needed Camden. All I wanted was for him to hold me and tell me that everything was going to be okay and that we'd find her. I was going to call him but I was pulling up to my mom's house and I didn't because I wanted to go in and search for Sarah.

When I got through the front door, my mom was sitting on the couch, leaning forward with her elbows on her knees and tears running down her face. She was on the phone with someone, but she told them she had to go when I walked in.

"Tell me everywhere you've looked," I demanded.

She set her phone down beside her, and she started listing off every place she'd already been. The longer she spoke, the more infuriated I got with her. It was like she kept running her mouth, and we were wasting time that we could have been out searching.

"What are we going to do? I called the police, and they said that they are sending out some officers in the neighborhood to look, but what if we don't find her?"

I held my hand up. I was done. My blood boiled over, and I had nothing else but unadulterated hate for my mom right now. "What are we going to do if we don't find her? That's not going to happen. She's going to be found and when she is, you are going to be getting yourself some help. There will be no more going out, no more partying, no more random guys, no more drinking, you will stay at home with your *eight-year-old child*, and you *will* be the responsible parent that you are supposed to be. I'm sick of picking up your slack Mom. I don't care if you have to go to counseling, or quit your job to be at home with her." I had ticked off each point on my fingers. "Enough is enough!"

"Do you really think scolding me right now is going to solve anything?"

I bent over at the waist and got in her face. "You *LOST* Sarah! Get off your fucking high horse and give me a little humility for once." I heard the front door open and Macie came into the living room. "I'm going out to look for her. Stay here until you hear from me or the police." Her mouth opened and closed like a fish. I swear if she said anything else to me I would be too tempted to slap her.

Macie looked at me sympathetically, and we walked to the front door. "Come on, we can go over to the school and see if she's hanging out over there."

"Do you think we should split up and cover more ground?" My chin quivered and tears pooled in my eyes. Fear was crashing into me in waves.

"No, I don't think you can drive right now. Just get in my car and we'll find her. I'm sure she's fine," she said comfortingly.

In the car Macie was trying to reassure me that Sarah was just being a typical eight-year-old, and that kids ran away from home all the time. They might, but most only did it out of defiance. Sarah likely took off because she was sick of being ignored. Nothing could placate my guilt.

"I told Dodger what was going on, and he said he would check the roads between your house and the apartment."

"Okay." I kept my eyes on the sidewalks and yards that we drove past, praying to whatever higher being I could think of that she was unharmed. It was dusk and darkness was creeping in with every passing minute. I felt like I was on the verge of hysterics. We'd been out searching for over an hour when I told Macie to stop by the apartment so I could see if Camden was out searching and to check if Sarah was in the area.

When we pulled up I told Macie I'd be right out. I took the stairs two at a time. Yanking the front door open, I was immediately greeted by a teary-eyed Sarah, and Camden sitting in front of her talking to her. My legs went weak, and I nearly passed out from relief. She looked over at me and shot up from the couch. She ran to me, and I dropped to my knees in time for her to crash into me sobbing. I bawled. My only thought was that she was safe, as I was breathing her in. I squeezed her tightly in my arms, and I stroked my hands down her wild curls. Camden had gotten up and looked down on us as he leaned against the breakfast bar.

"Where have you been? Do you have any idea how scared I was? How scared Mom was?"

"Mom doesn't care."

I pulled her back, grasping her upper arms. "Yes she does, Sarah. I know she may not show it like she should, but she does care. We've both been worried sick about you. Why would you just leave like that? You know you can't go anywhere without an adult with you. How did you even get over here?"

She lifted her shoulders. "I rode my bike."

"You what!?" I screeched.

"I had my helmet on, I was being safe."

"No Sarah, you weren't safe. At no time is it ever okay for you to leave the house without someone with you and go anywhere, let alone ride your bike several miles away. I don't care if you had on a helmet or not."

"I'm sorry." My tone was getting her upset all over again, but I didn't care. I wanted her to be upset, I wanted her to feel even just an ounce of the fear I'd been feeling for the last two hours.

Breathing in deeply I tried to calm my frazzled nerves. "Listen, we don't have to talk about it right now, but when we get home, Mom, you, and me are all going to sit down and talk. I think we need to make some new arrangements."

She nodded and wiped her nose with the back of her hand. "K."

I stood back up and faced Camden. Narrowing my eyes I gritted through my teeth, "How long had she been here?"

He tilted his head to the side as though he were confused by my confrontational tone. "It's been maybe fifteen minutes. She knocked on the door, I let her in, and tried to get her settled before I was going to give you a call."

My fingers flexed then dug into my palms. "Don't you think that's the first thing you should have done? Call me crazy, but we've all been driving around trying to find her, and you could have put me out of my misery fifteen minutes ago?"

"Keegan I think you need to settle down and take a breather. She's fine, she's safe, everything's okay."

"No Camden! Everything is *not* okay!" I screamed. Tears were pouring out of my eyes at a steady pace, and I wanted to wring his neck. "Don't you get it? Everyone has been out looking for her; me, Macie, Dodger...the *police*! You should have called me."

He narrowed his eyes, and his stance became rigid. "You're upset, and if you want to take it out on me, then fine. But I did what I thought was best, so I suggest you calm down and not get even more worked up."

I saw Sarah look up at me out of the corner of my eye. If she wasn't here, I would be digging through the kitchen drawers for a murder weapon right about now. Instead, I resolved myself. Turning toward the stairs, I started to make my way up to my room. In my closet I pulled out a duffle bag and began throwing all of my clothes in, not caring if they were folded neatly.

"What are you doing?" Camden asked from the doorway.

"Leaving."

He felt him come into my room and approach me from behind. "Why?" He sounded confused.

"Because I need out, I need to step away to get a break from everything." I went back to my closet and collected more things.

His arm shot out, and he grabbed my wrist. "Would you stop for a minute and *talk* to me?"

I faced him. "What do you want to talk about, huh? Do you want talk about the fact that you didn't think of me *again* when there was something that was obviously important? Or how about that you conveniently didn't tell me about Bree when knowing that you had a sister is a pretty big fucking deal. Or maybe even that I told you that I loved you for the first time and you had nothing to say about it." My chest heaved as air rushed out of me, and I broke out into a full on sob.

He tried to bring me into him, but I yanked my arm away. It pissed him off. "So you're just running away. You're not even going to give me the chance to talk to you, is that it?"

"You've had plenty of chances to tell me the shit that you've kept from me. Clearly I'm not a vital person in your life. You place your value in other things, and I'm too far down on your list of 'what Camden gives a shit about' for you to care."

He moved fast. Ripping the clothes out of my hands and throwing them against the wall, he clasped the back of my neck and made me look him in the eyes. I'd never seen him so angry in all the time that I'd known him. There was no mistaking the intensity of his words when he spoke. "You ever say anything like that to me again, I can promise you this is done. You've never been low on my priority list, and if you ever were, believe me you'd know it. I do things in my own way. You needed to take some time to process how you felt about me. That was fine, I was giving you that time. But in no way was that a reflection on *my* feelings. Was I wrong for not telling you about Breslin? Hell yes I was wrong, and I regret it. Should I have called you when Sarah came knocking on the door tonight? Yeah, probably. But everything I do Keegan, I do it in my own way. It's not because I'm trying to be mean, or facetious, or blatantly hurtful. I'm about done with you lashing out at me because you're pissed off. If you haven't noticed I'm not a very tolerant man. It fucking ends now. So you either get on board and deal with how I am, and I will try to make a concerted effort to be more open with the shit that comes my way, or you walk away. I won't stand here and let you accuse me of not caring, when I actually care more than you could imagine."

His fingers were digging into my hair, and I was panting so hard that my lips were dry. I felt so bewildered by his words that I wasn't even sure how to respond to him. Instead I stayed silent going over every word, processing each one so that it made sense. Apparently it was the wrong thing to do, because Camden abruptly let go of me and took a step back. His eyes bounced back and forth between mine. The one emotion that was so easy to read from him was pain. Somehow in my silence I'd crushed him and now he was the one pulling away. My heart lurched and I wanted nothing more than to say, 'wait, I love you. Let's not do this, can we just start over?' But I didn't. My feet were plastered in place as I watched him close his eyes and take a deep breath. When he opened them again, he shook his head at me and walked out. Without a care that Sarah was downstairs or that Macie might still be in the car, I flung myself onto my bed and curled into the fetal position and cried.

Camden left me.

CHAPTER NINETEEN

THE NEXT MORNING I WAS LYING in my bed staring at the yellow walls. Walls that Camden had painted for me because he was trying to do something nice, something to show he cared. The fact that I had a bag packed beside my bed was weighing heavily on me, but the idea of walking out of the apartment not knowing when I'd be back made me want to hurl myself off a cliff. If I walked out on Camden, that would be it. He wouldn't forgive me, and there'd be no coming back. There was a light tapping on the door before it was opened and in walked a showered and refreshed Bree. I thought she had left town already but apparently not. *Lucky me.*

"Hey, mind if I come in?" she asked.

Uncurling myself, I scooted up the bed and pushed my hair behind my ears. "No, come on in." I really wasn't in the mood to talk to anybody, and certainly not her. I might know who she was now, but that didn't mean my brain was yet computing that she wasn't the enemy. I should get to know her though. Camden protected her, he loved her, and he was a part of her, because they shared the same DNA. And anything that was Camden, I loved.

She came and sat down next to me, stretching out her long toned legs and getting comfortable next to me like she'd known me her whole life. "How're you holding up?"

"Fine I guess. Just happy that my sister is safe."

She nodded. "Yeah, I heard about that. That must've been pretty scary."

"Yes it was, more than you know." I was fidgeting with my blankets.

There was an awkward silence that loomed between us, and neither one of us were speaking. She glanced around my room and smiled. "Like your room. I have the same colors in mine."

I didn't know how I felt about us sharing the same tastes. Maybe that was why Camden picked what he did. "Thanks," was all the response I gave her.

"So this isn't awkward at all," she said sarcastically.

I had to give her credit, she was trying. I smiled over at her. "I'm sorry, I'm just not much for talking right now."

"I figured as much, which is why this might be perfect timing for me to do some talking, if you're willing to listen."

Intrigued, I sat up a little straighter. "Okay."

She started off by telling me about her mom, how she never was around, and how she made Bree feel like she didn't want her. "It wasn't like that all of the time though. We'd have moments where she'd come home with all the ingredients to bake cookies, and she wanted to spend time with me. Or we would camp out in the living room and watch cartoon after cartoon laughing. It was like she wanted to love me, she just didn't know how. Paul, my dad, he didn't realize she had been depressed when the courts gave her half custody. He's told me, had he known, he would have never let me live there. Paul's a good man.

It's where Camden gets it from. In fact that whole family is good people."

"They're your family too." I pointed out the obvious.

"Yes, but as you grow older, you question things that were done to you, and how having a different life would have led you in a different direction. I don't blame Paul or Donna for my childhood. They tried to get me to come live with them, but for some reason, I just couldn't leave her. I'd become the parent, and she was the child I raised."

Wow, didn't I know that feeling? Sitting here next to her it felt like every word that was pouring out of her mouth were words that I was supposed to hear, to relate to. Our childhood stories alone were so similar you'd think we lived side by side in the same world. Except, I didn't have a dad who wanted me. If I'd had one who was like Paul, I probably would have a lot more questions about my life and how different it could have been.

"Bree, I'm sorry for how I treated you, and the things that I said outside of the restaurant the other day. I had no idea who you were, and I'd kind of snapped. That's never happened to me before," I offered.

"It's cool. He should have told you. I knew he was dating someone, though I didn't know how serious you two were, but I should've known he would have kept it from you unless I gave him permission to tell you. See, that's the thing about Camden, he's loyal to a fault. He never spills secrets, even if it could ruin everyone else around him. I know that I have three other brothers who would drop everything for me if I asked, but Camden has always been the one who reaches out to me. He's the one who acts more like the big brother versus the little brother. I rely on him too much, and I wished I wouldn't have asked him to help me. It's caused a shit storm of a mess, and I'm very sorry about that."

I shook my head. "No, don't blame yourself. He should have told me, just like he should have told me about a lot of things. But I guess you're right about Camden being tight lipped about stuff. It's just that it's 'mum's the word' with him all the time, and all I want is for him to feel comfortable enough to talk to me."

She reached over and grabbed my hand. When I glanced up at her, I wanted to burst into tears. She looked so much like Camden, I couldn't wrap my mind around it. How did I not see it in the photo? Well, I guess if I wasn't looking for it, how could I have?

"He does feel comfortable enough with you. He loves you Keegan." I was about to argue, but she stopped me. "No, just listen to me. I've watched him grow up and date girls here and there. Do you know how many he's ever brought home?"

"No."

"Zero. Do you know how many he's stuck with for as long as he's been with you?"

"Huh-uh."

"Zero. And do you know how many he's told that he loves them?"

Tears sprung to my eyes and I said, "No."

"None, Keegan. He's never said it to another girl."

"But he's never said it to me either."

"Do you think he even needs to? Camden sees something in you that is clearly special, and I see it too. You're different than the other girls. He pushes and tests those that he lets in, because he wants to know that they will fight for him, like he will fight for them. Oh boy did you fight." She laughed. "He needs someone like you who'll give him a challenge. I knew that Camden was never going to settle for a girl who was shallow or vain. He likes other qualities...qualities that are real. Give him another chance, Keegan, he deserves one, and so do you."

The corners of my eyes had crusted dry tears, and now they were wet again. "Thank you for talking to me. Your brother is pretty special to me, and I think you're pretty great as well." I paused. "Wait, what are you going to do, you know, about the whole baby thing?"

She exhaled loudly. "That's the question of the year isn't it? I think I'll be heading back home to let the guy know and make a decision from there. I never thought I'd be in this position, but I am so I guess I better face the music."

I squeezed her hand. "Good luck, Bree. I know you have other people to talk to, but I'm here if you need someone."

"Thanks," she said as she got up from the bed. Before she walked out the door she faced me. "Keep him on his toes slugger. He deserves you." Then she walked out.

I'd kept my bags packed but didn't leave. I went over and over in my head some things that Camden had said. He told me that I needed to get on board with him, that he was set in his ways. Camden had never done relationships, especially ones where his girlfriend was already living with him. At what point did I not cut the man some slack for that? It was a big adjustment for the both of us. At twenty-five years old, he'd been doing things on his own for quite some time, and now he was having to make adjustments to almost every part of his life for me to fit in. If he didn't find me worth it, he wouldn't have. In my heart I knew this, but waiting for my brain to catch up wasn't so fun. My instincts were screaming at me to give him the chance that he deserved. If I walked out, that would have been it for us. I decided I was going to stay and fight for this, for us, because we deserved it. I loved him. Camden consumed me, and as scary as it was, it was still the best feeling I'd ever felt.

He had been gone for two days now. I'd texted Dodger after the first night to ask if he'd seen his brother, to which he responded that he was at his house, and he didn't know how long he'd be there. I felt sick that Camden wanted to be away from me. If this was what it was going to be like not having him around, I didn't like it at all. I was barely functioning as it was, but with each passing hour my heart was screaming at me to run to him. It was nearing midnight on night two when I'd passed out on the couch. I woke up to the sound of the lock clicking on the front door and the sight of a very disheveled looking Camden walking in. His hair was all over the place, his t-shirt was wrinkled, and if I had to guess, I'd say he had probably worn the same thing two days in a row. My heart skipped a beat at the sight of him. He looked out over the living room as though he were searching for me. The moment our eyes met, it was like I could breathe again. Rising from the couch, I went to him. Without hesitation he opened his arms to me, and it was like he was welcoming me back home. I pressed my face into his hard chest and let him wrap his enormous arms around me like a present. His scent invaded my senses, and I did everything I could not to climb up his body and cling to him like a monkey. He buried his nose in my hair, and he fisted a handful of my hair. We stayed this way; not speaking, not moving, just simply being, for quite some time. It could have easily been thirty minutes that we held each other like that when I felt it was time for us to talk.

"Please don't leave me," I mumbled into his neck.

"Never," he stated, squeezing me tighter.

"You were gone for a while. I wasn't sure if you were going to come back, or if you wanted me to leave before you got back."

"You're ridiculous. I just needed to work some things out in my head, is all. This all just went south really quickly and before I got a chance to fix anything, something else happened."

"And have you worked out the stuff in your head?"

"For the most part. Seeing you is making it better though. These last couple of days have been hard."

"For the record, I don't think I could ever walk away from you Camden. You're sort of my person. I kind of like you."

I heard him chuckle sleepily. "Good, cause I'm pretty sure I kind of like you too. But we do have a lot that we need to talk about Keegan."

Loosening my hold on him, I said, "Come upstairs with me?"

He nodded, taking my hand and walking upstairs. In his bedroom, we both stripped down and climbed into his bed. Once we were settled, we were lying down facing each other, our feet tangled together, and our faces only inches apart.

"I'm sorry for yelling at you, Camden. You didn't deserve how I treated you, or not letting you explain yourself to me. I've not been very understanding lately, and I think I've been scared that you'd get too close and then realize that I wasn't worth it."

"That's never going to happen. It wasn't until I met you that I knew that something worth it even existed. I think you and I are just going to have to work on a learning curve. Because we already live together, we have to do things differently. I'd never change us or our situation, but we both are still making adjustments. As long as you know that I'm in this with you and I'm not leaving, everything will be fine. I told you, you'd be the girl that could ruin me, and I meant it." He lifted one of my hands and placed it over his heart. "Do you feel this?"

"Yes."

"It's yours. It's not beating for anyone else, just you. I love you too Keegan. I didn't get the chance to say it back to you, because I think I was more shocked when those words left your beautiful lips than anything else. Never in my life did I think I'd find the girl who turns me upside-down and changes the way that I do things or how I think. Then in walked you, this blond-haired girl with the brightest blue eyes, and you've knocked me off my axis ever since. Our world spins a different way, and I like that."

My heart stuttered in my chest. Bree was right. But didn't I already know that? Camden Brooks just told me he loved me. Me. The girl who never dared to dream past getting a nursing degree and having a stable environment. I smiled the biggest smile I think my face had ever made, and he reciprocated. Somebody pinch me because I thought I was dreaming.

"No more not trusting, no more secrets, no more hiding. I promise to tell you everything, even the dirty ugly secrets about myself, but I want to know the same about you. To know everything there is to know about a person is a powerful thing."

"Agreed."

Sighing deeply I said, "I'm going to need your help with something."

"Name it, you've got my undivided attention."

"I need to go speak with my mom about Sarah, and I have a feeling it's not going to be pretty. Come with me?"

He cupped my cheek while he held himself up with one arm. "Of course."

My heart melted. "K. We'll go tomorrow afternoon while Sarah is at a birthday party."

"No problem, whenever." He bit his lip, and I recognized that playful look in his eyes. "What sort of dark ugly secrets do you have? Share one right now. Aaaand go!"

I laughed. "Okay well, it's not really a dirty secret, but I'm really strange about peanut M&M's. I eat them in threes. One goes in each cheek to get warm and melted, while I suck on the third one to get the candy shell off. Then I just rotate them around as I eat them."

"You are weird." He poked me in the side, and I squirmed away.

"Stop it, I'm not that bad. What did you expect me to say, I like to chew my toenails off, and I keep them in a plastic baggy in my closet?"

His eyes got wide. "Shit, do you do that?"

"You don't?"

He got quiet, and I busted out laughing. "Okay that's a break-upable offense. Just saying. If your toenails have been in your mouth at any age past childhood, we're going to have problems. I can't kiss a girl who might have foot fungus on her tongue."

I shoved his shoulder. "Shut up."

He took hold of my wrist and pinned it above my head, causing him to lean over the top of me. The lightheartedness instantly heated up.

"You ever going to push me away again?"

"Probably, but it's what I do."

He gave me a half smirk. "Smart ass. Do you trust me?"

"Without a shadow of a doubt." And I did.

He brought his lips to mine and kissed me reverently. I soaked it in like I was basking in the sun after a long harsh winter. He was my warmth, my comfort, my home. The way that he touched me while we took our time loving each other was a new experience. We weren't just doing it out of greedy passion, it was because we'd moved to the next level together. I knew I'd love Camden until I no longer existed on this earth. No one would ever make me feel the way that he did.

I'd called my mom to let her know that we were coming to talk with her. She had agreed that some things needed to be resolved, so I was hoping that she had an open mind about all of this. When we pulled up, I took a moment to steel myself for whatever kind of shit storm I was about to walk in on. I figured Mom would be in a defensive mode, but that was okay, I was prepared to deal with it.

Camden got out of the car and came around to my side. Opening my door, I got out, and he placed both arms on either said of me, caging me in. "You good?"

I nodded my head.

"I'm telling you this right now, Keegan, if she so much as raises her voice at you, I'm going to step in and say something. No way will I be able to keep my mouth shut."

Looking into his brown eyes, I could see he was serious. "Okay."

"K."

Dropping his arms we walked to the front door and I let us both in. It was weird that when I came back now, this house no longer felt like my home. It was just the place I used to live. Walking down the hallway I saw Mom sitting in the living room waiting for us.

"Hi Mom," I said, walking to the couch to sit down and get comfortable.

She gave me a tight smile. "Keegan, Camden, I'm glad you both came. Would you like something to drink?"

Why was she being so formal? "No, I'm good Mom. I just want to talk and then we have some things to go do." She tipped her chin down and waited. "Okay, so you already know how I feel about you leaving Sarah alone by herself, but I need you to look me in the eyes and tell me that you will be home with her when she's here. She's too young for you to leave her here so you can go to your boyfriend's house."

"I don't have a boyfriend."

"Well, whatever. I don't really know where you go, but it needs to stop. If you need to leave, at least call me to see what I'm doing. It's likely that Sarah could come over and hang out at the apartment until you pick her up."

Her lips thinned. "I thought that's why you moved out. So you could get some space from us."

My forehead wrinkled. "What? No! I left because I needed to separate myself from you, from this house, from everything. Being here was hindering my progress at school."

"So you did want to get away from us."

"No, not us mom, you."

She gaped at me. Camden took hold of my hand and laced his fingers with mine. It was his silent way to let me know he was here.

"And what did I do that was so terrible that you felt the need to run away."

I rolled my eyes and growled in frustration. "Are you even listening to me? Mom, I left because you were relying on me to be the parent. I was the one who made dinner every night, I was the one who made sure she did her homework, and I was the one who tucked her in at night. Where were you? Oh that's right, you were having another late evening at work. It was too much for me. My schoolwork was suffering, and you knew how important this degree was to me. Sarah has a mother… it isn't me. Be the parent." Wow that felt good to say.

Sitting back she crossed her arms. "How come you are just now telling me this?"

"I'm not. I've told you plenty of times, you just never listened. But after this latest incident with Sarah running away, I'm done with it. Something needs to give here or

I'm going to have to do something drastic." I didn't know what, but I figured I'd throw it out there.

"I don't know what you want from me."

"It's simple." I leaned forward and started ticking off my fingers one by one. "Be home when Sarah's home. Make sure that she is ready for school the next day. Feed and clothe her. And let her know that you love her. Children aren't complicated creatures Mom, if she knows that you love her and that you want to spend time with her, she will forgive you for everything that's already happened. It's just the kind of kid she is."

Tears welled up in her eyes, and she closed her mouth. I hoped that I was getting through to her. She had to have known that this wasn't acceptable behavior for a responsible parent. After some time she finally responded with, "Okay."

Blowing out a breath I didn't think that was what I expected to hear, but either way, I was good. "Also, I'm not telling you that you can't go out, or that you don't deserve to go out. But please, let me know. I'll rearrange things in my schedule, and she can come over."

"Okay."

Feeling as though things needed to end here before something else came up and caused us to backpedal, I stood up and walked over to her. Bending down I wrapped my arms around her shoulders and hugged her as best I could. "I love you, Mom. I know that having kids changed your life, but we're here." I felt her nod against my hair, and I pulled back. She gave me a small smile, and I took that as my cue to leave. Looking at Camden he stood from the couch. When Mom followed us to the front door, my dark and broody man couldn't help himself. He turned around and addressed my mother.

"Rowan, I know that you love your girls because well, who wouldn't. But I'm going to tell you this once, and I hope you take it to heart. Keegan has given you simple guidelines to help keep her sister safe. If at any time you can't stick to them, you should know that we will be coming to get Sarah, and she will be living with us from now on."

Mom's mouth dropped open. I think mine did too. He nodded his head at her before he put his hand on my lower back and led me out to the car. Oh Camden, you are full of surprises. But I couldn't have been more in love with him for standing up for me, and the most important person in my life. Getting in the car I grinned at him.

"You are a ballsy son of a bitch, you know that right?"

"Yep."

"Did you mean it?"

"Every word." He gave me the weight of his russet eyes and winked at me before we pulled out of the driveway.

God he made me happy.

EPILOGUE

One year later...

"Alexis Peabody." *Clapping*
"Miranda Pearl." *Clapping*
"Keegan Phillips." *Clapping*

I GOT UP FROM MY CHAIR and made my way across the short stage that was set up outside. Shaking the Dean's hand, he passed me my diploma. When I turned to face the audience I saw my whole family waving their signs and snapping photographs. Everyone that I loved was here, Camden's whole family, my mom, my sister, and Macie. I'd finally done it. After four years of intense work, over one hundred hours of clinicals, and a lot of lost sleep, I had finally received my Bachelor's in Nursing. This had to be one of the most proud moments of my life. I sought Camden out in the crowd. He was standing with his hands in his pockets, and he looked downright delectable in a pair of cargo shorts and white button-down shirt. But the look on his face was priceless; it oozed pride, admiration, and love. He didn't need to clap or cheer for me. No, that look said it all. He knew what I'd gone through to accomplish this, he'd been with me through the worst parts. I caught him winking before I went to take my seat and wait out the rest of the ceremony.

Last year I decided to enroll in an accelerated program that had nearly doubled my workload but would help me graduate in half the time. It was something new that the college was doing, and we were sort of the guinea pig class. I'd gone back and forth with doing it, because I knew I would have to quit my job, and going out would no longer be an option. My whole life would revolve around school. Camden was the deciding factor for me. He had sat me down after I'd been accepted into the program, and he said that I needed to do something for myself, to prove to myself that I was capable of bigger things. Naturally I fought him on it because…well, it was what I did. And of course, he won as per usual. I wasn't happy about no longer paying for my portion of the rent, but Camden assured me that he didn't mind and that I could pay him back in other ways. I didn't quite know what he meant until later that night he showed me exactly what he was talking about. Talk about unforgettable.

When the final speech was given and the ceremony ended, I made my way through the crowd to my man. As soon as I met Camden's eyes he started moving toward me, plowing through groups of people that were keeping me from him. It was like he was making a path for me to walk. People saw him coming and got out of his way. I leapt into his waiting arms, and he lifted me off the ground in a crushing hug. Even just the smell of him, that clean soapy scent of his skin, made me feel like I was home and gave me comfort. Lifting my head I placed my forehead against his.

"Congratulations Blue."

"Thank you." I smiled.

He held me in the air, my feet dangling for some time as people walked around us. We were having a moment and nobody was going to interrupt it. He kissed me on my nose, then tenderly on my lips. It was a sweet lingering one that made me all melty.

"You finally have your degree that you've worked so hard for, what are you going to do now?"

I pulled my head back and put my finger on my chin. "Hmmm…join the circus?"

He chuckled. "Always the wise ass."

"Always." I grinned at him. Kissing him quickly I squirmed for him to set me down when I noticed the rest of the family was coming to greet me.

When I was placed on my feet, I was quickly lifted back up in another suffocating hug by Dodger… and then another by Turner. Poor Wrigley didn't stand a chance when Camden stepped in front of him and simply stated, "No." I giggled and slapped his arm.

Macie shouldered her way through all of the boys like a boss. "Move it y'all, she was my friend first." We embraced, and I soaked in every ounce of love and support I was being given. Seriously, could a girl get any luckier?

"Oh man, I've gotta stop or I'm going to cry." I spoke into her hair.

"Suck it up ya big baby!" She slapped my ass, and I heard Wrigley give a whoop. "I'm proud of you Keegan. You deserved this."

Sniffling I said, "Thank you. Love you Mace."

"Love you too."

The rest of the family came up, giving me words of wisdom and expressing how amazing they thought I was. Just when I thought my heart would explode from happiness, my mom approached me. We have, for the most part, worked out our differences. Sarah was content and getting the attention that she deserved, and that was all that really mattered to me. The strain on our relationship was slowly diminishing, and I could see that she was making a genuine effort to make things right. I didn't know if it had been my words, or Camden's that gave her the wake-up call that she needed, but I was just pleased that she was trying. Looking at her now, I knew that everything would be alright. We would be alright.

Mom cupped my face in her hands and smiled at me. It was the same smile that was my own. "You did well baby girl. I can't believe that I was blessed to have a daughter like you." A tear rolled down her cheek. "You've grown into a beautiful young lady, Keegan. I'm proud of you."

The dam was opened, and my eyes shed tears. "Love you Mom. It's always you and me, always." I hugged her, knowing that I would remember this moment for the rest of my life.

Camden placed his hand on the small of my back indicating that it was time to go. We were heading over to his parent's house for a lunch celebration and then play a round of baseball. What would a gathering at the Brooks' house be if there wasn't baseball? I walked over to one of my classmates that I'd grown closer to throughout the year, and let her know we were leaving. I'd found out that Annabelle Keaton was a loner. Not that she didn't have friends. In fact she had a lot of friends, but halfway through the semester she told me that her parents had passed away in a car accident and that she'd been on her own since she was sixteen years old. Maybe that was why we got along so well. We both had to be independent long before a child should have to be. Either way, I wanted us to celebrate our day together, with a family that I knew would welcome her. Annabelle told me that she was going to grab her bag, and she would follow all of us over in her own car. I nodded, and we left for the house.

Donna had food all ready to go by the time we got there, so we loaded up our plates and sat down to eat. Chit chat was in full swing, and we were all having fun talking and teasing each other just like we normally did. I smiled that Annabelle was chatting away with everyone like she'd never missed a meal with this group.

"So Annabelle, what sort of nursing are you interested in?" Turner asked.

She looked up at him as if she were confused. He hadn't spoken a word to her since I introduced them, and his sudden interest took her by surprise. Clearing her throat she said, "Possibly sports medicine, or labor and delivery."

"Those two couldn't be any more different ends of the spectrum. Which one are you leaning toward?"

For some reason she looked over at me before she answered. "Uh, I'm not too sure actually. I was kind of hoping to apply wherever Keegan was."

The side of his mouth tilted up, and for the first time since knowing Turner, his eyes sparkled. "It's not like two girls getting up and going to the bathroom together. You don't have to work in pairs, so tell me which one would be a better fit?"

Annabelle frowned at him, obviously frustrated by his question. "Well if you're going to hold a gun to my head and tell me which one to choose I'd say sports medicine. But I've heard there will be several openings in L&D so that's likely where I'll go."

"Hmmm," was all he said in return.

The two of them stared at each other a few short beats before Turner looked away and joined in the conversation down the table. Annabella seemed wholeheartedly confused. She sought me out to see how I took that whole exchange, but I simply shrugged. I had no idea what to think of it. I briefly wondered if Turner was interested but quickly threw that out the window. Turner was a serial dater, and Annabelle was definitely not his type. She was a total stunner in the looks department, but she was sweet; never one to lay her cards out on the table too soon, which was what he'd expect from her.

"Time to hit up the field ladies and gents!" Wrigley announced as he stood up from his seat and cracked his knuckles.

"You're not driving the golf cart, Wrig. I know that's what you're after." Paul interjected. "You and your friends screwed up something with the motor, and I swear it's going to cost a couple hundred dollars to get it fixed. What were y'all doing? Racing?"

He stared at his dad like it was obvious. "Well, yeah."

"You're going to work that off, boy."

"Yes sir," Wrigley said. All the boys chuckling at their youngest brother's idiocy.

Once we were all out on the field we picked teams. As it turned out, it ended up being a boys versus girl game. Might not seem fair to some, but the way I looked at it, the girls were smaller and faster, and I conveniently left out smarter too. Didn't want to start an all-out war by stating the obvious. The game got started, and we were on our second inning. The boys were up by two, and I could tell Macie was getting pissed. I was pitching, as per usual, when Dodger stepped up to the plate. Macie was acting as catcher, and I knew she was going to start up with the distraction.

Readying himself, Dodger stood in position, and I was just tossing the ball when Macie said, "Did you know that when a girl first looks at a man, her eyes automatically go to their crotch?" Dodger swung too low, and he missed the ball. "Strike one," she said with a smirk.

He looked down at her with a glare. Unfortunately shortly after Camden and I worked out our issues, Macie and Dodger broke up. He wasn't moving as fast as she'd liked, and he wasn't willing to bend to her rules. It's been pretty ugly between them, but the sexual tension could drown a person if they got too close.

I underhanded the second ball, and Macie spoke loudly. "A man's lips are also apparently the same color as his tip." I snorted at her blatant attempt to make him miss...which was actually working. "Strike two."

"Macie, I swear to God, if you don't shut up..."

He looked away before he saw her devilish smile spread across her face. I shook out my shoulders to prepare myself for the third pitch. "You know, I've worn out the batteries on my vibrator for the second time in a month. Maybe I need to go find a replacement. Like an actual dick." The bat whooshed through the air as he swung for the third time and struck out. Macie stood up and dusted off her knees. As she walked past him, she bumped his shoulder. "Better luck next time, champ."

If looks could kill, I would suspect that Dodger would have loved to throttle her right about now. Chunking the bat into the fence, he stormed off the field to go take a walk. Oh man, those two were going to need to settle some of their shit before we got together like this again. The family shouldn't have to deal with their drama when we're trying to have a good time.

"Mace, come on!" I scolded.

"What?" She decided to act innocent. I just shook my head, and we went on with the game.

On our last inning, it was the girls up to bat. Annabelle was at home plate readying herself to hit the ball. On the first pitch, she landed a solid hit. It went low to the ground between second and third base to the outfield. She took off running while we all shouted and cheered. We needed her to score to tie up the game. Paul was throwing the ball back when she rounded herself out to third base. Unable to stop her momentum, her foot caught on the lip of the base, and she tripped and fell forward. Landing hard, she immediately grabbed a hold of her ankle and was wincing in pain. I went around the fence to get to my friend, but Turner was running up to her side to see what he could do. What Annabelle didn't know was that Turner was finishing up medical school, and he was a practicing doctor at UGA Medical for sports medicine. He was kneeling by her as I jogged up to see if I could help.

"Can you roll it this way?" he asked as he watched her attempt to move it.

The grimace on her face said that it hurt too much. "Oh my gosh, how embarrassing! I'm so sorry for ruining the game."

"Hush. You didn't ruin anything. Accidents happen all the time, plus you're wearing flip flops, so that didn't help at all."

"Turner, lecturing her isn't helping anyone. Can you at least tell if it's broken?" I argued.

His jaw clenched, and I watched as he reached down and gently picked up her foot like it was a bird with a broken wing. Tenderly he felt her dainty foot before he said, "Doesn't feel like there's anything broken, but you're going to have to sit out the rest of the game. In fact I think you need to go back to the house and get some ice on that before it starts swelling."

She swallowed and nodded at him. "Keegan, I apologize, I'm not normally this clumsy."

I shook my head. "No worries. I just hope that you're okay." Looking at Camden I asked him, "Can you come pick her up so she doesn't have to walk, and we'll get her loaded on the golf cart to take her back in?"

He was just coming over when Turner took it upon himself to lift her in his arms and make the trek to the vehicle. "I've got her," was all he said to me. Well okay then. The two of them took off, and I made note to ask him later why he was acting so strange. After Annabelle's spill, we decided to call it quits before anything else major could happen. Donna wanted to go see if she could help get Annabelle home, Wrigley had a party to go to, Mom and Sarah were headed home because it was getting late, and Macie and Dodger needed to get some space before one of them buried the other in the backyard.

I was ready to head in as well since it had been a really long day, and I wanted to put my feet up for a bit. Everyone had left, and it was just me and Camden. Meeting him out on the pitcher's mound, he pulled me into his arms and wrapped me up in his embrace. The strength of this man never failed to astound me. There was no safer place than right here in his arms. He kissed my forehead, and I leaned my head back to look at him. The warm chocolate of his eyes sucked me in like a strong undertow, and I was drowning in a sea of him. This was my favorite place to be.

"Did you have a good day?" he asked.

"I had a great day. I just can't believe I'm done. Now on to the next part of my life... being a grown-up."

He chuckled. "What about me, am I anywhere in those plans?"

"Not sure."

"Keegan," he said in warning.

"I mean, you are sort of bossy, and you leave your sweaty gym socks in the middle of the floor for me to pick up."

"And that's a bad thing?"

I crinkled my nose. "Are you kidding? Have you ever smelled your own socks?"

"Sure I have."

"Okay, I was kind of kidding, and ew!" I said on a laugh.

"You like it."

"If you think so..."

"What about the rest of your life? What are you doing for the rest of your life?"

His question took me by surprise. "I don't really know. Obviously I'll be applying at UGA Medical, and I think I want to work in L&D, but we'll see where the hospital can put me. I don't think I'm in any position to be picky about place- "

Camden cut me off. "No, I mean what are you doing, for the rest of your life?"

I cocked my head to the side, and I felt him brush his fingers through my long blond waves. I tried to understand what he was telling me but then it hit me. All of the air was sucked out of my lungs and I could tell he was reading me like a book and saw the realization in my eyes. Camden let go of me with one of his arms and reached into his pocket. He dug around and eventually pulled out a ring that was to die for gorgeous. It was cushion cut with diamonds surrounding the full carat in the center. The band was petite and feminine. As tears sprung to my eyes, Camden took ahold of my left hand and held it up to his chest. I could feel the steady rhythm of his heart as he started to speak.

"I can't tell you how proud I am of you, Blue. You've accomplished your goals and achieved the first of many dreams. You inspire me every day to strive for more and do better. Not only in my own life, but in our lives." His chocolate colored eyes dazzled with humor and love. "I've been waiting for this moment since I think you first walked into my apartment. You were the girl, the one who made me see everything differently. You've been defiant, stubborn, difficult, and an all-around giant pain in the ass." I giggled and wiped my tear filled eyes. "But…you've also been challenging, beautiful, open, and the most amazing person I've ever met. You were made me for Blue. You're my person. Marry me, let me show you how you should be loved for the rest of your life."

Oh my God was this real? Camden Brooks just proposed to me, and I felt like I was living in some alternate universe. Things like this just didn't happen to me. Nodding my head vigorously, I did the only thing that I knew I could. I screamed at the top of my lungs and said, "YES! Oh my gosh a thousand times, yes!"

Sliding the ring on my finger, Camden picked me up and spun me in a circle. His face was buried in my hair, and I was laughing with unrequited joy. Never in my life did I ever think that answering an ad for a roommate was going to lead me to the rest of my life. Camden filled me, every day, he showed me love, compassion, and humility. Over a year ago, I thought my purpose in life was going to be to help raise my sister, try and graduate with my class, and attempt to find happiness on my own. I've been blessed to find a man who selflessly supported me in every adventure I took on. It'd been quite the ride with Camden. Oh yes, he'd been full of surprises, but I wouldn't change it for the world.

Crushing his lips to mine, he pushed his tongue into my mouth and swallowed a low moan that seeped out. His fingers threaded into my hair, and I stood on my tippy toes, allowing him to consume me in every way possible. I smiled against his mouth as he kissed me, and he grinned as well. Pecking my nose in the way that he always did, he looked down at me.

"I love you."

"I love you too. So very much," I said.

"Good I'm glad."

"Hmmm…" I said contentedly. "Now what?"

"Well, now it looks like we have a wedding to plan."

"Yes, looks like."

The End

Be on the lookout for Turner's book, *Slider*, releasing in early summer 2014.

ACKNOWLEDGEMENTS

To my family. You know my usual spiel by now. I love you all, and thank you for putting up with my usual crap!

To my editor Jenny, who dealt with my whining and extended deadlines, I think I scored big with you. You proved to me that you know your stuff, and this book is best I've ever written, and I definitely think that's because of you. Thank you for helping me bring this book to the next level. I couldn't have done it without you.

Shawn, you waltzed into my life like a tornado and blew me away with everything that is *you*. You helped make this book what it is, and I hope I did you proud. It still blows my mind that I found someone that fit the character I'd thought up in my head before I even knew who you were. You shaped and molded Camden for me as I went. Thank you for being so incredible, for giving me up-lifting words when I wanted to quit, for being a support that I never expected from a cover model. You were a huge surprise and one that I hope I have in my life for years to come. You're special Mr.! I love you to pieces!

Bayli, gah...there aren't words for what you mean to me. Your friendship is so important to me as I've travelled through the indie world, and outside of it. You critiqued this book and helped me remember to stay on point when I'd start to stray. I love that you loved my characters as much as I did. Best friends, critique partners, and table partners for life.

To my beta readers...you know, all 6 of you. Thank you for taking time away from your families and reading as I went along. Some of you got Bender in chapters, some of you got the book when it was done. I appreciate every single one of your kind words and pointing out things that I couldn't see when writing. Beta readers are the back bones of my books, and I adore every single one of you.

To Golden, you mad genius you. I love the way we work together. All 3 times we have come together, you've taken my ideas and ran with them. I appreciate that you have let me come into your space and make little adjustments with the models as something new hit me. Your brilliance has given me some of the best photos that I, as an author, could ask for. You're the very best in this business, and I can't wait to see what else we can come up with together.

To Kassi, you ma'am are the mastermind of my teasers. What an incredible person you are to have in my corner. Not only do you deal with my demands of being creative for me, you also format my books, created a cover for me for my other novels, and I tortured you with looking at my photos of my models. lol *winkie face* Seriously though, I'm so happy that I finally got to meet you, and you are just as sweet in person as you have been to me online. Here's to more work together.

To the bloggers & readers that gave Bender a chance and helped me advertise it. THANK YOU! I am one

BENDER

person and I can only reach so far. Without your help, Bender might only end up in the hands of like...10 people. Lol. Your continued support is always appreciated.

Made in the USA
Charleston, SC
12 June 2014